MW01139534

THE PROF CROFT SERIES

PREQUELS

Book of Souls

Siren Call

MAIN SERIES

Demon Moon

Blood Deal

Purge City

Death Mage

Black Luck

Power Game

Druid Bond

MORE COMING!

DEMON MOON

A Prof Croft Novel

by

Brad Magnarella

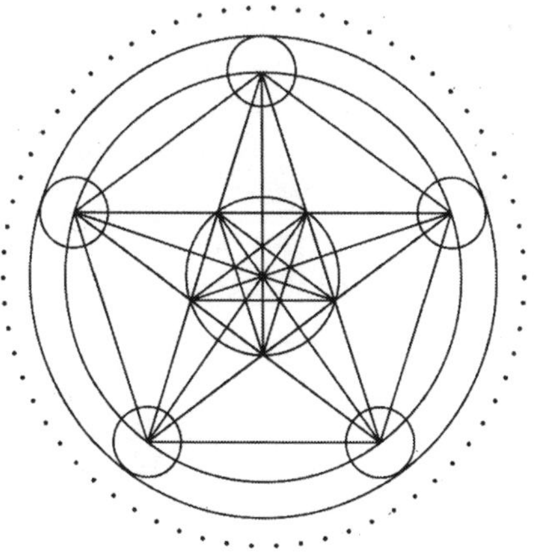

Demon Moon

A Prof Croft Novel

www.bradmagnarella.com

ISBN-13: 978-153547-537-2
ISBN-10: 1-535-47537-4

Cover art by Damon Freeman
www.damonza.com

First Edition

Printed in the U.S.A.

For my parents

1

I blew out a curse as the first droplets of rain pelted my face and punched through my magic. As if I wasn't already running late.

Making an umbrella of my coat collar, I stooped into a run, skirting bags of garbage that swelled from the fronts of row houses like pustules, but it was no use. The downpour that blackened the sidewalk and drove rats from the festering piles also broke apart my hunting spell.

And it had been one of my better ones.

I took refuge on a crumbling porch and shook out my coat. I was in the pit of the East Village, and it stunk. Except for a flicker of street light, the block was midnight dark, the building across the way a brick shell, hollowed out by arson. Not the domicile of the conjurer I needed to stop. Or more likely save.

Assuming I could find him now.

"Seguire," I said in a low, thrumming voice.

Most hunting spells worked like a dowsing rod, pulling the user toward the source of something. In this case, taboo magic. But reliable hunting spells, such as those needed to navigate New York's convoluted streets, required time to prepare. And even then they were delicate.

"Seguire," I repeated, louder.

Though the storm was already sweeping off, the spell refused to take shape again. I swore under my breath. Magic and moving water made poor bedfellows. And here I'd dropped a fat hundred on the booster: ground narwhale tusk. Sunk cost, I thought bitterly as I hustled back to the sidewalk. There were a lot of those in wizardry, my svelte wallet the proof.

Splashing in the direction I'd been pulled before the cloudburst, I gave up on the hunting spell and resorted to twenty-twenty vision, scanning passing buildings for signs of life.

As the sidewalks thickened with larger mounds of garbage, the rats became more territorial. I knocked aside several with my walking cane. The soul eaters that hunkered like shadows in the below-ground stairwells weren't quite so bold. They watched with hollow eyes before shrinking from the protective power of my necklace, in search of weaker, drug-addled prey. Luckily for them, post-Crash New York was a boomtown for chemical addiction.

Unfortunately for me, the financial crash had also made a growth stock of amateur conjurers.

They tended to be men and women seeking lost money or means—or simply some meaning where their prior faith, whether spiritual or material, seemed to have failed them. Understandable, certainly, but as far as my work went, a royal pain in the ass. Most mortals could only access the nether realms, and shallowly at that. In their fat-fingered efforts, they called up grubby creatures better left undisturbed. Ones more inclined to make a sopping meal of a conjurer's heart than grant his material wishes.

Trust me, it wasn't pretty.

Neither was the job of casting the charming beings back to their realms, but it was the job I'd been decreed. I had some nice acid burns and a missing right ear lobe to prove it. A business card might have read:

Everson Croft
Wizard Garbage Collector

Nice, huh? But unlike the city's striking sanitation workers, I couldn't just walk off the job.

Small messes became big messes, and in magical terms, that was a recipe for ruin. The apocalyptic kind. Better to scoop up the filth, drop it down the hatch, and batten down the lid. Plenty of ancient evils lurked in the Deep Down, their senses attuned to the smallest openings to our world. Human history was dotted with near misses, thanks in part to the vigilance of my lineage.

The thought of being the one to screw up that streak was hell on a good night's sleep, let me tell you.

At Avenue C, I rounded a small mountain of plowed trash and shuffled to a stop. A new scent was skewering the vaporous reek, hooking like a talon in my throat. A sickly-sweet scent, like crushed cockroach or...

Fear spread through me as I raised my eyes toward the source: a steep apartment building with a pair of lights burning near the top floor. Dark magic dissipated above the building in a blood-red haze.

I *was* too late. And whatever the conjurer had summoned was no cockroach.

“Crap,” I spat, and launched into a run.

The smell was distinctly demonic.

2

I stumbled into a blacked-out lobby, raised my ironwood cane, and uttered, *"Illuminare."*

White light swelled from an opal inset in the cane's end to reveal an upended concierge's desk and graffiti-smeared walls. The single elevator door opposite me was open. I moved toward it, noting the message sprayed over the burned-out elevator lights: "STEP RIGHT IN," an arrow inviting riders into a carless shaft. I peeked down the two-story plunge to a subbasement, where I could hear something large thump-dragging around.

No thanks.

I hit the stairwell and took the steps two at a time. The cloying smell from the street sharpened in my sinuses, making my eyes water. I had smelled demon before, but in Eastern Europe, years ago—the near-death experience had marked my passage into wizardhood, in a way.

But no, never here. Not in New York.

Which meant a seriously evil conjurer had slipped under the Order's watchful gaze. I considered sending up a message, but that would take energy I couldn't afford at the moment—not to mention time. The Oracular Order of Magi and Magical Beings was an esteemed and ancient body. Accordingly, they made decisions at a pace on par with the Mendenhall glacier.

That, and I was still on their iffy list for what had happened ten years earlier, during the aforementioned demonic encounter. Never mind that my actions (which, okay, *had* involved summoning an incubus spirit) saved my life, or that I was only twenty-two at the time.

So yeah, the less contact with the Order, the better, I'd since learned.

Between the third and fourth floors, the stairwell began to vibrate. At the fifth floor—the one on which I'd observed the lights from outside—the vibrating became a hammering. I pulled the stairwell door open onto a stink of hard diesel and understood the commotion's source: a gas-powered generator. At the hallway's end, light outlined a door.

I was halfway to the door when a woman's scream pierced the tumult. Jerking my cane into two parts, I gripped a staff in my left hand and a steel sword in my right. A shadow grew around the door a second before it banged open.

The man was six foot ten, easy. Blades of black tattooing scaled his pin-pierced face, giving over to an all-out ink fight on his shaved scalp. Leather and spiked studs stretched over powerful arms holding what looked like a pump-action shotgun.

The sorcerer's bodyguard?

He inclined forward, squinting into the dim hallway. The screaming behind him continued, accompanied now by angry beats and the wail of a guitar. I exhaled and sheathed my sword.

Punks. The literal kind.

"Hey!" Tattoo Face boomed as I retreated back toward the stairwell. "You're missing a kickass set. Blade's only on till two." Then as a further inducement: "Half cover, since you got here late."

I sniffed the air, but the generator's fumes were still clouding over the demon smell. I couldn't fix on a direction. I returned to Tattoo Face, shouting to be heard. "Do you live here?"

He shrugged as he lowered the shotgun. "Live. Squat."

"Seen anyone strange in the building?" I peered past him into the hazy room of head-bangers, the pink-haired singer/screamer—Blade, I presumed—standing on the hearth of a bricked-over fireplace. I decided to rephrase the question. "Anyone who looks like they don't belong?"

Behind all of his ink, the punk's face was surprisingly soft, almost boyish, but it hardened as I stepped more fully into the generator-powered light. I followed his gaze down to where my tweed jacket and dark knit tie peeked from the parting flaps of my trench coat. Beneath his own jacket, he was wearing a bandolier of shotgun shells.

"You a narc or something?" he asked.

I shook my head. "Just looking for someone."

His eyes fell further to my walking cane, which, not to polish my own brass, was at definite odds with someone six feet tall and in his apparent prime. My hairline had receded slightly, but still... Tattoo Face frowned studiously, as though still undecided if he could trust me.

"I help people," I added.

After another moment, he nodded. "Strange guy showed up a couple of weeks ago. Hauled a big trunk upstairs." He raised his eyes. "Unit right above ours. Talks to himself. Same things, over and over."

I sprinted back to the stairwell, not bothering with the usual pretense of a trick knee to explain the cane.

Tattoo Face seemed not to notice. "Blade's on till two!" he shouted after me.

I raised a hand in thanks for the reminder, but I was still mulling the *talks to himself* part. The *over and over* sounded like chanting.

Add them up and I'd found my conjurer.

3

On the sixth floor, the demon stink was back. And gut-rottingly potent. I called more light to my cane and advanced on the door at hallway's end, weathered floorboards creaking underfoot.

The knob turned in my grasp, but one or more bolts were engaged. Crouching, I sniffed near the dark door space and immediately regretted the decision. "Holy *hell*," I whispered against my coat sleeve. The sickly-sweet scent burned all the way up to my brain, like ammonia.

Drawing the sword from my cane, I pointed it at the door and uttered, *"Vigore."*

A force shot down the length of the blade and snapped the bolts. The door blew inward. With another incantation, the light from my staff slid into a curved shield. I crouched, ready for anything, but except for the vibrating coming from one floor down, the space beyond the door was still and silent.

I tested the threshold with the tip of my sword. It broke the plane cleanly, which meant no warding spells.

Odd…

I entered, sword and glowing staff held forward. The unit was a restored tenement that, like many in the East Village, had been written off in the Crash's rumbling wake and left to die. Shadows climbed and fell over a newspaper-littered living room. I crept past sticks of curb-side furniture and a spill of canned goods before ducking beneath a line of hanging boxer briefs, still damp.

Hardly the evil-sorcerer sanctum I'd imagined.

I stuck my light into one of the doorless bedrooms, the silence tense against my eardrums. A thin roll-up mattress lay slipshod on a metal bed frame, dirty sheets puddled around its legs. A cracked window framed the bombed-out ruin of a neighboring building. When a pipe coughed, I wheeled, my gaze falling to a crowded plank-and-cinderblock bookcase.

In the light of my staff, I scanned book spines that might as well have read "Amateur Conjurer." Abrahamic texts, including a Bible, gave way to dime-store spell books and darker tomes, but without organization. Spaghetti shots in the dark. Someone looking for power or answers.

So where had the demon come from? More crucially, where had it gone?

In the neighboring bedroom, I flinched as my gaze met my own hazel eyes in a mirror on the near wall. *Gonna give myself a fricking heart attack.* Opposite the mirror, an oblong table held a scatter of spell-cooking implements. A Bunsen burner stood on one end, its line snaking to a tipped-over propane tank. Beside the tank, a pair of legs protruded.

I rounded the table and knelt beside the fallen conjurer. Parting a spill of dark, greasy hair, I took in a middle-aged male face with Coke-bottle glasses that had fallen askew, magnifying his whiskered right cheek. I recognized some of the conjurers in the city—or thought I did—and I'd never seen this guy. I straightened his glasses and patted his cheek firmly.

"*Hey*," I whispered.

The man choked on a snort, then fell back into his mind-shattered slumber. He was alive, anyway.

I raised my light to the protective circle the man had chalked on the floorboards and no doubt stood inside while casting his summoning spell. A common mistake. Chalk made fragile circles. And a circle only protected spell casters capable of instilling them with power. That excluded most mortals, who weren't designed to channel, much less direct, the ley energies of this world.

They can damn sure act as gateways to other worlds, though.

My gaze shifted to a second circle near the table's far end, this one with a crude pentagram drawn inside. From a toppled pile of ash and animal entrails, a glistening residue slid into an adjacent bathroom.

Crap.

I felt quickly beneath the man's army surplus jacket and exhaled as my hand came back dry. The only reason he wasn't dead or mortally wounded was the recentness of the spell. Demonic creatures summoned from deeper down underwent a period of gestation, usually in a dark, damp space, to fortify their strength. They emerged half blind, drawn by the scent of the conjurer's vital organs, from which they derived even more potency.

That I'd arrived before that had happened was to my advantage. I hoped.

Rising, I crept toward the bathroom.

4

The trail turned dark red over the bathroom's dingy tiles, gobbets of black matter glistening in its wake. By now I was more or less desensitized to the smell, thank God. Through the half-open door, my light shone over a dripping faucet. The end of a free-standing tub glowed beyond.

With a foot, I edged the door wider.

The trail climbed the side of the tub, spread into a foul puddle, then climbed again. This time into a torn-out section of tiling between the shower head and the hot and cold spigots down below.

I adjusted my slick grip on the sword handle. The creature was inside the wall.

My sword hummed as I channeled currents of ley energy. With a *"Vigore!"* I thrust the sword toward the hole.

Tile and plaster exploded over my light shield in a dusty wave. A keening cry went up. In the exposed wall, wedged behind oozing pipes, I saw it. The creature had enfolded its body with a pair of membranous black wings. From a skull-sharp head of bristling hair, a pair of albino-white eyes stared blindly. Before I could push the attack, the creature screamed again.

The jagged sound became a weapon. Waves as sharp as the creature's barbed teeth pierced my thoughts and fractured my casting prism. I was dealing with a shrieker. A lower demonic being but ridiculously deadly—even to wizards.

Awesome.

My light shield wavered in front of me, then burst in a shower of sparks. The energetic release thrust me backwards as the room fell dark, my right heel catching the threshold. A squelch sounded, followed by the shallow splash of the thing dropping into the tub.

I flailed for balance but went down. My right elbow slammed into the floor, sending a numbing bolt up and down my arm. When metal clanged off behind me, I realized I'd lost my sword.

Beyond my outstretched legs, claws scrabbled over porcelain.

I kick-scooted away, sweeping an arm back for my weapon.

Wings slapped the air, the wet sound swallowed by the shrieker's next cry. Abandoning my search, I thrust my staff into the darkness above my face. The end struck something soft. A claw hooked behind my right orbital bone before tearing away, missing my eyeball by a breath.

I felt the shrieker flap past me, still clumsy in its just-summoned state. No doubt going for the conjurer. But if I was going to stop it, I had to do something about the damned screaming.

Blood dribbled down the side of my face as I sat up. Praying the shrieker wasn't rounding back on me, I jammed a finger into each ear. With the screaming muted, I repeated a centering mantra.

Within seconds, the mental prism through which I converted ley energy into force and light reconstituted. A white orb swelled from the end of my staff, illuminating the apartment once more. I quickly touched the staff to each ear, uttering Words of Power. Shields of light energy covered them like muffs, blocking out the shrieker's cries.

I scooped up my sword and raised both sword and staff, expecting to find the shrieker hunched over the splayed-out conjurer. But the conjurer was alone, the shrieker nowhere in sight. The animal entrails were missing from the summoning circle, though, meaning it had fed.

Not good.

I raised my light toward the windows to ensure they were still intact. Remembering the blown-open front door, I hurried to the main room, terrified the creature had gotten out and into the city's six-million-person buffet. I ducked beneath the clothesline and felt the newspapers at my feet gusting up. I spun to find the abomination flapping at my face.

"Vigore!" I cried.

The wave-like force from my sword blasted the shrieker into a corner of the ceiling. It dropped onto a radiator, then tumbled wetly to the floor. I repeated the Word, but the shrieker scrabbled behind a wooden chair and darted into the bedroom. The chair blew apart in its stead.

I pursued and, guessing the creature's next move, aimed my staff at the near window. *"Protezione!"*

The light shield that spread over the glass held long enough for the shrieker to bounce from it. The shrieker launched itself at the window beside it, but I cast first. More sparks fell away as it beat its wings up and down the protected window like a flailing moth.

"You're not going anywhere, you little imp."

Only it wasn't so little anymore. The bed jumped when the shrieker dropped onto the headboard, taloned feet gripping the metal bar. The white caul over its eyes was thinning, too, goat-like pupils peering out. As I crept nearer, the creature's appearance stirred in me equal parts fascination and revulsion. Its wings spread to reveal a wrinkled body mapped in throbbing black vessels.

Okay, now it was just revulsion.

The shrieker put everything into its next scream. The light energy over my right ear broke apart. A sensation like shattered glass filled my head. Hunching my shoulder to my naked ear, I threw my weight into a sword thrust and grunted as hot fluid sprayed over me.

The shrieker fell silent, staring at me as though trying to comprehend what I had done. Its eyes fell to the sword, which had skewered its chest and driven a solid inch into the wall behind it. But it wasn't enough to physically wound such creatures. They had to be dispersed.

"Disfare," I shouted, concentrating force along the blade.

The shrieker's wings trembled, then began to flail. Unfortunately, the more power it took to summon a creature into our world, the more power it required to send it back. And the homeless appearance of the conjurer aside, some damned powerful magic had called this thing up.

"Disfare!" I repeated, louder.

The shrieker thrashed more fiercely, the tarry fluid that bubbled from its mouth drowning its hideous cry. But its form remained intact. And I was pushing my limits, a lead-like fatigue beginning to weigh on my limbs. The shrieker's wings folded down, and a pair of bat-like hands seized the blade.

"What the…?"

The creature gave a pull and skewered itself toward me.

"Hey, stop that!" I yelled pointlessly.

I pressed my glowing staff against its chin, but with another tug, the shrieker was an inch closer. It snapped at my staff with gunky teeth, then swiped with a clawed hand, narrowly missing my reared-back face.

I considered ditching my sword, but then what? I wasn't dealing with flesh and blood here. The second the shrieker came off the hilt, it would reconfigure itself, becoming larger and more powerful. And if it overwhelmed me, the conjurer would be next, followed by the head-bangers one floor down. An image of the party as a bloody scene of carnage jagged through my mind's eye.

"DISFARE!" I boomed.

A tidal wave of energy burst from my mental prism, shook down the length of my arm, through my sword, and then out the creature. I squeezed my eyes closed as the creature's gargling shriek cut off and an explosion of foul-smelling ectoplasm nearly knocked me down.

There was a reason I'd waterproofed my coat, and it wasn't for the shiny look.

I opened my eyes to a steamy, tar-spattered room and exhaled. The shrieker was gone, cast back to its hellish pit.

But at a price.

The edges of my thoughts swam in creamy waves, a sensation that heralded the impending arrival of Thelonious. That incubus spirit I called up a decade ago? He was still around, clinging to my spirit like a parasite. Despite that he was thousands of years old, I pictured him as a cool cat in black shades and a glittering 'fro—probably because he shared a name with a famous musician. And my Thelonious had a jazzy way about him. As long as I didn't push my limits, I could keep him at bay. Cross that line, and I became a vessel for Thelonious's, ahem, festivities.

And yeah, I'd just crossed that line.

More creamy waves washed in. I would have to work quickly.

The demonic gunk was evaporating as I drew my sword from the wall. I cleaned the blade against the thigh of my coat, resheathed it, and then returned to the fallen conjurer. Still out. I shone my light over his table, pocketing samples of spell ingredients for later study.

"But where oh where is the recipe?" I muttered.

I stopped at the flaky ashes of what appeared to have been a piece of college-ruled paper. The spell must have contained an incineration component, meant to destroy evidence of its origin.

"Naturally."

Sliding my cane into the belt of my coat, I stooped for the conjurer. "Up you go," I grunted. His head lolled as I carried him into the bedroom. I set him on the mattress, arranged his arms and legs into a semblance of order, then shook out the sheet and spread it over him.

His mortal mind was blown, but not beyond repair.

I touched my cane to the center of his brow and uttered ancient Words of healing. He murmured as a cottony light grew from the remaining power in the staff. The healing would take time, which was just as well. In a few more minutes, I wouldn't be in much shape to question him.

"I'll be back in a couple of days," I told the snoring man.

The creamy waves crested, spilling into my final wells of free will. There was no good place to go now except away from people. I was turning to leave when my—or I should say, Thelonious's—gaze fell to the space beneath the bed. A half-full bottle of tannic liquid leaned against one of the legs.

I felt my lips stretch into a grin. *Bourbon*, Thelonious purred in his bass voice.

My final memory of that night, the fire of alcohol in my throat, was tottering down a hallway toward a shaking generator and the siren screams of a pink-haired punker named Blade.

Ooh, yeah...

5

Swollen eyelids cracked open onto a room wall-papered in album jackets and cast in the gray light of morning. I was on a mattress on the floor, no doubt in the punk rockers' apartment. I managed to extricate my naked torso from a tangle of sheets and sit up. The room revolved, making my brain hurt.

"Sweet Jesus," I muttered, dragging a hand through my salt-stiff hair, then clamping my temples.

A mean smell of smoke lingered in my sinuses and beneath it, the cloying stink of last night's shrieker. Not a pleasant combo, especially when you threw in a cheap eighty-proof hangover.

At least the apartment was quiet, everyone probably still asleep.

I drew the sheets from my legs. Evidently, I'd managed to retain my boxers and a single gray sock. That didn't always happen. *Oh, wait.* I looked again. The sock wasn't mine.

Time to go.

I stood and began shuffling around in search of my clothes and cane. My goal was to get at least ten blocks away before anyone awakened. Lord only knew what Thelonious had gotten up to last—

"Morning," a woman's voice said.

I wheeled to find pink spikes of hair jutting from a narrow tube of bedding at the mattress's far side. The hair framed a face that, despite its resting surliness and dozens of painful-looking piercings, possessed a hard beauty.

My cheeks burned with blood. *Did we...? Had we...?*

She must have read my panic. "Relax." Thin, tattoo-stained arms emerged from the sheets and stretched overhead. She continued to speak as she yawned. "I don't do charity cases."

I felt my brow furrow. "Charity?"

She smacked on the last of her yawn. "I did fix your eye, though."

My hand floated to where the shrieker had gouged me. The place beside my right brow was padded with gauze and tape. "Thanks?" I said.

"Your stuff's over there." She jutted her spade-shaped chin, also pierced, at a wooden dresser in the corner. My clothes were folded neatly on top, my cane lying horizontally over the stack. "But let's get one thing straight. *You* were responsible for the strip tease, not me."

Not knowing how to respond, I nodded meekly. I heard her resettle on the mattress.

"Hey, listen," I said, shaking out my trousers and stepping into them. I'd already swapped the gray sock for my own. "Blade, right? Whatever I did last night, Blade, I'm really sorry. I'm not normally like that."

I buckled up and patted my pockets, relieved to feel my wallet and keys. That didn't always happen, either.

"I don't know too many who are," Blade said in a smoky voice. "You're a real original."

"What exactly did...? Forget it. I don't want to know."

She smiled mysteriously and propped her elbows behind her. "So, what's your name?"

Inventing one felt like too much work. "Everson," I replied.

"And where does Everson dwell?"

"West Village." I jerked my head, though I had no idea which direction was which.

"Really?" Interest glinted in her dark eyes as she watched me configure my tie into a Windsor knot. "You strike me as, I don't know, more Midtown. When you're sober, anyway."

"I actually—" A dreadful realization struck me. I grabbed my mechanical watch from the dresser and stared at its face. "Oh, crap."

"What's the matter?"

"I'm late." I snatched up my coat and cane and made for the door.

"For what?" Blade was sitting up now, sheets pressed to her stark breastbone.

"My morning class."

Her brow wrinkled. "You're a student?"

"No," I called back. "Professor."

6

It was a quarter past eight when I slipped into the hallowed halls of Midtown College, the first classes of the day already underway.

I stopped off in the faculty bathroom upstairs, where I kept a spare toiletry bag, relieved to find the room empty. There hadn't been time to go home, and I already knew by my reflection in the subway's scratched-up window that I looked a wreck. The bathroom mirror confirmed this with even more candor.

In the space of a minute, I pulled a wet comb through my hair, washed my puffy face, and jagged a toothbrush around my mouth. I finished with a few drops of Visine in each eye. The demon gunk had evaporated from my coat, but the same couldn't be said for the blood on my jacket collar. Rubbing it with a wet paper towel only smeared it around.

Maybe it was time to stow a spare set of clothes up here as well.

I arrived at my classroom to find Caroline Reid sitting at the head of the circular arrangement of desks, lecturing on something. Which was to say she was covering my ass again. She glanced over and caught me watching her through the door window. Her lips tensed into a smile that barely dimpled her cheeks and fell far short of her blue-green eyes.

Caroline was a brilliant scholar of urban history and affairs. Her classroom/office was adjacent to mine, which I think we both considered my blessing and her burden. More than once I'd entertained the thought of being more than friends, but I was smart enough to know *that* feeling wasn't mutual. Besides, she was currently seeing some accountant stud—an oxymoron, I know.

Caroline stood and smoothed her coffee-brown slacks as I opened the door. "And with that, I'll hand off to Professor Croft," she announced.

"Much obliged, Professor Reid," I said. "Truly."

She looked over my stained and crumpled shirt as she approached, her own shirt a neat beige blouse, waves of golden hair shifting over the shoulders. I adjusted the knot of my tie, as if it made any difference.

"Heads up," she whispered, when she'd drawn even. "Snodgrass is on the lookout for you again."

My stomach sank at the mention of our department chairman, but I didn't let it show.

"Appreciate the warning," I whispered back. Her faint honey scent reminded me that for the last ten hours I'd inhaled nothing even remotely pleasant—and no doubt smelled the part.

"Just be careful," she said.

"Will do. And hey, I owe you for..." I nodded toward the classroom.

"All right, but this is the last time." She raised her slender eyebrows. "I'm serious."

She'd been threatening to let me hang for more than a year now, but I didn't dare point that out. Instead, I thanked her again, bowing slightly. She gave a final tight-lipped smile that said, *You're better than this*, before stepping out. That stung. Of course she knew nothing about my second job and how close the greater East Village had come to being shrieker meat.

I exhaled as I closed the door behind her and cane-tapped toward my students.

All six of them.

In the wake of the Crash, graduate students were less willing to spend their tuition money on courses entitled *Ancient Mythology and Lore*. I couldn't exactly fault them. There wasn't a glut of job openings in the field, something our department chair was all too happy to point out.

But the Order seemed to believe the course might attract natural magic users who, for various reasons, had fallen through the cracks. Indeed, given the current budget crunch, the only thing keeping me employed at Midtown College were my research grants, all of them from foundations just stuffy-sounding enough to discourage scrutiny. I'd long interpreted the grants as measures of the Order's pleasure with my work. Lately, though, the amounts had been dwindling. And teaching was my sole source of income.

"All right." I clapped my hands once and eased into a seat still warm with Caroline's heat. I'd left my satchel with all of my notes at home, and hadn't the faintest what was on the syllabus for today. "How did the reading go?"

I was already checking out as I asked, contemplating last night's demonic summoning and who might have supplied the conjurer the spell and to what end and what I would need to do to find out. It was serious business. I finally noticed the students' puzzled faces.

"What reading?" one of them asked.

"Oh. The, ah..." I twisted around to face the chalkboard I sometimes wrote on. Whatever I'd last scrawled up there was dated September 14, and it was now late October. "Didn't I...?"

"We're still working on our literature reviews," another student spoke up, sparing me further bumbling. "For our term papers?"

"Right." I remembered now. "Excellent. And how are those going?"

I directed the question to a young woman sitting to my right. To my knowledge, no magic-born types had passed through my door, but every semester saw at least one overachiever. This semester it was Meredith Proctor.

"Me?" she asked, straightening her cat-eye glasses.

I nodded in encouragement. She was the one undergraduate student in my graduate-level course, and for good reason. She had the gift of gab and the smarts to back it up. Once she got going, I'd be able to slip back into problem-solving mode, *hmm*ing here and there in pretended interest, asking open-ended questions. It made me a less-than-exemplary professor, but there was demon magic afoot.

Meredith cleared her throat. "Actually, I found your thesis paper in the library—on the roots of medieval European beliefs?"

"Extra credit if you burned it," I said to laughter.

"No, no, it was fascinating." She blinked beneath her brunette bangs and leaned forward. "I was hoping you could tell us about it."

Well, that went nowhere fast.

"Please?" she pressed.

The paper to which she was referring had been a biggie, actually, placing me on the academic map. I still took a certain pride in it, even if it had chaffed some religious denominations. "Well, as a graduate student, I'd heard stories of an abandoned monastery deep in the Carpathian Mountains. Its founding monks were rumored to have transcribed several ancient texts believed lost. For my PhD dissertation I went to Romania in search of them." I shrugged modestly. "Lo and behold, the stories were true."

"That is so cool," the lone male student, a goateed beatnik, said.

The other students nodded, faces rapt. Wizards' tales tended to have that effect. I hadn't told them the entire truth, though. I actually went to Romania looking for a certain occult book I hoped would uncover the mystery of who my peculiar grandfather had been—and who I was. Finding the other works in the monastery's vault of forbidden texts had been a happy accident.

Meredith raised her hand, a hint of boldness in her fluttering fingers. "I was especially intrigued by your theory of that one legend being a precursor to the stories of the seven deadly sins."

"Ah, yes. *The First Saints Legend*."

I could see by the students' intent faces that I was going to have to give at least a Cliff's Notes version of the legend. I began by presenting an overview of the period in which the story had its oral roots, in ancient Rome. The legend was later transcribed into Latin, deemed heretical for challenging the Biblical stories of Satan and Michael, and then lost to history.

"I read where a coalition of church leaders attacked your findings," Meredith said.

"Well, not physically," I replied, to another flutter of laughter. "But, yes, that's one of the occupational hazards of scholarship in our field."

"So what's the legend, Prof?" the beatnik asked.

"Right." I checked my watch. "In the earliest days, nine elemental demons were said to inhabit the world. They seeded discontent, sowed misery, and terrorized humankind. Not exactly stand-up guys. In response, the Creator sent nine saints, their virtues the antitheses of the demons' sins."

As I spoke, the students settled in. I felt the ley energy in the room drawing toward their circle of desks, as though listening too. I wasn't calling that energy. A wizard's story-telling voice, coupled with an interested—and, yes, impressionable—audience, was usually all it took.

"For hundreds of years," I continued, "the two sides battled until there remained only three demons and three saints. They battled for a millennia more. Demons held the advantage during the dark of night, the saints during the day. Similarly, the demons gained ground in the winter months, when the world turned dark and brittle." A subtle chill descended, and Meredith hugged her arms. "The saints did the same in the summer months, when light and life prevailed."

Though I didn't describe the battle in words, I could sense my students slipping out of time, experiencing the struggle on a deep limbic level. Their pupils expanded beneath hooded eyelids.

"At last, they agreed to an accord," I said. "Both sides would retreat from the world and no more involve themselves in matters of humankind. But it was a trick. Following the agreement, the demons slew two of the saints." Several students flinched. "The third and most powerful of the saints, Michael, escaped. He represented Faith. Through his strength and virtue, he ultimately overcame and banished the three remaining demon lords: Belphegor, Beezlebub, and, finally, the terrible demon Sathanas, who represented Wrath."

"Sathanas was the precursor to Satan," Meredith said in a distant monotone.

"In the traditional sense, yes," I replied. "Saint Michael's work wasn't done, however. During their time in the world, the demon lords had taken many human concubines, their offspring precursors to the night creatures: vampires, werewolves, ghouls, other monstrosities. In answer, Michael wed a peasant girl, and they began a family of their own. Their sons and daughters became the progenitors of powerful lines of mages meant to balance the darkness of the night creatures."

I wasn't about to tell my students that I was a descendant of one such line. But it was true—on my mother's side. Sensing I needed to wrap up, I began expelling energy from the circle.

"So, the *First Saints Legend* gave rise not just to later versions of the seven deadly sins—even though there were nine original demons—but to many of the creature and magic myths that persist to this day. Indeed, they're all around us." *Much more literally than you kids realize*, I thought, glancing at my watch. "Oops, we went over again."

I clapped sharply to break the remaining energy in the circle. The students started as though coming out of trances, which they were.

"Keep working on those lit reviews," I said as they stood and gathered notebooks and backpacks. "I have to cancel office hours tomorrow, so we'll meet again Monday afternoon." That would clear my schedule to follow up on last night's summoning and learn exactly what I was dealing with.

I waited for the students to file out, Meredith's gaze lingering on me from the hallway, then grabbed a folder of ungraded student papers from my desk, tucked it under an arm, and aimed for the door myself. I had just locked up when a prim voice sounded behind me.

"Well, if it isn't the elusive Professor Croft."

Recalling Caroline's warning too late, I closed my eyes and exhaled through my nose.

"Professor Snodgrass," I said.

"Can you can spare a minute, I wonder?"

Not really, you self-important jerk.

"Yeah, sure."

7

With a priggish clearing of his throat, Professor Snodgrass settled behind a behemoth desk that swallowed his five-two frame, making him look like a boy playing in his father's office. In many ways, he was. Family connections, and not scholarship, had elevated him to chairman of the history department. He adjusted his plaid bow tie, then clasped his small fingers on the desktop.

"We have a problem, Professor Croft."

"Is that right?" I dropped into one of the ridiculously steep wingback chairs facing him.

"Several, I should say. For starters, you were late to your own class again."

"The subway broke down."

His right eyebrow arched. "Your colleagues had no trouble arriving on time." He gave a pointed sniff. "They also managed to arrive without the stink of alcohol emanating from their pores."

"That's aftershave," I lied again. "Purchased from a street vendor, granted."

"And yet, you're clearly unshaven," he said, touching his smooth chin. I remembered my own jaw as it had appeared in the restroom mirror: steel-blue with bristles. He had me there. "And how do you explain the rumpled condition of your suit—didn't I see you in the same one yesterday? Or the unsightly stains on your collar. We have a professional code of appearance, you know."

I lifted a gunky shoe. "Do you think it's cheap keeping these kickers shined?"

I wasn't typically such a smartass. Or as much of one, anyway. My headache and underslept state had a lot to do with it. That and the fact he'd chosen the morning after a demon summoning to re-air his list of petty grievances—an event that would have reduced a man like Snodgrass to a shitting wreck.

Although Snodgrass was my boss, he had little power in the matter of hiring and firing, thank God. That responsibility rested with the college board. Whether or not they shared Snodgrass's low opinion of my character, they certainly liked the grants I hauled in. Not to mention that my student reviews were generally stellar. That no doubt irked Snodgrass all the more. His department meetings put grown men and women to sleep, so I could only imagine what his students thought of him.

"I'm glad you find this all so amusing, Professor Croft," he said. "But some other concerns have come to light that go more to the heart of your role at the college." Snodgrass, who agitated easily, remained oddly composed. No lip twitching or obsessive fingering of his little oval glasses. Instead, he gave a knowing chuckle, which I did not like.

I fought the urge to swallow. "Such as...?"

"Well, you already know how I feel about your course. Ancient mythology and lore hardly qualifies as academia. It comes across as pop scholarship and more than a little ... occultish."

I rankled at the suggestion, even coming from him. History might help explain the mundane world, but it was mythology that lent insight into the forces that *supported* the mundane—

"Given the present budget constraints," he continued, "as well as dwindling interest in your course, I made my recommendation to the board that it be dropped from the catalogue."

"Again?" I feigned a yawn.

His lips pinched, but not in irritation. He was trying not to grin.

That got me. Against my better judgment, I pushed back. "And I'm betting the board reminded you that I bring in half the research grants of this department."

"Oh, let's not exaggerate," he said, clucking his tongue. "It's more on the order of thirty percent—and trending down. And there have been no grants so far this semester, am I correct?"

"They're pending," I muttered.

"But yes, the board *is* impressed by your grants. I'll give you that. What they're far less impressed by, however, is news of your criminality."

"My what?"

He lifted a stapled-together packet from a neat wire tray and tossed it forward.

Heat spread over my face as I lifted the packet from his desk.

"Last summer you were picked up at an apartment in Hell's Kitchen," he said. "The scene of a murder. You were in an intoxicated state. When you sobered, you claimed to know nothing, remember nothing. And yet the victim's blood was on your hands and clothes. The NYPD had their theories, but without a murder weapon or apparent motive, there was little they could do except charge you with obstruction. You're currently serving a two-year probation."

Hand to my frowning chin, I read over the police report, even though I already knew it line for line. Long story short, I had failed to get to a conjurer in time, then exhausted my powers banishing the tentacled creature he had called up—not unlike what happened last night. Only in the Hell's Kitchen case, I failed to escape the scene before Thelonious took over and evidently discovered the liquor cabinet.

I could feel Snodgrass's smirking eyes on me as I flipped to the court order.

I had foolishly believed these reports would remain buried beneath a growing mountain of unprocessed paperwork. Like most city services, the criminal justice budget had been slashed to the bone. Dysfunction and backlogging, problematic even in the best of times, had rocketed to new heights. For almost a year, the reports *had* stayed buried.

Meaning the son of a bitch had gone digging.

Snodgrass brushed the stiff lapels of his double-breasted suit with the back of a hand. "Shouldn't you have reported all of this to the college?" he asked.

I opened my mouth to suggest there was more to the story, but he cut me off.

"Save it for the board, Mr. Croft. I've proposed a hearing for Monday morning. You'll have an opportunity to make your case then. I suspect it will take more than another grant—or even a stack of fawning reviews—to convince them of your fitness to continue teaching here." His eyes sparkled with delight. "The board takes such matters *very* seriously."

I turned to the last page of the court order, which enumerated the conditions of my probation: remain in the state, no drugs or alcohol, consent to searches... The next item hit my memory like a cattle prod. I jumped from the chair. Snodgrass flinched back, as though I intended to knock him from his perch, but that wasn't where I was headed. Cane in hand, I spun toward the office door.

"Professor *Croft*," he scolded, recovering himself. "I haven't dismiss—"

"Save it, chief. Gotta run."

The window glass gave a satisfying rattle as I slammed the office door behind me. But it didn't change the fact I was late again. This time for a meeting with my probation officer.

8

At the entrance to the subway station, I drew a deep breath. It was partly in anticipation of the stale-urine odor but more so that I had, well, a phobia of going underground. A skin-prickling, airway-constricting, almost full-blown anxiety. Not something I was proud of. The origins of the phobia weren't entirely clear. My therapist and I had been trying to get to the source before wizarding became too costly for me to afford him any longer. I still had his card somewhere.

I plunged down the stairwell and, approaching the turnstile, exhaled at the sound of a south-bound train squealing toward the station. Movement helped the condition. I swiped my transit card, hurried onto the platform, and boarded a rear car.

Edging to the back of a compartment crowded with the barely making it and the beaten down, I checked my watch. My meeting was at ten. If the track was clear, I'd be no more than fifteen minutes late. Not terrible—assuming my officer was in a good mood, which happened sometimes. If I had a cell phone, I could have called him, but wizards and technology? Yeah. Payphones were a surer bet, but I wasn't toting any change. Plus, there was no guarantee I'd get through the warren of extensions to his office.

If nothing else, it gave me something more immediate than my demotion to the bread lines to worry about.

At Fourteenth Street, the train lurched to a crawl. The Broadway line and its east-west services had been out for more than five years, doubling traffic on the Lexington line. Promises to have the routes restored had run into budget shortfalls, not to mention the mysterious disappearance of a team of surveyors. All sorts of theories had been floated regarding their fate—they got lost, suffocated on the foul air, etc.—but the stark, bone-crunching truth was that the defunct tunnels were now infested with ghouls.

Not my beat, thankfully.

At the stop for City Hall, I burst up into the gunmetal light and dodged the traffic on Centre Street. Beyond the municipal building, the cube-shaped fortress of One Police Plaza took shape. I was joining the line at the pedestrian checkpoint when a Bronx-sharp voice called from my right.

"You're a half hour late."

I spun and nearly fumbled my cane. The woman striding toward me was dressed in a no-nonsense suit, black blouse, midnight hair pulled from a striking Latin face, one that managed to appear youthful and veteran at the same time. That was what Homicide did to a third-year detective, I supposed.

"Technically, you're in violation of your probation."

She would know. She was the one who had arrested me.

"Detective Vega," I managed. Hooking a thumb back the way I'd come, I stammered, "The subway, ah, hit a snarl."

"Save it." She seized my wrist with a small but manacle-tense grip. "Let's go."

I was resigning myself to arrest—could the day get any crappier?—when I noticed she was marching me away from the thirteen-story headquarters. I stumbled to keep pace, even though I had a good foot of height on her. My cane wasn't doing anything for her sympathy, apparently. We arrived beside a scraped-up sedan parked over the curb. Opening the passenger side door, she all but swung me inside. I raised a finger. "Um, where exactly are—?"

She slammed the door.

The driver side door cannoned opened, and she dropped behind the wheel. "I had the pleasure of meeting your department chair last week," she said, throwing the gearshift into drive. The car jumped from the curb and into traffic. "He told me you're a professor of the arcane?"

So that's where Snodgrass had gotten the report.

"Ancient mythology and lore, actually. It's a graduate-level course." Or *was*.

Detective Vega gave no sign she'd heard me as she swung south onto Park Row and switched on the siren. Cars honked and edged from her path. She accelerated, knocking past an obstinate taxi. Not even a backward glance.

"How are you with ancient languages?"

"Huh?" When I realized I was white-knuckling the door handle, I relaxed my grip and brought both hands to my cane. "Ancient languages? Not bad. I mean, I'm fluent in a couple, familiar with several others."

"Good."

I waited for more, but her dark eyes remained narrowed on the traffic in front of her. It was the same ruthless look she'd fixed on my court-appointed attorney while testifying against me last fall.

Police Plaza disappeared behind us. "Hey, uh, what about my meeting with the probation officer?"

Instead of answering, Detective Vega lowered her window. We were entering the shadow of the barrier that separated the Financial District from the rest of Manhattan. I dipped my head to take in the grim concrete span. Following the Crash, public outrage had fallen on the banking class. Detonating bombs around their buildings had become a popular pastime.

Now Wall Street featured an actual wall again, even if it was located a few blocks north, on Liberty Street. No small irony there.

At an entrance for official vehicles, Detective Vega held up the ID that dangled around her neck. Armored guards in shield sunglasses looked from her to me, then motioned us through with assault rifles. The skyscraper-lined corridors beyond were strangely silent.

"There's been a murder at St. Martin's," Detective Vega said.

I stiffened. "The cathedral?" Sited on a fount of ley energy, it was the oldest and among the most powerful places of worship in the city.

"No, the Caribbean island," she replied, giving me a dry look. *And you're a professor?* it seemed to ask. I'd gotten that look a few times. "I'm not going into details other than to say the rector's body was found in the church sacristy this morning. There was some writing at the scene our language people couldn't make sense of. They're thinking it's ancient."

Well, that explained things. “And you want to see if I can decipher it?”

“Boy, you’re sharp.”

“What are you offering?”

When her eyebrows pressed together, I remembered how quick she was to anger. “Excuse me?” she challenged.

“You’re contracting my services, right? Shouldn’t there be a fee or something?”

While it was true I could use the extra money, this was about getting some things straight. First, probation or not, I wasn’t hers to muscle around. I had enough going on in my own life at the moment. Second, we weren’t friends. I didn’t owe her any kindnesses. Especially since she was the reason I was about to get drop-kicked from Midtown College. If she wanted her back scratched, she was damn sure going to run her nails up and down mine.

Hmm. Probably could have phrased that better.

“Your *fee*,” she said evenly, “is me not collaring your ass for failure to show. How’s that sound?”

I shook my head against the rest. “Nice try.”

“What?”

“You didn’t know I was going to be late. You parked with a view of the checkpoint well before I showed up. Forty minutes, I’m guessing.” I nodded toward the hood. “Engine was cold.”

She glanced over as though taking some measure of me.

While it was true wizards possessed an enhanced awareness, catching subtleties that most overlooked, I was presently blowing an ass-load of smoke. I had no idea what temperature the engine had been.

“It doesn’t change the fact you were late,” she said.

She'd bought the bluff, but I could see she wasn't going to budge on her position.

"Well, what were you *preparing* to offer?" I asked.

She blinked twice quickly. A tell.

"All right," I said, drumming my fingers over my cane as I thought aloud. "You had no intention of paying me. I'm on probation, a criminal. I know how that would look—even inside the NYPD. I get it. So, I'm guessing it was some kind of commutation of my sentence?"

Another rapid blink.

"A year?" I pressed, my heart already accelerating at the possibility. A year would take care of the second half of my probation. I'd be a free man. And if, come Monday's hearing, I was no longer under the NYPD's thumb, I might actually have a crack at saving my job.

"A month," Detective Vega countered sharply.

My hope shattered like a clay pigeon. I could see in her set expression she wasn't going to let herself be talked into a full year. She already hated that I'd made her feel transparent. My mistake, I realized now.

We were slowing past a police cordon and into a mayhem of squad cars that fronted St. Martin's. Detective Vega knifed into a too-small space and twisted to look me full in the face.

"*If* whatever information you provide leads to an arrest," she said, "I'll consider upping it to six."

I understood some wizards could peer into souls. It wasn't a gift I possessed—or even desired, for that matter—but I *had* developed a decent ability to read people. And what I saw beyond the façade of Detective Vega's hard eyes was the bone-weary fatigue of a detective whose resources were being stripped at the same time murders in the city were soaring. She needed all the breaks she could get.

"A year," I tried again.

"Six months."

I glimpsed something else, but before it took on contours, Vega turned and banged her door into the squad car beside ours. Conversation over.

After edging out, she paced toward an approaching officer who looked to be managing the outdoor scene. When she pointed back in my direction, I squeezed out too, though with less property damage. I stood with my cane, peering at the cathedral's stately bronze doors, then up the soaring Gothic spire shimmering with ley energy. Back down, to the right, tombstones stood in the gated churchyard I used to play in. I had attended St. Martin's as a boy, when my family still lived in the city.

"Hey!" Detective Vega had finished signing in with the officer and was waving for me to follow.

I eyed the wrought doors of the cathedral again, sweat breaking across my upper back. I mentioned my phobia of being underground? Places of worship were almost as anxiety-causing. In this case, though, it wasn't that such places repulsed me, but that I seemed to repulse them.

"Croft!" she snapped.

I watched her watching me, one hand bracing the strong curve of her cocked hip. Her NYPD shield glinted at her belt, and I could see the bulge of a sidearm holstered beside it, beneath her jacket. Six months was no guarantee of salvation, but it *was* half my remaining sentence.

I took a deep breath and made my head nod.

"Coming."

9

My legs seemed to be hauling large iron balls as I ascended the three steps leading to the set of bronze doors. Detective Vega powered right between them, but I had to stop.

In addition to being places of worship, religious houses had a long history of providing sanctuary against evil. The longer-standing the house, the stronger the protection—especially if the house stood on a fount of ley energy. The protection was felt most palpably at thresholds, and St. Martin's threshold was all but thrusting me back into the street.

It wasn't that I was evil, but I had that little Thelonious problem. He wasn't demonic, per se, but as an incubus, he gave off a similar vibe. And thresholds weren't in the business of splitting hairs.

I peered past the doorway into the vaulted interior. Detective Vega was already passing through a propped-open set of glass doors to the deep pew-lined nave, where police personnel consulted and a few robed church officials drifted in monastic sorrow. Realizing I wasn't behind her, Vega turned and gestured sharply.

"*Croft*," she whispered.

At the sound of my name, one of the church officials raised his head and moved toward me. He wore a white tunic over a long black cassock. What looked like a grieving stole, heavy and dark, draped his neck. When his face swam from the gloom, I recognized him.

"Is that Everson Croft?" he asked, stopping a few feet from me. His parted red hair was going white, I saw. And he sported a trim beard now, denser around his lips, like an unintended goatee. But his eyes were the same seashell blue I remembered from childhood.

"Father Victor," I said, smiling.

He had been in charge of the youth programs when I attended, and I remembered him as good-humored and kind, a natural with kids. He had risen in the church ranks since, and word on the supernatural street was that he performed shadow exorcisms. My kind of guy.

"Please, I still go by Vick," he said. "How long has it been? Fifteen years?"

"Closer to twenty." I caught myself stubbing a toe against the concrete. Even though Father Vick's tone wasn't the least bit insinuating, my long absenteeism still stirred up a cloud of guilt. I struggled to meet his eyes. "Listen," I said, "I'm really sorry about your rector."

I hadn't known the man. The rector from my time had retired, his replacement coming from another diocese.

Father Vick nodded. “Yes. A terrible thing.”

“I’m actually here to help with the investigation, as a consultant.”

I peeked past him to where Detective Vega appeared on her last nerve.

Father Vick stepped to one side and made a humble gesture with his arm. “Please, do come in.”

At those words, the threshold relented. Invitations to enter calmed them. A clammy wave of nausea rippled through me as I stepped inside, but it was better than being burned like a square of toast. Even so, I felt a good chunk of my wizarding powers fall away.

That was something else thresholds could do.

Father Vick placed a comforting hand on my upper back and guided me into the nave. Something about his touch, which hummed with the supernatural power of faith, and the fact he was two inches taller than me, evoked memories of being a young parishioner here.

“Thank you,” I said, the sanctity of the cathedral reducing my voice to a whisper.

“I know you have work to do,” he said, “but I hope we’ll have the opportunity to catch up soon.”

He slipped a card into my hand as he left me with Detective Vega.

“Old friend?” she asked when he was out of earshot.

“Something like that.” I tucked his card into my pocket.

“Well, don’t get too cozy. At this point everyone in here’s a suspect.”

I snorted. “Reminds me of another case.”

She shot me a dark look. We both knew the NYPD hadn't had sufficient cause to try me. But in their nigh-impossible campaign to clear cases, all sorts of protocols were being skirted, if not sledge-hammered. Though I hadn't been charged with murder, getting the obstruction charge to stick had no doubt been sufficient to toss the case into the "good enough" basket.

"Here," she said, clipping a plastic card to my coat lapel, the big NYPD letters stamped in yellow.

"Am I being deputized?"

She frowned. "This way."

I followed her down the cathedral's center aisle. To either side, muted light fell through steep Gothic windows. Ahead of us, a majestic stained-glass window glowed softly. During services, I used to study its depiction of hallowed saints and angels, one of them my forebear, Michael. The sections of colored glass seemed to endow them with magic. With that pleasant memory came others: the smells of starched suits and faint perfumes, the warmth of the cushioned pew beside my Nana, her hand absently stroking my hair.

Grandpa had never joined us, for reasons I wouldn't understand until much later.

We climbed the wooden steps to the chancel, ducked under a ribbon of police tape, and rounded a cloth-draped altar. A pair of policemen stood guard at a door on the left. A table beside them held a set of cardboard cartons.

"The body's still inside, but it's covered," Vega told me. "We're waiting on forensics, so you'll need to put these on."

She had been yanking disposable gloves and shoe covers from the cartons and now shoved a pair of each into my hands. She had everything on before I'd even figured out the gloves. I had just pulled on the second shoe cover when a hairnet snapped over my ears. Detective Vega, in a blue hairnet of her own, stuffed my stray strands beneath the elastic with a studious frown that might have been endearing if she weren't going about the job so roughly.

She stood back and looked me over. "I hope I don't have to tell you that anything you see or hear is strictly confidential. You tell so much as your cat, and the deal's off. Got it?"

"Got it," I said.

I was pretty sure Detective Vega wasn't aware I owned a cat—much less one that talked.

"At least we know blood doesn't bother you," she muttered.

She was referring to the fact I'd been stained in it when she arrested me. *Good one, Detective.* Without waiting for a response, she stepped past the policemen and into the sacristy.

10

I was only aware I'd begun to submit to the calming power of the cathedral when the room into which I followed Detective Vega blew the gathering quiet from my cells. I leaned against my cane, faint and breathless. Something must have come over my face as well.

"You all right?" Vega asked. "Need a mask?"

I shook my head. The smell of death was bitter, but it wasn't that. I blinked and moved my gaze over the small room a second time.

The white sacristy, where the holy services were prepared, was blood-smeared and ransacked. Cabinets had been opened, drawers ripped from their slots, candles, chalices, and vestments spilled. To my right, old ritual books had been removed from a vault and torn asunder, the brittle pages scattered. On the other side of the room lay the murdered rector.

I had seen bodies before—I didn't always get to amateur conjurers in time—but this wasn't a case of a nether creature feeding to sustain its form. No, the scene spoke to fury, and something far more troubling. Glee.

My ears picked up the police chatter outside, apparently filling in a newcomer:

"...gold chalice..." "...face beaten to a jelly..." "...don't hardly look like a person."

The white sheet covering the rector's body featured a spreading red-brown stain over a misshapen mound of head. At the end closer to me, the dusty soles of formal shoes were splayed downward.

Though I cleared my throat, my next words came out as scratches. "Where's the writing?"

Detective Vega stepped toward the body, the first time I'd seen her do anything gingerly, and lifted the sheet. I tilted my head. Having something to analyze helped. The words had been drawn vertically on his white-robed back, left and right sides. The ink of choice appeared to have been the rector's blood.

"Aren't there any photos?" I asked.

"They're being rendered," she snapped. "Mean anything to you?"

"Well, your people were right. It is ancient. A precursor to Latin, in fact."

"What's it say?"

I pulled a flip-top notepad from a coat pocket and slid a short green pencil from its metal spiraling. "The language isn't one of my fluencies, unfortunately." I wrote down the message, letter for letter. "It's going to take a bit of research."

Vega's eyebrows did the collapsing-down thing again.

I shrugged a *sorry*.

"You done?" she asked from her stooped-over position.

I looked over the writing once more and made a couple more notes. Despite the chilling medium, the penmanship had a certain elegance. Farther up the tent Detective Vega had made of the sheet, I glimpsed what looked like a sticky flap of scalp. I looked away and nodded quickly.

Outside the room, we dropped our bits of protective covering into a trash bag.

"How long?" she asked.

"To figure out the message?" I made a puttering sound with my lips. "A couple of days? It's a rare language," I explained before she could voice the protest gathering on her face.

She sighed harshly. "Any idea who else in the city would know it?"

"I'll add that to my honey-do list."

She fixed me with another warning look as she reached inside a jacket pocket. "I'm taking you at your word." Her first two fingers returned with a business card, which she held an inch from my face. "A 'couple of days' is Saturday. I'll expect a phone call by then. You don't want me to come looking for you."

"I can think of worse things." I flashed a grin.

The juvenile comment kept her chocolate-brown eyes on mine, which enabled me to accept the card with one hand while unclasping and hiding away the NYPD tag with the other. Classic misdirection.

Detective Vega didn't notice. After telling me I could find my own way home, she left me for her investigative team. I looked around for Father Vick as I descended the steps of the chancel, but the nave was empty now of church officials. Maybe they were being questioned.

At the bronze doors of the cathedral, another uncomfortable wave rippled through me, but my powers were back. Which got me thinking. The murder probably hadn't been the work of a supernatural entity. Even if one had managed to get itself invited into the sanctuary, the threshold would have stripped its powers. It wouldn't have been able to maintain its form inside.

So we were dealing with a human. And given the excessive violence of the act, likely someone with a vendetta against the rector. But then what did the message mean?

I pulled out my notepad as I started toward the Wall and re-read my translation:

Black Earth

Yeah, I'd held back on Detective Vega. But to get those six months wiped, I needed to not only interpret the message but point her in the direction of an arrest. And that second part *was* going to take time. Fortunately, I had a resource in mind. I'd get that ball rolling while I worked on how and why a shrieker had been summoned the night before. Which reminded me, I would need to alert the Order.

I peeked back at the receding Cathedral of St. Martin, a beautiful, if haunting, anomaly amid the towering edifices of mammon, and sighed. Something told me it was going to be a long next few days.

Thank God for Colombian dark roast.

11

I performed a quick check of my warding spells—all intact—before fishing out my keychain. Home was a walk-up apartment on West Tenth Street, its top floor small and square, like the top tier of a wedding cake, making it invisible from street level. Naturally, it was the floor I lived on.

I turned the three bolts, gold, silver, and bronze, stepped over my threshold, and immediately felt better. There was no greater contentment for a wizard than returning to his sheltered domicile—especially when the twelve hours I had been away felt like twelve days.

Contrary to other dimensions of my life, I took obsessive-compulsive pride in the order of my loft space. And thanks to New York's current vacancy glut, the rent was ridiculously reasonable, even for someone on my pay grade.

Of course, that could change come Monday.

For now, though, the industrial-chic apartment was home. I took in the space: high-ceilings with exposed beams, arched, double-story windows, and large throw rugs over stained concrete floors. A plush couch and chairs huddled around a flagstone fireplace, which I kept stoked from October to April. Beyond the kitchen, a ladder climbed to a second-story library and laboratory. There was plenty of open air for magic to move about. And in those rare instances when magic escaped my hold (hey, practice before mastery), the crooked West Village grid broke up the energy before it could do any real damage.

That gas explosion on Bleeker Street last month? Wasn't me.

As I hung my cane on the coat rack, a rattling snort sounded. On the divan beneath the west-facing window, a large mound of orange hair stirred. Ochre-green eyes slitted open followed by a yawning mouth of sharp teeth.

Damn, I'd woken the cat.

Her tail end heaved up before shifting ponderously and settling back down. I stood still and waited for her eyes to close again—they did that sometimes—but they stayed watching me.

"You smell like crap," she said.

"And it's nice to see you, too," I replied.

"Where the fuck have you been?"

"Hey! What did I say about the language?" It really was something I'd been trying to train out of her—without much success, obviously. Tabitha was, well, Tabitha: a succubus spirit who had been called up by an amateur and would have devoured *both* our loins had I not channeled her into a stray cat. Unable to decapitate the cat, per succubus-destroying protocol, I took her in. A questionable move, I'll admit. But that was five years ago, and

I still had all my parts. The Order had been none too happy, but what else was new?

Anyway, since then Tabitha had become less seductress and more harpy—and at forty pounds, a *lot* more harpy.

"Well?" she pressed.

"Well, things became a little more involved than anticipated." I walked over to the kitchen, set the paper bag from the corner grocery store onto the counter, and began unloading it. "That summoning I set out for last night? It ended up being demonic. The fight left me drained, meaning Thelonious time. Ha. I'm sure *you* can imagine. That made me late for class, then late for a meeting with my probation officer. Well, the second was Snodgrass's fault. The jerk." I set the canister of coffee down harder than I meant to. "Oh, and get this—if I can't help solve a murder by the end of the weekend, there's a great chance I'm out of a job."

I caught myself verging on full drama-queen. I looked at Tabitha for some sign of support, but her head had settled back onto her paws, eyes closed. At forty pounds, she was also becoming narcoleptic.

"Did you at least remember my milk?" she asked languidly.

I held up a bottle of raw goat's milk—twenty bucks a pop—and gave it a bitter shake. Tabitha's tastes weren't cheap. Between that and the brandy-sautéed tuna steaks, she ate better than I did.

"And warmer this time," she said, turning away.

"Not before you report on your tours."

"All's quiet," she murmured.

In exchange for room, board, and her life, Tabitha was supposed to tour the broad ledge of the level below every two hours and report anything unusual on the street. To say her compliance was spotty was putting it nicely.

"How about that Thai restaurant going in across the way?" I asked. "Gaudy sign, huh?"

"Hideous."

"There is no Thai restaurant."

"It was raining. I couldn't see very well."

She wasn't even trying to sound convincing.

"Yeah, last night and for like ten minutes!" I took several calming breaths. Tabitha's no-craps-given attitude had a way of spiking my blood pressure. "Look, it's for both of our safety. Not everyone holds me in as high esteem as you do. And anything strong enough to smash through my wards isn't going to turn gooey at the sight of a house cat. Especially one so ... galling."

Tabitha yawned.

I placed the bottle in the fridge and closed the door. Tabitha could get into a lot of things, but not the fridge.

"No report, no milk," I announced.

The cat didn't stir for a full minute. At last, she sighed heavily.

"Maybe I won't come back," she muttered, dropping from the divan with a graceless thud. At the neighboring window, she shot me a final slitted look before shifting her rump and squeezing through the cat door.

Tabitha not coming back would do wonders for my savings, but it was only noise. Besides the pull of endless goat lactose, she didn't have the strength to break through my wards. Not that she'd ever tried. Like a tired married couple, we'd developed a begrudging dependency on the other. She would be as disappointed to never see me again as I would to never see her.

Of course, you'd have to tear out a few nails to get either one of us to admit it.

I poured half the milk into a small pot on the stove and lowered the burner to a guttering flame. Then, licking a finger, I decided to take advantage of the cat's absence to make a call. (Tabitha had an annoying habit of providing background commentary.) I carried the desk phone from the counter to my favorite reading chair and rotary-dialed from memory. For wielders of magic, mechanical telephone switches trumped microchips every time. I'd fried more than my share of the second.

"Hello?" Caroline's pleasant voice answered.

"Working late, Professor Reid?" I teased.

The voice fell flat. "Hi, Everson. Working, yes, but it's not even two o'clock yet."

"Really?" It felt much later, but I decided that saying so would make me sound like a loafer. Not an impression I wanted to reinforce, especially since I was preparing to ask her for another favor.

"What did Snodgrass want?" she asked first.

Though my colleague had lowered her voice to a whisper, her concern came through loud and clear. I felt a stab of guilt for evoking it and decided to play things down.

"Oh, you know. 'Your class size is too small. You're not a real historian. You're a disgrace to academia.' Same old refrains."

"Are you sure that was all?" she asked skeptically. "He was practically skipping after your meeting."

The image made my face burn. "The man probably found a discount on paperclips."

Caroline laughed into the phone, a beautiful, effusive sound that always cheered me up. I imagined the backward spill of hair, the point-perfect dimples in her cheeks. She cleared her throat. "So, what's up?"

“Well, without being allowed to say too, too much, something happened at St. Martin’s Cathedral last night, and—”

“You mean the murder?” she asked. “Isn’t that awful?”

“You know about it?”

“My dad told me.”

Of course. Caroline’s father worked as an attorney for the mayor’s office. I’d met him once, a barrel-chested man, iron hair combed back in severe lines, somber face. To hear Caroline tell it, he was the last honest broker in City Hall. That took brass. I wasn’t sure whether to envy the bastard who would one day ask for his daughter’s hand, or fear for the bastard’s life.

“Right,” I said. “Well, I was consulted for my knowledge of arcane languages—there was some writing at the scene, you see.” Oh, if Detective Vega could hear me now. “But I need some more info.”

“What kind?”

“Well, like who might have something against the church or rector.”

For time’s sake, I’d decided it was going to be easier to narrow down the suspects and see if I could link any to the message, versus starting with the message and performing the equivalent of a city-wide radial search. Caroline understood the city and its web of power brokers as well as anyone.

“I can think of a few,” she said after a moment, “but let me look into it.”

“Is lunchtime tomorrow too soon? We could meet at your favorite deli. My treat, of course.”

“That should be fine.”

“Hey, ah, I really appreciate you doing this.”

"Well, it's nice to see you taking something seriously."

She left out the *for a change*, but it was there, in her tone. Moments like these were when secret wizarding tended to suck the most. There were no explicit rules against my telling people what I did, but the less who knew about my other life, the better—for their sanity as much as for my safety. I didn't have time to dwell on the question after we hung up. While Caroline was working on her list, I would need to get started on the shrieker case.

But first things first...

My cat had been right about one thing, I thought as I shed my coat and shoes and shuffled toward the shower.

I did smell like crap.

12

My first stop upstairs was a table that held a hologram of the city. Purchased from an architect friend of Caroline's, it was as marvelous to me as any magic. From the great upthrust of downtown to the relative plains of the Villages to the spires of Midtown and the wilds of Central Park, it was all there: every street and structure, built to scale.

And fortunately, all presently dim.

Through magic, I had bound the hologram to a series of wards placed throughout the city by the Order. If the wards detected so much as a whiff of taboo magic, a red gas light appeared. The light effect was accompanied by a fog-horn, more psychic than auditory, so I could hear it even when away from home. It was then up to me to hunt down the offender.

Last night the ruins of the East Village had lit up like hellfire. That should have tipped me off to the magic's demonic nature.

I stepped over a silver casting circle and emptied what I'd gathered from the conjurer's apartment onto an iron table that ran along the railing of the loft space. The spell elements I inspected were common. The power for the spell must have been in the ritual and incantation.

I turned around to a steep wall of mundane books.

"Svelare," I said.

In a rippling wave, encyclopedias and classical titles became magical tomes and grimoires, the majority of them handwritten in lost languages, centuries old. Some of the very titles I labored to keep out of the hands of amateurs. I scaled the rolling ladder, walked my fingers over binders, and returned with a small stack of reference books dealing with demonology and subterranean beings. I spread the books over my corner desk and spent the next several hours deep inside them, emerging only for swallows of coffee.

When I closed the final book, I had some answers. Namely confirmation that the amateur conjurer hadn't acted alone. A shrieker summoning required the power of a magic born or a higher demon. And since there didn't seem to be any of the second bandying about, I was putting my money on the first.

I drew a piece of parchment paper from a drawer, dipped a quill in lampblack ink, and began penning my report to the Order.

To the Esteemed Oracular Order of Magi and Magical Beings,

Re: Amateur Magic/ Summoning
Urgency: High

(They were very particular about how these were to be composed: part Jane Austen, part inter-department memo.)

I. Practitioner: Apparent AMATEUR. Middle-aged male of minimal means. Name unknown. No identification found. Domicile apparently settled by occupation versus lease or purchase. Due to post-conjuration mental state, AMATEUR could not be immediately interviewed. Healing initiated.

II. Location: Avenue C, East Village, New York City, United States

III. Source of Magic: Unknown at this time (see above, I). AMATEUR appears to have conjured from common components, but spell was incinerated, likely to obscure origin. ADVANCED MAGIC USER suspected. Plan to interview AMATEUR following full restoration of senses. Estimated recover time: forty-eight (48) to seventy-two (72) hours.

IV. Creature summoned: SHRIEKER

V. Outcome: Banished

(I decided it better to leave out the specifics, especially the part about Thelonious.)

Unless otherwise instructed, I plan to pursue the investigation into the origin of the spell and will report further discoveries as I attain them.

Humbly Submitted,
Everson Croft

I reread the report and, satisfied it was sufficiently informative and deferential, folded it into a six-sided disc. At my lab table, I waved the hexagon over a silver cup with a plum-colored flame: my direct line to the Order.

"Consegnare," I said.

The report smoked, then went up in a bright flash.

The flame in the pot shifted to orange before returning to its plum-colored hue, telling me the message had gone through. The tension in my neck and shoulders let out a little. There would be more work on the case, but I would have the Order's muscle in my corner—even if it was the slow-twitch variety. And who knew? Maybe this would be my break, the case that would promote me from the wizarding basement, as it were. Ten years was starting to feel like long enough.

I checked my watch, surprised at the late hour. It was nearly ten.

"Don't bother fixing dinner." Tabitha hopped onto the end of the iron table and collapsed on her side. "I fended for myself."

"Fended?" I asked before spotting the tuft of gray feathers stuck to a corner of her mouth. "*Pigeon?*"

"What else is a girl threatening to be shoved out the door supposed to do?"

Translation: *See how low you made me go.*

I snorted a laugh. “So it’s gone from ‘Maybe I won’t come back’ to ‘He’s throwing me out’?”

“Gotta survive somehow,” she went on in her hurt voice, as though she’d been done a terrible injustice. She stopped talking long enough to tongue-probe a back tooth. “I think I cracked a molar.”

Translation: *You made me crack a molar.*

I didn’t need to look to know her molars were fine, but since ninety percent of any relationship was knowing when to argue and when to accede... “I’m sorry,” I said. “Let me see about putting some magic to it.”

“You’ll just make it worse,” she pouted, turning her head away.

The other ten percent was knowing when neither one did any good.

I sighed and began returning the research books to their dusty slots. I could feel her succubus eyes on the back of my head. “Aren’t you going to ask for my report?” she asked after a moment.

“Do you have something?” I said from the ladder, trying to appear more interested in the title of the book I was holding. When her voice took on that dangling quality it meant she *did* have something.

“Oh, I might’ve caught someone watching our building.”

Cold fingers brushed the back of my neck. “Man or woman.”

“Hmm. You can never tell these days, can you?”

I turned. “Which did it *look* like?”

Tabitha licked a paw and began combing it over an ear. After several passes, she blinked up at me. “Did you say something, darling?”

"Man-looking or woman-looking?"

"Couldn't see much beneath the coat, but given the long hair ... woman-looking."

I flipped through a mental Rolodex of women who might come calling—or who even knew where I lived. Of course, there were locating spells for the second, assuming the female in question had a magical bent. But I narrowed it down to the mundane: Caroline Reid or Detective Vega, one bearing a gift of info, the other coming to demand it. But why not just walk up? Or call, for that matter?

"When?" I asked.

"Couple of hours ago."

"What did she look like?"

"Average in every way."

I leveled my gaze at her. "If that were any less helpful, it might actually be helpful."

Tabitha gave a self-satisfied smirk.

"Young or old."

"Young but older-looking."

"Blond-haired or black?"

"Brunette."

I could tell Tabitha was tiring of the game because her eyes had closed and she was giving responses more freely. But I was no closer to who the woman might have been. Based on hair color, Reid and Vega were out. Still, call it wizard's intuition, whoever it was *had* been watching for me.

I would need to find out why.

"All right, if she shows up again, try to pick out a defining feature or two." I slid home the last book. "Better yet, let me know right away." I turned and found Tabitha fast asleep.

I shook my head, but maybe it was time for me to do the same. After the day I'd had, I could use a solid twelve. Back at my desk, I grabbed my empty coffee pot and mug. The downstairs lights were glowing warmly up the unit's tall windows. Somewhere on the Hudson, a ship's horn sounded.

No, wait...

I spun to face the city hologram, and nearly choked.

Not a ship's horn, my alarm. The hologram was glowing that hellfire red again.

This time in two places.

13

The narrow streets of Chinatown were deserted when the cabbie dropped me off forty minutes later. I tipped him the requisite one hundred percent for the after-dark run—the "danger premium," New Yorkers called it.

Aptly named, I thought as the cab motored off. Of course most New Yorkers didn't know what horrors *truly* lurked in the dark, lured by the city's vortices of ley energy and, more recently, a muddy fog of despair.

I took a moment to get my bearings. The street that bustled with commerce by day was now an aisle of rolled-down steel doors, business names painted across the top in red Chinese characters. Some were accompanied by Oriental signs against evil. Above, lights glowed in solitary apartment windows.

As I began walking, I noted that the sidewalks were infinitely cleaner than those in the East Village, thanks to the crime syndicate that ran the neighborhood. Besides dealing in the usual vices, the White Hand profited by taxing local businesses and residents for "protection and services," which evidently included trash pickup. Of course, failure to pay meant your head would be in the next day's pile.

The White Hand didn't care for outsiders, either, especially after dark. I would need to tread carefully.

I was on the block where the ward had been triggered. The hunting spell I cooked up had been necessarily hasty—and I'd had to make two of them, the second for the alarm up in the One Forties—but with no rain in the forecast, it had a good chance of holding together.

At that thought, a fish-like force wiggled my cane, tugging me northward. I obliged at a run.

Half a block later, the force twisted me into an alleyway stretching between two restaurants and ending at a Dumpster. Chunks of pavement were piled up against the Dumpster's brown metal side, as though someone had jack-hammered down to a water main and left the mess for somebody else to clean up. I slowed and sniffed the air. The demon stink from the night before remained a stale after-scent in my sinuses, but it seemed I was picking up a fresh wave.

Not as powerful as the night before, but...

Ahead and to my left was a green door, pieces of glass glinting over its stoop. Beside it lay a twisted window cage. I raised my eyes to the dark socket of a window two floors up. From the jagged outline of broken glass, the same blood-red haze I'd seen the night before was leaking out.

I drew my cane into sword and staff and peered around, heart thumping rabbit-hard in my chest. The alley was still, but whatever had been summoned was loose in the city, dammit.

I blew open the locked green door, entered a narrow stairwell, and ascended quickly. At the second floor, I opened a door off the landing and held out my lit staff.

"Good God," I muttered.

Inside the apartment's one room, I assessed the grisly scene at a glance: the spell circles, done in salt this time, the familiar ingredients, the burned parchment, the gunky trail leading beneath the kitchen sink and eventually to the window, where the shrieker had flapped to freedom.

I went to the fallen conjurer.

His mouth was agape, his dark eyes rolled upward, as though trying to see something atop his head. Or maybe he hadn't wanted to watch what was happening down below. His ribs shone pale white around the hollowed-out bowl of his torso. The shrieker had consumed everything.

With gloved hands, I searched through his pockets for identification. Nothing there, but in a wallet on a back table I found a driver's license. The face was a match.

"What did you get yourself into, Chin Lau Ping?" I muttered as I copied his name into my notepad.

By his other IDs, I gathered he'd driven an intercity bus. I took a final look at the photo before returning the wallet to the table. The trim-haired man couldn't have been more different than the East Village vagrant, and yet the two had somehow gotten their hands on the same spell. Despite needing to get to the other summoning, like an hour ago, I made a quick circuit of the apartment.

Something had to link the two.

I stopped at a bamboo bookcase with a mirror on top and shone my light over the titles. But it was the standard amateur fare: religious texts, lay spell books, an encyclopedia of channeling and divination. Nothing that would contain the dark secrets of demon summoning. And why shriekers?

At the window, I peered past the broken frame into the night. I listened for bloody screams but heard only distant car horns and sirens. With any luck, the creature had gone into a second gestation.

I would need to alert the Order of the development, but first I had to get uptown.

I returned to the alley at a run, shoes crunching over the broken window glass. I sensed movement an instant before my vision exploded in stars. The blow only registered as I was landing on my face.

Something solid had struck the back of my head.

14

I twisted and blinked up at my attacker. The looming figure was hard to make sense of. It was as though someone had taken the chunks of pavement beside the Dumpster, assembled them into the proportions of a large human, and endowed them with life. I peeked past the figure. Sure enough, the pavement pile was gone.

Wonderful. I was dealing with a golem.

With a low moan, the golem raised a giant fist. I might or might not have screamed as I threw myself from its trajectory. Pavement exploded behind me. I gained my feet and staggered backwards, sword out. The blow had turned my legs to noodles, but my mental prism remained intact.

"Vigore," I cried.

The force from my sword destroyed the golem's right arm, which went knocking down the alleyway. But though the golem rocked back, its legs held fast. It lumbered forward and swung its remaining arm. I got my light shield up in time, but the concussion from the backhand sent me into a brick wall, dealing my head another lovely smack. The alley tilted one way and the other before I could stare it straight again.

"Forza dura!" I shouted.

With my prism wavering, the force wasn't up to the task of a charging golem. Though chunks blew from its torso, the creature hardly slowed. I wheeled and staggered toward the mouth of the alleyway. I needed some kind of backup, but from whom? The city was sprinkled with magic users, but I had no idea who did and didn't belong to the Order—which was just how the Elders seemed to want it.

As I cleared the alley, an idea struck me: Canal Street, just north of here. A branch of the defunct Broadway line ran beneath it.

I veered right. Seconds later, the golem's smashing footfalls fell in behind me.

Pumping my cane like a relay baton, I remembered an account of a dark sorcerer using golems to protect his spell-casting sanctum. That had to be it. Someone knew last night's shrieker summoning had been thwarted. Looking to avoid a repeat, he had not only arranged for tonight's twin summonings at opposite ends of the city, but placed a golem at the closer one, perhaps as a component of the shrieker spell, for any wizards who might come sniffing around. My stepping over the conjurer's threshold had probably triggered the animation.

But how had the person known I was closer to Chinatown than to Harlem? Unless he knew where I lived. I thought of the brunette woman Tabitha had seen watching my building.

Did the woman play a role in this? Was *she* the sorcerer?

I snuck a peek over my shoulder and regretted it. The thing was less than a half block away and gaining, its clunky strides literally eating up concrete. But I'd reached Canal Street. I took a hard right and began squinting ahead for...

There!

I aimed my sword toward the subway vent that took up half the sidewalk. With a shouted Word, I blew it from its foundation. Tight-roping the ledge between the sudden hole and a storefront, I gathered more energy to my prism, hoping to hell the golem would play follow-the-leader.

When I turned, it was. Sort of.

Instead of veering around the hole, the golem had chosen to stretch a clunky leg across. I aimed my sword at its front foot.

"Vigore!"

As foot touched sidewalk, the golem's leg erupted at the shin. With a surprised moan, the rest of the golem plummeted from view—only for stony fingers to reappear and seize the ledge. But a second Word demolished its hand, and I watched the golem crash-bang down into the foul-smelling void.

Head still ringing, I stooped over to catch my breath. Then I replaced the steel grating over the hole and hemmed the mess in with some nearby construction barricades that littered the city. Far below, the retching, rumbling battle was already underway. Ghouls versus golem.

With any luck, my new friend would land a few solid shots before being torn apart. In any case, it was on its own.

I had a ride uptown to catch.

15

As it turned out, I hadn't needed a hunting spell to locate the site of the second summoning. The small army of police cruisers did the job for me.

"This you, buddy?" the cabbie muttered as he pulled over. "Christ."

He hadn't been too happy about the address. Following the Crash, Hamilton Heights had fallen as hard as any neighborhood and was neck-and-neck with the South Bronx for most homicidal.

"You mind waiting?" I asked. "I won't be long."

The man's pouchy eyes jerked from building to building as though bullets were going to fly from them at any second. "Sorry, pal," he said, shaking his head at the extra twenty I held out. "I'm as hard up as anyone but not *that* hard up."

As the cab U-turned and took off back south, I hurried toward the crime scene, an unadorned brick apartment building, twenty-odd stories high. Several residents had gathered out front as police appeared and disappeared through the building's entrance. I eased up to the edge of the crowd and stood behind an older couple, both in thick night robes.

"What's going on?" I asked.

"Flash got himself killed," the man said without turning.

"Murder?"

"Big old messy one," the woman said.

"Someone tore into Flash good," the man took up again. "Super found him after we complained of some ungodly screaming from his unit."

I imagined a similar scene to the one in Chinatown.

"Did they catch the guy?" I asked.

"Nun-uh." The man cocked his head up. "Broke out through the window, must've went down the fire escape."

"Either that or had wings," the woman put in, "cause the man live twelve stories up."

Yeah, nastiest wings you ever saw, lady. Which meant we had two shriekers on the loose.

"What sort of work did Flash do?" I needed to find some sort of connection between the conjurers, a common cause. That the couple seemed to know the latest victim was to my good fortune—not something I fell into very often.

But instead of popping off another response, they turned around for the first time. Beyond their glasses, I watched squinting suspicions take hold. *So long, fortune.* Not only was I foreign to the neighborhood, but my face was freshly banged up. I followed the man's gaze to my gloves, both bloodstained from patting down the Chinatown conjurer.

"O-officer!" the man called over a shoulder as he backed his wife away. "Officer!"

"Now wait a minute," I said, showing a palm.

Bad move. Now the woman could see the blood. She responded with a piercing scream.

That would get someone's attention. Lowering my head into the shadow of my hunched-up collar, I wheeled and strolled south, Mr. Nonchalant himself. I kept an ear trained on the excitement of voices behind me. When I picked out "white man" and "killer," I decided to speed my pace.

To an all out sprint.

"Stop!" a woman's voice called.

Sorry, Officer, but being nabbed for a probation violation is bad enough. Being nabbed with the blood of another stiff on my hands, and without a good explanation of how it got there? Yeah, not gonna happen.

I rounded the corner of the building as a pair of cracks sounded behind me.

Of course, you could just shoot me dead.

For the second time that night, I was in full flight mode. I narrowed my sights on a south-facing entrance to the same apartment building. But instead of ducking inside, I pressed my back to the ninety-degree angle the jutting entrance made with the building's brick siding.

Holding my cane at chin level, I whispered a Word: *"Oscurare."*

As the police officer slapped around the corner into view, the white opal in my cane absorbed the immediate light. The shadow I stood inside turned darker, more obscuring.

Slowing, the officer snapped on a flashlight and held it level with her firearm. The beam swept side to side, then shot under a pair of stripped cars leaning curbside. Ninety-nine percent of the current force would have said, "The hell with it," backed away, lived to police another day. Hamilton Heights at night was no place for a cop to be caught alone. But it seemed my pursuer belonged to that hallowed one percent who still believed in Serving and Protecting.

Lucky me.

At that thought, the beam glared across my face. The officer began running my way.

Not *officer*, though—*detective*. As in Vega.

I felt explanations bunching up in the back of my throat, none worth a spit. To Detective Vega, I was just another degenerate in a city running over with them—not someone trying to help clean up the mess. Nothing I said would change that. Even in the dark, I could see her glossy black eyebrows creasing sharply down.

But she wasn't hitting me with the light anymore. The beam was trained on the entrance I was hidden beside. She hurried past my spot and disappeared. I listened to a large door shake but remain locked. Detective Vega huffed out a sigh. The beam swung around, this time into the street.

My knees buckled in relief—until a pair of male officers came running up, their own flashlight beams wavering dangerously close. I stiffened straight, wondering how long I could hold the spell.

"Find him?" the larger officer asked.

"I think he went in," Vega said from just out of sight. "Locked the door behind him."

"Want us to do a top-to-bottom," the other one asked, clearly uncomfortable with his own suggestion. Beside his partner, he looked like a twelve-year-old. They had chosen a spot five feet in front of me to hold their end of the meeting. If I reached out with my cane, I could have goosed either one.

"No." Vega joined the meeting in profile. "I want you to check on one of our probationers, make sure he's home."

You cannot be serious.

"What's the name?"

I closed my eyes. *Please, not—*

"Everson Croft," Vega said. "The address is in the system. West Tenth, I think."

"We're on it."

As the officers took off, Detective Vega gave the street another pass with her light. I'd tried to keep my cane concealed while fleeing, but I hadn't been careful enough, it seemed. She must have seen it. At least my cane was doing a better job of concealing *me* at the moment.

Detective Vega lowered her light. Something in the disappointment, if not defeat, of the gesture poked me square in the sympathy center. My own night wasn't going much better. Under different circumstances, I might have pulled her into a hug. Then again, Vega didn't strike me as a cuddler.

Gun in hand, she stomped back toward the front of the building, a muttered threat trailing behind her.

"And if you're *not* home, Croft..."

All right, sympathy time over. If I didn't want to learn the second part of Vega's threat, I needed to figure out how to race a speeding police cruiser one-hundred thirty blocks south.

And win.

16

I ran south for several blocks before cutting west.

I'd already eliminated the subway as an option. Too unreliable. My plan was to flag a cab, empty my wallet onto his lap, and have him turn the West Side Highway into his personal Autobahn. The police cruiser had taken off down Fredrick Douglass Boulevard a minute before, bottoming out at an intersection. I was gambling they'd hold that course, hopefully hit a traffic snag or twelve from Midtown south.

But for my plan to work, I needed a taxi. I pulled up wheezing at the edge of St. Nicholas Park, where the danger factor lessened slightly, and peered down the street to the glowing entrance of a metro stop.

Not a single cab.

"Oh, c'mon," I shouted in frustration, "it's not even a full moon!" Our wooded parks had a bit of a werewolf—or bloodthirsty feral dog—problem, depending on who you talked to.

I sized up the few cars parked along the curb. Even if I could've hotwired one, I wouldn't have known how to drive it. (Hey, I grew up in the city). That left hijacking the next vehicle that happened to pass. Or acting like a wizard.

Ducking tree branches, I hurried up a cement staircase into the park. The path it led to was little more than a crumbling line of pavement, quickly swallowed by a decade's worth of overgrowth. Joggers, bikers, and strollers—not to mention the Department of Parks and Rec—had long since abandoned St. Nicholas to its new denizens: an assortment of shadow creatures and the occasional junky desperate enough to shoot up back here.

I didn't go far, veering off path to scrabble over an eruption of boulders. Inside, I discovered a small dirt-packed clearing. As any druid would tell you, mineral-rich stones made good energy containers. I kicked aside some soiled clothing, drug needles, and what might have been a human femur and looked around. It smelled like a Porta-Potty, but the space would do for my spell.

Using the tip of my sword, I drew a man-hole sized circle in the dirt and inscribed my family symbol inside: two squares, one offset at forty-five degrees to look like a diamond. I connected the corners with four diagonal lines and scratched a sigil at each end. From inside my coat, I pulled out a tall vial of copper filings and sprinkled them along the furrows. To connect the circle to the spell target, I removed three keys from my jangling chain—one gold, one silver, one bronze—to correspond with the three locks on my door. I arranged them near the edges of the casting circle in a triangular pattern and stood back.

The spell would require energy, and lots of it. That was where I had to be extra careful. I couldn't afford to let Thelonious through the door. Not tonight, and *definitely* not out here, where night hags were rumored to wander. Thelonious had chased skirts more putrid, believe me.

"All right," I said, shaking my arms loose.

I was about to attempt a projection spell, one that would manifest a walking, talking likeness of me at the target. Besides requiring a healthy dose of energy, they were tough as hell to get right, especially over long distances. Even then, they were ephemeral. Though I'd practiced the spell countless times, I could count on one hand the number of times I'd put it into actual practice.

Let's just say the results had been a mixed bag.

I stepped into the center of the circle and, feet together, began to chant an ancient Word that translated into *home*. As the sound vibrated in my core, I pictured the inside of my door as vividly as I could: the molding, the glass peephole, the brass knob. I imagined the feel of the shag rug under my feet, the cavernous space of the loft at my back.

With every chant, ley energy surged voltage-like through my mental prism, down my body, and into the casting circle. There it coursed along the lines of my symbol, glowing whiter, gaining strength.

Within minutes, it became a self-sustaining force.

"Oikos," I repeated.

A high resonance began to ring from the door keys. A moment later, the inside of my door wavered into being, a ghost image over the blacked-out park. I was taking shape in my apartment. I channeled more energy, imagining away my bulky attire, replacing it with the cottony feel of pajamas and the loose grip of tube socks.

"Oikos."

I was putting the finishing touches on my bed-headed coif when a knock sounded.

"Mr. Croft?"

I'd managed to beat the police officers, but only just. I waited the requisite ten seconds for them to imagine me waking up, climbing out of bed, crossing the room...

A harder bout of pounding. "Mr. Croft, it's the police."

"Coming," I called, my voice strange-sounding, as though I were hearing myself from the opposite end of a tunnel.

I extended a pajama-clad arm forward and twisted the bolts, the hard feel of them also seeming to arrive from a hollow distance. The two officers I'd been hiding from only a short time before appeared in the opening doorway. I blinked between them blearily.

"Mr. Croft?" the larger one asked from a lumpy boxer's face.

"Last time I checked." I read his name tag. "Officer Dempsey."

The two officers took a moment to examine me, no doubt lining up my features with the stats and mug shot on their dashboard computer. The other one's name was Dipinski, which also seemed to fit him. Something in their stares told me I wasn't dealing with the department's sharpest tacks. From experience, I knew that could cut either way.

"Help you with something?" I asked.

Dipinski, whose eight-point police hat barely reached the height of my chin, stepped forward. "Have you been home all night?"

"I have, in fact." I stifled a fake yawn and gestured vaguely behind me. "Was grading papers till about ten and then conked out."

Their eyes darted past me as though eager to find something amiss. I turned with them, mostly out of curiosity. The apartment, superimposed over the park's boulders, was as neat as I'd left it, Tabitha curled up on her divan, dead to the world. That was one less worry, anyway.

"Well, consider this a random audit," Dempsey said.

His partner aimed a finger up at me. "We come after eight at night and you're *not* in, you're in violation of your probation, bud. And then guess what? We're going to take a little ride."

Yeah, and had I goosed you with my cane back there, dipshit, you'd be duck-walking in those little polyester pants.

"Got it," I said.

Dipinski glared at me as though trying to decide whether my curt response was meant as an insult. While it was true I held him in roughly the same regard as a peanut, I just needed these guys gone.

At last he lowered his finger and began to back off. That was when the image wavered.

Spent energy was leaving the spell, dammit, and I was in no position to resume incanting. Though I managed to steady the projection by force of will, Dipinski had caught the disruption. His small, freckled face pinched into a squint. Once more, the spell tried to tremble away.

"I don't believe it!" his partner exclaimed, seeming to choke on his own breath.

I drew back before realizing he wasn't looking at me. Following his floating finger, I found Tabitha stretching and rising to her haunches.

"Is that a ... *cat*?" he asked.

"Yeah," I said, struggling to hold the spell together. "Name's Tabitha."

"Good gawd!" The fit of laughter that seized Dempsey sounded like dry heaving.

Dipinski gave a mean smirk. "You've got a real chubber there, Croft." Apparently, my plus-sized cat trumped a man flickering in and out of existence. As noted, not the sharpest tacks.

"Chubber?" Dempsey said, coming up for air. "That's the biggest fucking cat I've ever seen!"

That got Dipinski giggling.

Tabitha dropped from the divan, ears pinned.

"Hey, look, fellas," I whispered, trying to close the door enough to block her from their view and vice versa. "The cat gets a little weird around ... you know ... people she doesn't know."

Dipinski wiped an eye with a finger. "Bet that'd change if I showed up with a Christmas ham."

Their laughter verged on hysterical now.

"You'd better bring the whole damn pig!" his large partner wheezed.

"You'll do nicely," Tabitha hissed from right behind me.

"All right, thanks for stopping by." With what energy remained in my failing projection, I slammed and locked the door on the officers before Tabitha could sink her claws into them.

The image buckled and broke apart. I fell from the circle and landed seat-down in the dirt, blinking around at the sudden darkness. The scent of burnt copper hung in the cool air.

I sat a moment, waiting to see whether Thelonious would be paying our world a visit. But though the creamy light moved briefly around the edges of my thoughts, I had retained enough power to prevent him from breaking through. And expended just enough to keep my ass out of the clink.

I rose shakily, collected my singed keys, and swept the bottom of a shoe over the smoking circle. Some night. Two dead conjurers, two escaped shriekers. And I had a bad feeling that no matter what those two buffoons reported to Detective Vega, that image of me fleeing was going to remain stuck in her head. I wasn't sure what the implications would be. Certainly nothing good. If I'd had poorer outings as a wizard, none came to mind.

I returned to the street in a sulk, too slow to hail the on-duty cab motoring past. A moment later, the light over the metro entrance turned off. Sighing, I aimed myself south and started for home.

17

"I am *so* sorry," I said as I slipped into the seat opposite Caroline Reid at the small deli table.

She was sitting arrow straight, which was her peeved posture. I seemed to make her do that a lot. In my defense, I trudged sixty blocks last night before finally snagging a cab. Back home, I had to calm Tabitha, who had been deep into scheming Dempsey's and Dipinski's murders, update the Order on the shrieker situation, and then shower and treat my injuries.

By the time I crawled into bed, it was almost four a.m.

"I don't get it, Everson," Caroline said. "*You* arranged this meeting."

"I know, I know, but—"

"*You* needed my help."

"Right, and I—"

"And yet where would you be if I hadn't called?"

The correct answer was still in bed. It wasn't my alarm, but the brassy ring of the telephone that had awakened me, Caroline wanting to know where in God's name I was. That had been an hour ago.

"Look ..." I took a breath. "I know this is no excuse, but I had a rough night."

"You seem to have a lot of those. And while you were out doing ... whatever it is you do, I was home working on this." She hefted up a thick manila folder and gave it a shake. "For you."

"And I appreciate that. I really do."

Lips compressed, she dropped the folder in front of me and stood.

"Hey, where are you going?"

"I have office hours in fifteen minutes." She fixed her purse strap over a shoulder. "Some of us take our responsibilities seriously."

"And I don't?"

"No, in fact. And you lied to me."

"*Lied?*" I was honestly at a loss. "About what?"

"Your meeting with Snodgrass. I know about the hearing."

Oh. Which meant she also knew about my probationary status.

When I didn't say anything, she shook her head and turned to leave.

"Wait." I caught her slender wrist. It was a bold move given the hole I was already in, but she stopped. When she faced me, the hardness in her blue-green eyes told me I had roughly ten seconds to make my appeal.

"Okay. I was arrested last summer," I said, releasing her carefully. "Wrong place, wrong time. Throw in a stressed public safety system, and I got two years probation on no evidence. I kept it from the college, probably the wrong move, but Snodgrass found out. As things stand, I'm in a tough spot, true. *But,*" I tapped the folder, "if I can point the NYPD in the direction of the cathedral murderer, my remaining probation gets halved. And with that, I can at least make a case to the board. I think they'd look favorably on a professor using the tools of his profession to help solve a crime. Good recruiting pitch, too."

Carolina snorted dryly. But in her softening stance, I could see that if she didn't believe me, she really wanted to. That was a start. She let me guide her back to the table and scoot her chair under her.

"What are we going to do with you?" she asked tiredly.

"Well, this will definitely help." I indicated the folder as I sat.

"Not that." She reached forward and brushed my sleeve. "Your coat's inside out."

I looked down. Damn.

"And what's with the bandages?"

A waiter came over, sparing me from having to explain my injuries. I fixed my coat and ordered a coffee. Caroline asked for a refill of hers.

"Shall we?" she asked, clearing her throat and opening the folder of what she'd compiled. "I have about five minutes before I'll be late." When she scooted nearer, her clean scent washed around me. "I came up with two names. Fist, Arnaud Thorne, CEO of Chillington."

The groan in my thoughts must have seeped out because Caroline looked up. "Know him?"

"By reputation," I replied, which was mostly true. Arnaud

Thorne epitomized the worst of investment banking. Cold, soulless, rapacious—the standard tags. His was one of a cabal of firms that had secured a nice pre-Crash profit betting against New York municipal bonds, undermining the city's ability to pay its mounting debts. In the Crash's smoking aftermath, the same firms swooped down on City Hall. Headed by Arnaud, they offered to manage the very debt they'd rendered worthless—but at crippling interest rates. They now had their teeth fixed firmly in New York's jugular, ensuring themselves a steady stream of tax dollars for the next fifty years. New York, in turn, had become their mindless slave.

All very fitting considering the same investment bankers were vampires.

"Why Arnaud?" I asked.

"Because St. Martin's Cathedral sits on prime real estate," Caroline replied, turning some pages over. "Here are the lawsuits Chillington Capital filed to have the cathedral's downtown block converted to commercial. The church and a collective of preservation groups fought back. When the lawsuits failed, Arnaud shifted his sights to the rector. I have it on reliable authority the two met last month. Arnaud offered Father Richard a small fortune to convince the diocese to abandon the downtown location. Richard said no."

"And yesterday morning he's found beaten to death," I finished.

Holding a knuckle to my lips, I leafed through the evidence. Vampires valued material assets but mostly as a means of self-preservation and control. Arnaud's interest in the property probably had more to do with the fount of ley energy it sat on—

energy he could tap. I doubted Arnaud had committed the murder himself, though. He would have lost his powers at the threshold, if not been incinerated. Vampires didn't fare well in holy spaces. And St. Martin's was about as holy as they came. Of course, he could always have hired a thug to do the job.

Still, I needed a connection between Arnaud and the message on the rector's back. With last night's hoopla, I hadn't had time to research *Black Earth* or what it might mean.

"Who's the other one?" I asked, not sure I wanted to know.

"Wang Gang."

"Wang Gang?"

"He also goes by Bashi. He took over the Chinatown crime syndicate two months ago."

Something squeezed my stomach. "The White Hand?"

She nodded. "The former boss died in July."

"I *did* hear about that. Natural causes, right?" I'd read about it, actually, an image of the man's crinkly face and wispy white hair appearing beside the article. It hardly seemed fair that someone responsible for so much fear and death should be allowed to drift peacefully from his mortal coil.

Caroline continued. "Following a bloody struggle, the youngest son emerged on top. But where his father kept a kind of order, Bashi has spent his first weeks as boss sowing chaos, exacting revenge for every perceived slight."

"And one of his beefs was with the church?"

"St. Martin's took in ten girls last year who escaped a White Hand brothel. The young women had seen their handlers paying uniformed police officers and so feared going to the law. St. Martin's gave them sanctuary until they could be spirited from the city. Let's just say Bashi took it as a personal affront when he found out. Before becoming boss, he was in charge of the prostitution rings."

"And the church didn't stay quiet," I said, recalling another news item I'd read.

"No," Caroline affirmed. "The church took the lead in trying to end the exploitation. Father Richard organized a community task force, offered money to informants, put pressure on the police department to crack down."

I nodded grimly. The story fit with murder as revenge. And because the White Hand was a mortal organization, the threshold wouldn't have been an obstacle. What didn't fit, however, was the message. When the White Hand left their mark on a crime scene, it wasn't in early Latin.

I flipped through photo-copied articles on Wang Gang and the White Hand until I arrived at the back of the folder. "So these two?"

"In New York, every office comes with a dozen or more spokes of conflict, but from what I was able to find, Arnaud and Bashi look the most damning."

Or damned, in the first case, I thought.

"What about within the church?" I asked. I was thinking about what Detective Vega had said about everyone inside being a suspect.

"St. Martin's wasn't afflicted with the political or liturgical conflicts you sometimes see in powerful religious institutions. At least not openly. Fathers Richard and Victor worked well together as rector and vicar." Not realizing Father Vick had been promoted to vicar, I made a sound of interest. Vick the Vicar. "Father Richard was well-regarded within the church hierarchy and larger interfaith community, popular with his parishioners..."

I must have been watching Caroline with a little too much admiration because her cheeks began to color. She checked her watch, as though to give her eyes something to do.

"Now I really do have to get going," she said.

Shoot, I thought. "Just one more question. Have you ever heard of 'Black Earth'? Maybe the name of a fraternal organization, an underground society, something like that?"

If it existed, there was a good chance Caroline would know. She maintained an eclectic network of contacts throughout the city. Whether her contacts were cultivated for research purposes or something more, I wasn't sure and had never asked. Sometimes the best way to safeguard one's own secrets was to allow your friends theirs.

But a comma-shaped wrinkle was forming between Caroline's brows. "Not ringing a bell. I can ask around."

"No, no, please don't." The last thing I wanted was for her to draw the attention of a dangerous group, especially if it had a supernatural bent. "More of a tangential question, really." I forced a chuckle. "Not related to this here."

"Mm-hmm," she said, sounding unconvinced.

I stood up as she did, dropping a few bills on the table and tucking the thick folder under my arm. It suddenly occurred to me neither of us had eaten. Geez, and here I'd offered to treat her. "Oh, hey, can I get you a salad or sandwich from the cooler to take back with you?"

"No worries. I packed a backup lunch."

"Backup...?"

When she patted my unshaven cheek, it was as though to say, *I know you by now.*

"Okay, well, I owe you," I said lamely.

She gave a smile that could have been interpreted any number of ways and made her way toward the front of the deli. The afternoon light through the windows, though muted, enveloped her in a lovely aura, capturing my feelings for her in that moment. I opened my mouth, not knowing what I was going to say. But when it came to me and Caroline, there were only three words.

"Sorry!" I called. "Thanks again!"

18

An hour later, having decided to begin with the vampire Arnaud, I was on a subway pulling into the heart of the Financial District.

I exited with a bevy of men and women in professional attire. Past the turnstiles, steel barriers herded us toward a checkpoint. We were inside the Wall. I watched those ahead of me showing their passport-like IDs. At a table beyond, an armed guard was rifling a man's briefcase while a second guard performed a rough pat down of a harrowed-looking woman.

I swallowed and fingered the police ID I had, ahem, forgotten to return to Detective Vega. I was still debating whether or not to use it when my turn came up.

"C'mon, c'mon," a guard grunted, holding out a hand. He wasn't your typical paunchy retired cop. With his walnut-knotted frame and shaved head, the man looked like a special ops agent. They all did. And why not? The titans of finance could afford the most lethal.

Almost reflexively, I jerked the NYPD card from my pocket. The guard snapped it from me and held it in front of his shield sunglasses—worn underground as well, apparently. Through the window of a booth to his left, I could see someone inspecting an X-ray scan of my body.

"What's your business?"

"The, uh, St. Martin's case."

"This doesn't say who you are," he growled.

I fumbled for my wallet. "Everson Croft, Special Consultant to the NYPD." I finally managed to free my Midtown College ID, which I held up as well.

The guard wasn't interested. He slapped the NYPD card against my chest, hard enough to alter my heart rhythm, and shoved me toward the inspection station. I stumbled against the metal table, where I was rudely deprived of my cane. I watched the guard inspect either end and then try to pull it apart. *Good luck, buddy.* A family charm held it closed. More worrisome, though, were the hands prodding my personal areas and digging into my pockets.

"What's all this?" the guard asked when he'd finished.

I looked at the items lined up across the table and cleared my throat. "Well, that's for hydration, of course." I indicated the Evian bottle of holy water. "This is a mineral supplement," I said of the vial of copper filings. "Supposed to be good for circulation. My notepad's there. And that..." My eyes shifted to the small bag of rice. "Well, after I finish up here, I'm going to try to make it to a wedding. You know, shower the happy couple when it's over." I gave a small eye roll to suggest I thought the practice as silly as they probably did.

Neither guard cracked a grin. For several troubling seconds, their shielded gazes remained fixed on my face. Then, as though coming to some sort of psychic agreement, they gave a simultaneous nod.

"Get your shit and get out of here," the nearer one grunted.

I obliged and was soon hurrying up the steps, just as thankful to be past the checkpoint as I was to be above ground. On street level, giant skyscrapers funneled powerful winds down Broadway. My coat flapped like wings. Tilting my head back, I spotted the landmark building that housed Arnaud's offices. He owned the entire tower, as well as several others in the Financial District.

Five minutes later, a pair of young men in brass-button suits were opening the building's front doors for me. Vampires didn't mess with wards. They kept blood slaves instead—as much for a food supply as security. I nodded at their ageless faces and stepped from the batting winds.

The deep lobby felt like a tomb. The young woman at the crescent-shaped reception desk smiled a little too earnestly as the doors closed behind me, sealing out the sun and inducing a bone-deep chill.

"Welcome," she called in a lilting southern accent. "How may I help you?"

"Good afternoon." I walked up and stood the NYPD card on her marble desk. "I'd like to have a word with Arnaud, if I may."

"Do you have an appointment?"

"For police business?"

"All meetings require an appointment, sir, official or otherwise."

I knew Arnaud had leverage in this city, but wow. "All right, let's make one for say ... fifteen minutes from now?"

She tilted her head in a show of forbearing. White-blond hair that had been brushed to a sheen fell over the shoulder of a pale scoop-neck blouse. She was beautiful in a way that wasn't quite right. Too porcelain. I suspected I had only to remove her stylish choker to discover the puckered cause.

"Appointments can only be made by phone," she said, "and require three to five days for approval."

"Three to five days?"

I didn't have three to five days. I had exactly one. I studied the receptionist in thought. It wasn't hard to imagine the young debutante she had been, stepping from the Port Authority Bus Terminal, suitcase in hand, dizzying dreams of theater in her head. Fury at Arnaud and his fellow parasites burned in my blood. If I'd had the power to restore that young woman, believe me, I would have.

Though the receptionist continued to show her perfect teeth, her smile seemed less inviting now, more menacing. In my peripheral vision, I noticed several young men I hadn't seen upon entering. They drew nearer, making it so my only move would be toward the door I had entered by.

"I'm sorry, sir," the receptionist said, her voice developing a not-so-subtle edge, "but you're going to have to leave."

She seemed to become taller, the bones of her jaw sharper.

I glanced around, tightening my grip on my cane. The young men, who could have been interns with their shiny side-parted hair and Brooks Brothers suits, drew nearer still. I felt Arnaud's cold eyes watching me from theirs, inducing a weakness in my core. I forced myself to straighten.

I had one more ace.

Splaying my right hand on the desk, I said, "My name is Everson Croft, grandson of Asmus Croft, Grand Mage of the Society of the Dragon. I demand the right to an audience with Arnaud Thorne."

As the powerful words shook from me and resounded around the marble room, the men stopped. The receptionist's eyes fell to my ring finger. The winged serpent embossed in thick silver appeared ready to lunge up at her. Inching back, she lifted a phone to her ear.

I'd thought that might get things rolling.

"Um, there's an Everson Croft to see you, sir." She listened, her large eyes never leaving my ring, but the phone call was for show. Arnaud had seen and heard all that she had.

After a moment, she hung up and shifted her gaze past me. "Show him up," she said, no longer smiling.

Without touching me, the group of men enveloped me and fell into a silent lockstep. I moved with them, as though carried by a cold, hypnotic force. As blood slaves, the men weren't vampires, but vessels for Arnaud. A brood mentality, along with superhuman speed and strength, were just a few of the perks that came with the position. Perhaps a modest stipend.

We boarded an elevator that lifted off with smooth, stomach-dipping speed. The slaves, who probably *had* been finance majors at one time, fixed their gazes straight ahead. In the brushed steel doors, I studied their faces, their dead eyes. I'd heard that vestiges of humanity remained inside them, clawing the walls of their bodily confinement, screaming for release or death. All very much to the head vampire's delight, I imagined.

I looked away, not wanting my compassion toward them to soften my guard. At Arnaud's word, the same poor souls would be clambering over one another to rip out my throat. I was a little surprised they hadn't tried yet.

At the top floor, we exited and proceeded down a hall of what appeared executive-level offices. Ahead loomed a stately set of doors, the steep wood oiled and dark. Outside the doors, ice-cold hands plied my cane away and stripped off my coat. They lifted away my necklace holding my charmed coin. Though I knew better than to resist, my heart pumped into full panic. All of the defenses I'd been counting on left with the departing men.

The blood slave who remained behind suppressed a smile. His face was youthful but his almond-shaped eyes were beginning to jaundice at the edges, betraying advanced age. His hair spoke to another era, the short black bangs combed straight down, like a monk's. *You can take the boy out of the Middle Ages*, I caught myself thinking.

He bowed and opened one of the two doors.

Every instinct in me was demanding I leave, and yet...

The dim room beyond the doorway released a smell of leather and musk. At the other end of what appeared either a large office or small library, a huge brown-tinted window cut a tall man's silhouette. For a vertiginous moment, the regal figure seemed to take his measure of me.

"Everson Croft," a silken voice said. "Please, do come in."

I was dimly aware of stepping over the threshold and onto soft carpet.

"You are either the most audacious human to request an audience," the voice said, with a hint of tragic humor, "or, my poor boy, you have simply given up on life." I only realized the figure had been standing with his back to me when he wheeled and a pair of predatory eyes flashed into view.

Behind me, the door slammed closed.

19

I watched Arnaud watching me. He wasn't as tall as he had first appeared. Neither was he wearing the long-tailed black suit I thought I'd glimpsed when he turned. His suit was light colored and contemporary, the pale oxford underneath open to a criss-crossing of thin chains. Mane-length waves of white hair fell from a center part, brushing a silky red scarf that draped his shoulders.

The newspapers called him *fashionable* and *rakish*. I found *vampiric* far more fitting. The black eyes that stared into mine held no humanity—and hadn't for hundreds of years.

"So, which one is it?" he asked.

My voice stuck in my dry throat. "I-I'm sorry?"

"Audacity or lost hope?"

Though Arnaud remained preternaturally still, I could sense a coiling in his muscles, as though he were poising to strike. I felt, too, that he *wanted* me to sense this. I stiffened in apprehension.

"Boldness or gloom? Because, you see, my boy, I have the cure for either."

I searched my peripheral vision for anything I might put between us, but the bookshelf-lined room seemed to have stretched out, the corporate desk and plush leather chairs suddenly far away. I felt naked without my confiscated items.

Arnaud gave a knowing laugh. "Rest assured, Mr. Croft, your accoutrements are quite safe."

Vampires weren't psychic, per se, but they could detect the chemicals humans emitted as a byproduct of fear. They also enjoyed inciting them, the hormonal aerosol being almost as nutritive for a vampire as blood. I could all but feel Arnaud's smooth tongue lapping up mine.

Gross.

"Security precaution, you understand," he was saying. "With so much nastiness and loathing out there, one can never be too prudent. But between us, a bag of rice could hardly be considered harmful, now could it?" When he laughed again it was with a hint of derision. "Or helpful, for that matter. As though spilled grains would drive one to such distraction he would fail to finish what he'd set out to do."

Okay, so I'd gone with an untested myth on that one. Holy water, however—

"But back to the question at hand." Arnaud took his first precise steps toward me, pupils gleaming. "Was it daring or despair that brought you? Or perhaps something of both? I am a granter of wishes, you know."

His velvet voice took on a low flutter of hunger as he crossed the office cleanly, effortlessly. In the next moment, he was too close. An oppressive atmosphere enveloped me. It was the enticing smell I'd picked up outside, but grown more penetrating and foul, as though it were covering up a stink of decomposition. I struggled to breathe, to think clearly.

"Oh, yes, *wonderful* wishes," he purred.

He was at my back now, circling. The atmosphere was the vampire's making, emanating from his pores like a toxic opiate. An intense drowsiness pulled at my mind with the promise of the warmest, most luxurious sleep.

"You are a little older than the boys I like to take in, but I would make an exception." Something walked over my scalp like spider's legs—his fingers, I realized. "Yes, I smell power in your blood, Mr. Croft. Pledge it to me, and I will grant you wealth, eternal life. You'll never want again."

I staggered to remain standing.

"One has only to ... *submit*," he whispered, the final word like a down pillow under my head. "There, you see?"

His fingers massaged my scalp in small circles. When a chilling breath brushed my throat, I realized in horror that I was offering it to him. Through thick eyelids, I watched his lips retract from an impossibly large jaw, the emerging fangs bunched together like a great white's. His fingers sank in, bracing my head, while his lower face disappeared beneath my chin.

The Pact, I tried to murmur.

I could feel the skin near my Adam's apple dimpling beneath needle-sharp points.

"The Pact," I managed.

Arnaud hesitated.

"You and the ... the Society of the Dragon," I forged on. "You made a pact with one another... to stop warring and join forces ... against ... the Inquisition."

I had discovered the story during my time in Romania, connecting it to the ring I'd found among Grandpa's possessions. A ring that had been inert for as long as I'd possessed it, but now pulsed around my finger.

Arnaud chuckled softly. "I'm afraid the Brasov Pact does not apply to descendants. Only to those who had an immediate interest in keeping the Church from lopping our heads from our bodies. Besides, that was more than four centuries ago. I trust there's a statute of limitation."

I'd been struggling my right arm up until my fist was level with his heart.

A strange Word swelled in the back of my throat: *"Balaur!"*

It emerged like a cannon ball, as though the ring had spoken it. An angry force exploded from my right fist, and Arnaud went flying. His body cracked into the far wall of polarized glass, head whiplashing back. But when Arnaud landed, it was on fingertips and the toes of his loafers. He growled at me through shanks of white hair.

"How *dare* you," he seethed, pain twisting the words.

Flaps of skin dangled from his face, as though it had been raked by a dragon's talons. I had to remind myself that the gleaming blood wasn't his. He hissed again as smoke rose from beneath the collar of his shirt.

"You burned me!"

"The ring burned you," I corrected him. I was in full possession of my language and limbs again, the torpor gone from my thoughts. "Punishment for violating the Pact. So, in essence, you burned yourself."

When Arnaud reared to spring, I brought my right fist up. His eyes shifted to the ring, and I watched the first shard of uncertainty take hold. The enchanted ring was no longer pulsing—I may have exhausted its charge with the blast—but Arnaud didn't need to know that.

He sniffed the air for the least apprehension, but I gave him none. "Can we talk now?" I asked with an attitude of impatience.

Arnaud scowled but relaxed and slowly rose. The smoke dissipated into a haze around his head. He straightened his jacket with indignant tugs, then fixed the scarf over his shoulders. When the smoke cleared, his face was intact again, the skin restored to its waxy state.

He paced over to a small bar, his back to me. On the other side of him, glass clinked and liquid splashed. I expected him to order me out, but when he turned, he was holding two poured drinks—scotch on the rocks, from the looks of them. He set one drink down on an end table beside a chair of oxblood leather and took the chair across from it: an invitation to join him.

I did so, going over and lowering myself to the edge of the soft cushion.

Arnaud took a sip of his drink, then gave his hair a toss as he sat back, the rakish billionaire once more. He opened a hand of slender fingers toward me. "*Now*," he said, as though we'd arrived at some understanding, "if you've come to talk, then get on with it. I'm a very busy man."

Not knowing how long his respect for the ring would hold, I decided to shoot to the point. "There was a murder at St. Martin's Cathedral," I said, "sometime Wednesday night."

"Ah, yes. Father Richard." He made a soft tsking sound. "A tragedy."

"Did you know him?"

"Indeed. We had an opportunity to talk last month."

"Oh?"

"Mr. Croft," he said with an edge of reproach, "if you insist on carrying on in this manner, with your surprised faces and little 'oh's, I am certain I can find a more productive use of my time. You know our history. You know my interest in the church property. Even now you're searching for an eye tick, some tell, to determine whether I was involved in his murder. Why the artifice? Certainly a man of your bloodline can come straight to it and ask."

"Did you have him killed?"

As he studied his drink, a smile touched the corners of his thin lips. I had played my hand clumsily, handing him back control, dammit. "There," he said, "doesn't that feel better?"

"Well?" I pressed.

"Why the sudden interest? The Church showed far less concern for your forebears, after all. Poisonings. Public burnings. Beheadings." Arnaud made the tsking sound again. "Nasty, nasty business."

"Is that why you want St. Martin's out of the Financial District?"

The Church had come down just as hard, if not harder, on Arnaud and his contemporaries. Had magic users and vampires not aligned, both would have been cleansed from Europe. Instead, they fought back, defeating the regional enforcers of the Inquisition. Arnaud and Grandpa went their separate ways, only to eventually wash up on the same Manhattan shoreline.

I mentioned how Grandpa never joined us at Sunday Mass? He had his reasons.

"In part," Arnaud replied at last. "But I have learned many things in my life, chief among them to not draw attention to my nature. Our kind inspires fear, yes, but also uncommon wrath."

Arnaud stood and, his glass dangling from his long fingers, strolled to the floor-to-ceiling window that cast the room in tannic brown light. Beyond and far below, I could see the wall that separated his domain from the rest of Manhattan. The streets beyond were clogged with cars and pedestrians, great knots converging on the checkpoints. For a moment, I saw the people as Arnaud must have—bearers of pikes and torches, castle-stormers.

"I like to keep my activities quiet, you see." He took another sip of scotch. "The brutal murder of one as exalted as Father Richard is anything but. Not that I regret what happened. If his death presents me with someone more amenable to financial pressure, well ... let's just say I won't demur."

"So you had nothing to do with the murder?"

"I believe I've answered your question, my boy."

He spoke with the self-possession of someone with nothing to hide, and I caught myself nodding.

"What about Black Earth?" I asked.

He turned to face me. "What about them?"

Them? I straightened.

"Are they a group?" I blurted before I could stop myself.

Arnaud's lips stretched into a wicked smile. Damn. He strolled back to his chair, this time sitting with his legs neatly crossed. He draped a wrist over his knee and jiggled his drained glass, making the ice clink.

"It seems I have something you want," he said.

"Not necessarily. I mean, if you know something about Black Earth that I don't, then—"

He silenced me with a raised hand. "The cat is already out of its foul little bag, Mr. Croft. Why, there it is now, scampering about, the rascal." His eyes darted around as though tracking it, then returned to mine. He studied me for a long moment, his gaze dipping once to my hand.

"The ring," he said.

I curled my fingers protectively. "Huh?"

"Yes. The ring for the information."

Though he sounded like someone proposing a simple business transaction, I sensed an underlying urgency. He didn't like the idea of an enchanted item out there that could hurt him. For my part, I didn't like the idea of *not* having that item. But with less than twenty-four hours to point Detective Vega in the direction of the killer, I needed to know what Black Earth meant.

"A renewed truce?" I counter-offered.

"The ring or nothing."

I studied the dragon embossed in the face of dark silver. I hadn't thought the ring was anything more than symbolic. In fact, I'd only brought it to get inside and, once here, to remind Arnaud of the Pact. Fortunately for my immortal soul, the power of the Pact had been bound inside the ring through enchantment. It was a powerful artifact, and one I might need again.

"I'm sorry, but I can't give this up," I said.

"Then it appears we're done."

Before I could come up with another offer, Arnaud stood and clapped his hands sharply. The blood slave who had ushered me in opened the door.

"Zarko," Arnaud said. "Please show Mr. Croft down and return his belongings." He rotated back to the window as though I had already been escorted out. Knowing further appeals would fall on deaf ears, I stood from my chair, drink untouched, and headed for the door.

I was nearly to the threshold when Arnaud spoke again. "I've become fond of you in our short time together this afternoon, Mr. Croft." The way his voice warped the word *fond* told me he'd become anything but. I turned anyway, alert in anticipation. "As such, I will tell you this. While the Pact may forbid me from coming after you, I cannot be held liable for the actions of my employees. No offense to good Zarko here, but they are rather mindless, after all. There is no telling what they might do if provoked."

"And what *might* provoke them?" I asked, edging from Zarko, whose pale lips had turned up at the corners.

"Remain on your side of the Wall, my boy, and I doubt you'll ever need know."

I clenched my jaw. In exchange for the vaguest acknowledgment that a group called Black Earth *did* exist, possibly even somewhere in the city, I'd relinquished my access to the bulk of downtown Manhattan—where St. Martin's just happened to sit.

"I won't make any promises," I muttered as I crossed the threshold.

"Well, then neither will I," Arnaud answered.

20

I left the Financial District on foot, dumping the bag of rice at the first garbage bin I encountered.

As I stepped from the Wall's shadow, I squinted around. I was still recovering from Arnaud's poisonous presence (the dull afternoon light outside his building had nearly blinded me), but part of my splintering headache arose from irritation at myself. That was what risking my life for nothing tended to do.

Well, not nothing, I thought as I tapped north. I felt I could safely cross Arnaud off the list of suspects. He was right. His survival had as much to do with amassing wealth and influence as keeping his vampiric activities on the down low. As badly as he wanted St. Martin's out of his district, he was resigned to doing so through legal action and bribery.

That left Wang Gang and the White Hand. Perhaps Black Earth was the name of an inner circle Caroline hadn't known about? I still thought it was a long shot, given the language of the message, but Chinatown was all I had. One small problem, however—I didn't have an in with the White Hand like I did with Arnaud. No family connections or...

The thought trailed off as an idea took hold.

Fifteen minutes later I was stepping beneath a string of paper lanterns and opening a door to a sharp *tring*.

A familiar pungency met me as I peered around. It had been years since I'd set foot inside Mr. Han's Apothecary (Midge's Medicinals in the West Village was more convenient), but it was much as I remembered. A tight maze work of shelves and small drawers packed with just about anything a spell-caster could want: roots, rare stones, ground bones, dried arachnids, some as large as my hand, seemingly empty bottles with labels like GOOD HOPE and INSANITY.

I could browse in here all day.

"That Mr. Croft?" an accented voice asked.

I turned to the small register in the front of the store to find a late middle-aged man with jet-black hair, a collared shirt buttoned to his narrow throat. Just the fellow I was looking for.

"Mr. Han! Hey, how are you?"

"Oh, you know, just *chilling out*." That must have been one of the first English phrases he'd learned because it was his answer to every inquiry into his or his family's well being. I expected him to ask about my long absence, but he shifted immediately to business. "How can help you? Have good, good sale on scorpion today." He nodded toward a fish bowl squirming with them.

"Oh, no thanks."

"Boar tail? Sloth wee-wee?"

For a moment I considered the second—it was great for encumbering spells—but I shook my head. "Actually, Mr. Han, I was hoping you could help me with a question."

"Have question?"

I looked around to ensure the store's emptiness before stooping toward his small counter. I studied the diminutive man, doubting his connection to the White Hand went any further than having to pay them a business tax. Even so, I would need to proceed with care.

"Does the name Black Earth mean anything to you?"

"Black Earth," he repeated sharply. He said nothing for several moments. By his blank face, I couldn't tell if he was even considering the question. But he was checking the name against a mental inventory because when he spoke again, he said, "Mr. Han no carry. Can order. Be here two week."

He thrust out a pair of fingers.

"No, no," I said with a chuckle. I'd always liked Mr. Han. "Black Earth isn't an ingredient. It's the name of a group, I think."

Another blank face.

"Maybe one associated with, you know, the *bosses*?" I looked around to suggest greater Chinatown.

"Boss? I only boss," he said. "Father boss before me, but gone. Son next boss, but lazy." He made a face of disgust and jerked his head to the right. "Play videogame but no learn business."

A pale green curtain fluttered over the doorway Mr. Han had indicated. Beyond, I could make out bursts of electronic gunfire.

"Need Black Earth today?" he said, getting back to my question. "Go to North Wood. Central Park."

Sensing the line of inquiry was only going to elicit more confused answers, I decided to shift to the shrieker case. I pulled out my notepad and flipped to last night's scribblings. I noticed my pencil was missing from the spiral binding, probably when the checkpoint guards had rifled my pockets.

"Do you know a man named Chin Lau Ping?"

"Chin drive bus."

Okay, so I had the right person. But because word of his death hadn't seemed to have hit the streets yet, I was careful to phrase my next question in present tense. "Does he ever shop here?"

"Chin come many, many time."

Sounded like another magic dabbler. I was trying to think of an appropriate follow-up question when Mr. Han turned toward the doorway to his living quarters and unleashed an explosion of Chinese. I looked in time to see a shadow recede from the other side of the diaphanous curtain. Mr. Han shook his head and returned his attention to me. "Chin funny man."

"You mean strange?"

"No, tell funny joke."

I couldn't match Mr. Han's delighted laughter as he related the impossible-to-follow story involving chopsticks and fried bull testicles, but I chuckled at what I guessed to have been the punch line.

"That's ... great," I said.

Hitting a dead end there as well, I rounded up a few spell items, including a vial of the sloth urine, and paid for them back at the counter. It looked like I was going to have to do my own research at home. Accepting the neat paper bag, I bid the apothecary owner farewell.

"Chill out at Mr. Han anytime!" he called after me.

21

Back home, I reclined in my downstairs reading chair and shook open the afternoon edition of the *Scream*. The cheap tabloid focused on crime and vice, hence the need for two daily runs. Indeed, while the big city papers were entering their second decade of declining ad sales and readership, the *Scream* was in boom mode with no signs of slowing.

On the second page, I found what I was looking for:

GRUESOME EVISCERATION IN HARLEM! SECOND IN CHINATOWN!

Though the three-column story was long on sensationalism and short on specifics, I picked out a few details. The Hamilton Heights conjurer had been twenty-eight-year-old Fred "Flash" Thomas. He'd worked at a fast-food joint in the neighborhood and was considered something of a prankster.

According to a neighbor, one of his favorite tricks had been to throw his voice to make it sound as though complete strangers were insulting one another. “Started more than his share of fights,” the woman was quoted as saying. “Probably what got him killed.”

Magic was what got him killed, actually. And with the voice projecting, it sounded as though he’d been dabbling in the art for a while. The article went on to list the city schools he’d attended, a couple of them reformatory, but nothing to help answer the question of *where* he’d picked up the spell.

The coverage of the Chinatown conjurer wasn’t much more informative. I’d gotten the man’s name and occupation correct, though it seemed little more was known about him.

“Given their ritualistic nature,” the article concluded, “the grisly killings are believed to have been perpetrated by the same sick, depraved individual.” My eyes wandered to a composite sketch below.

“Of course,” I said.

The staring eyes were too wide, the nose too large, and the lips too narrow, but I could imagine the back and forth as the elderly couple from the Hamilton Heights apartments described me to the police sketch artist. They’d even included the various scrapes and gouges on my face. My healing spell had all but taken care of those, fortunately, but the physical description of the man wanted for questioning was another matter.

“Six-foot to six-two male,” I read aloud, “dark brown hair, hazel eyes ... last seen running westbound on 142nd Street, near Fredrick Douglass Boulevard, carrying a wooden cane.”

Thank God my projection spell had worked last night. Then again, having the jackass duo of Dempsey and Dipinski as alibis was no guarantee of anything.

I thumbed through the rest of the paper. There was no coverage on the St. Martin's murder yet, which suggested the church had paid the *Scream* for their silence—another way the paper raked in revenue. Church officials no doubt wanted to be able to break the news to the parishioners themselves, and more gently.

The other murders in the last twenty-four hours were shootings, which was actually a relief. It meant the shriekers hadn't fed since being loosed. Maybe the Order had sent someone to deal with them.

I set the paper aside and checked my watch. The East Village conjurer remained under my mind-restoring magic, and would for another twelve to twenty-four. The man being my best source of where the spell had come from, I would need to be there when he woke up.

In the meantime, I could focus on the cathedral murder, which meant trying to learn what Black Earth meant.

Tabitha stirred as I passed her, the food plate and milk bowl beside the divan licked clean. I preempted my cat by saying, "Dinner after your tour."

"I've toured twice already, you tyrannical fu—"

"Language," I reminded her. "Anything to report?"

She yawned and flopped onto her other side. "Your admirer was back."

An electric jolt shot through me. "The woman?" I'd checked the outside of the building before entering but hadn't seen any average-looking brunettes watching. At least not in plain view.

"Still can't tell for sure," Tabitha replied.

"What time?"

"One, two o'clock. I don't know."

"Did you pick out any defining features like we talked about?"

"Yeah, two. She was standing across the street, and her feet were together."

On my last visit to the dentist I was told I grind my teeth. Hmm, I wonder why. "Look, if you're not going to try, then neither am I. How does water and Meow Mix sound?"

Tabitha sighed. "She was in a dark coat, hair past her shoulders."

I tried to align the composite with people I knew and came up empty.

"Next time you see her, come get me."

"Hard to do when you're never home."

"Just..." She had a point. "Look, I have a ton on my plate. More than *you'll* ever appreciate. All so we can continue to enjoy our present comfortable lifestyle, I should remind you."

Tabitha acted as though she wasn't listening.

"I'll be upstairs. *Working*."

As I climbed the ladder to my library and lab, my irritation with Tabitha gave over to puzzlement about who was staking out the apartment. I ruled out plainclothes detective, since Tabitha had first seen the woman yesterday, before the killings in which my unflattering likeness was now the chief suspect. That left ... who? Someone involved with the church murder? The shrieker conjurings?

The hologram of the city was dim, anyway, which was a relief. I needed it to stay that way. I didn't think I could handle another summoning tonight.

I got right to work on the church case, poring through several thick tomes for anything that might relate to the message. I was a good hour in when I found something. In a section on spell-craft in ancient Britain, my eyes locked onto the name of a group who practiced a druidic form of magic.

The monks had called themselves *Nigra Terra*. Translation: Black Earth.

I jotted down a page's worth of notes on the fierce group, then leaned back in my desk chair in thought. There were a few druid cults in the city who dabbled in nature magic. Blessing trees and animals, that sort of thing. Harmless, really.

But I'd heard rumors of a clandestine group whose activities were less well known. They hadn't been summoning nether creatures—the alarm would have alerted me. Still, they practiced in Central Park which was telling, given the beings that roamed those wilds. The druid group was either more powerful than the resident creatures or aligned with them, somehow.

I nearly tipped backwards in my chair as I remembered what Mr. Han had said that afternoon.

Need Black Earth today? Go to North Wood. Central Park.

Had he been trying to tell me something?

I was considering the question when the flame on my table erupted in a red-purple column. A folded piece of paper shot from the peaking flame, unfolding as it fell, fluttering to the table top. It came to a rest in the table's center, as neat as if someone had placed it there.

From the Order? A response within twelve hours would be lightening speed for them. I rushed over to the message anyway, hoping for an update on the shrieker situation.

To: Everson Croft

After reviewing your reports on the recent summonings, we hereby order you to cease pursuit of the matter and discontinue all magic use until further notice. This decree goes into immediate effect.

Signed: The Order

I staggered backwards as though I'd been punched in the throat.

"*What?*"

22

The Order had voiced displeasure with me in the past (the Thelonious issue remained a *really* touchy subject), but they had never taken away my practice of magic. Next to death, it was the harshest decree that could be handed down, reserved for magic users who drifted into the dark arts.

I stopped. *Is that what they think I've done?*

"Relax, Everson," I whispered. "Deep breaths."

I resumed pacing, respiring in through my nose and out through pursed lips. My heart continued to pound high in my chest. I reread the message. Calling me off the case I could understand. I could even see where the directive was meant to keep me safe. Demonic beings were beyond my present abilities, as my battle with the juvenile shrieker had attested.

But "discontinue all magic use until further notice"? What the hell?

Developed beyond a certain point, magic became as integral to a wizard as any vital organ. More so, magic became a lens through which we perceived existence and our place in it. I couldn't imagine my life without it. But the Order was demanding I do just that.

I tried to harness some hope to the final three words: "until further notice." Maybe this was a temporary stay, again for reasons of safety.

But a harsher truth was rearing up in my mind, and it went back to Thelonious. I'd already mentioned that, as an incubus, he belonged to a similar class of being as demons. It was why the threshold at St. Martin's wanted nothing to do with me. I was also beginning to suspect it was the reason for the Order's decision. After all, the spells had to be coming from someone or something with a strong link to the demon world. That didn't necessarily make me a suspect, but in the minds of the Order, it made me susceptible to manipulation or outright possession. As a wizard with an incubus problem, I was a handicap.

My heart settled. That had to be it.

I studied the plum-colored flame. Getting that assurance from the source would have been nice, but the arcane society to which I belonged—though felt more outsider than member—was rigidly hierarchical. A follow-up inquiry would either get me an identically-worded decree or be ignored altogether. Experience told me the second. I had a mentor I might have been able to tap, but I hadn't seen Chicory in almost a year. Judging by his scattered nature, I wasn't sure he went much higher up the ladder than I did.

Fine, I thought, balling up the Order's message and tossing it into the flame, where it incinerated. *I'll play along*.

In the meantime, there was the matter of my job at the college. To save it, I was going to need to make some serious headway on the cathedral case before I had to report back to Detective Vega sometime tomorrow. The druid cult in Central Park was a possible break, but I needed a motive for the killing. And for that I would need to talk to someone at St. Martin's. I fished in my pockets for the card Father Vick had handed me.

"Hello, Father," I said when he answered. "This is Everson Croft."

"Everson, it's so good to hear you."

"How are you doing?" I asked carefully.

"If I'm being honest, not well." He gave a forlorn laugh. "My faith is strong, but so too was my closeness to Brother Richard."

"I understand." I waited the appropriate beat before continuing. "I hate to ask at a time like this, Father, but could I stop by this evening to talk? I'm still helping out on the case and was hoping you might shed some light on a few questions."

"I'm not sure I can tell you anything more than I've already told your detective."

Right, I thought, *only I don't have access to Detective Vega's case file. She would erupt if she even knew I was talking to you.*

"Well," I hedged, "I'm pursuing a slightly different lead."

"In that case, I'll do whatever I can to assist. However, I'm conducting a special Mass this evening for church officials. Might we meet in the morning?"

I didn't like the idea of sitting on the case for the next fourteen hours, but what could I say?

"Is eight o'clock too early?" I asked.

"That will be fine, Everson. We can talk in the vicarage here at the cathedral."

"One more thing," I said before he could hang up. "Would you mind, um, meeting me at the front door?"

23

I couldn't sit on the church case that night, it turned out, much less sleep. Following several restless hours of tossing, I dressed, retrieved an antique item from my trunk, and grabbed my cane. Remembering the no-magic decree, I went back for my revolver, tucking it into the front of my pants.

Outside my apartment building, I peered around to make sure no one was watching. There was no one, period. Barely after midnight, and I had the street to myself. This was a very different New York than the one I'd grown up in. I tightened my coat against the cold and headed east.

Several blocks later, I slipped into Washington Square Park, its walkways and lawns also deserted. I ran my gaze along the curving lines of empty benches. Even the vagrants knew better than to sleep out in the open anymore. The sane ones, anyway.

A wet snort jerked my eyes toward a copse of dying sycamores. *Not deserted, after all*, I thought. When the wind picked up, a scent of sewage blew past. A moment later, a large hominid shadow separated from the trunks, ducking low branches. Crap. I looked around the see whether the ghoul belonged to a pack, but it appeared to have come up alone. Even so, avoidance was usually the best tactic.

I was backing away when the breeze changed direction, flapping my coat against my calves. The ghoul paused, raised its lump of a nose, and sniffed wetly. A moment later, a pair of yellow eyes fell toward me.

Wonderful.

The ghoul's jaw gaped as it began shambling toward me. My cane was halfway apart before I remembered the decree. Sighing, I swapped the cane for my revolver. I had become so accustomed to channeling and pushing energy that the gun felt cold and alien in my grip.

I took aim at the ghoul's head and squeezed. A pair of silver slugs slammed it sideways. The ghoul yowled and kicked through a line of benches. Wooden planks and iron flew up around its hulking body. My backward steps became an awkward jog, jostling my aim. My next shot missed entirely.

The ghoul loped into a run, anticipating its midnight snack.

I wasn't going to outrace it. Stopping, I set my legs in a shooter's stance and aimed with both hands. I tried to remember what the instructor at the firing range had taught me, oh, six or seven years ago. One of the ghoul's yellow eyes bobbed in and out of the revolver's sight, growing larger. I squeezed three times. The final crack sprayed fluid and snapped the ghoul's head back. Both hands flew to its right eye as the creature fell to the pavement, howling.

"Go on," I shouted, stomping my foot. "Get out of here!"

The ghoul thrashed up and scrambled off. They were survivalists first, man-eaters second. I waited until the creature's pained cries and smacking footfalls faded east before returning the revolver to my pants.

All right. I let out a tremulous sigh. *Back to business.*

Where the park opened out, I climbed into the dry wading pool and approached the central ring from which water used to fount. Washington Square Arch, no longer lit at night, loomed as a massive silhouette to the north. I knelt at the pool's center, dry leaves crackling beneath me, and wound a small music box. When I released the key, a tinkling melody rose into the night.

I set the box on the ring and whispered, "Effie."

I'd found the music box in an antique shop years before. Curious, I took it to a local diviner. She told me it had belonged to a girl who succumbed to yellow fever in the 1800s and was buried in the city's pauper grave. Her remains now rested among twenty-thousand others, roughly beneath where I was kneeling. Her spirit, however, was as restless as mine.

"That you, Everson?" an innocent voice asked, clear as a bell.

When I turned, the eight-year-old girl was standing behind me, eyes large and inquisitive. Plain brushed hair fell over the shoulders of the gown she'd probably been buried in, light blue with a broad ribbon fastened belt-like above her waist. Her shoes were simple clogs.

"Hi there, Effie."

"You brought me music box," she exclaimed, moving past me to stoop over her former possession.

I smiled sadly. Ghosts weren't souls. They were best described as living echoes, possessing the appearance and personality of the departed, but little in the way of free will. The more malignant ones could drive a person to insanity, true, but Effie's ghost represented the sweet end of the spectrum. My heart broke a little as I watched her attempt to pick up the box.

To distract her, I said, "What did you do today, Effie?"

"I tried making friends with a boy, but 'e wouldn't talk to me." When she turned, her lips were bent in an indignant frown. She was no doubt referring to a human boy without Sight.

"Probably a loser," I said. "What about the friends you already have?"

"They're a'right," she replied. "But Mary's gettin' plumb on me nerves with her tales."

"Ugh. Mary and her tales." I shook my head. "Hey, uh, speaking of your friends, I have a question I'd like you to ask them."

"Whut is it?"

"You know St. Martin's Cathedral downtown, right?" Fortunately, it was old enough to have been standing during Effie's time in New York. I watched her nod. "Good. I want you to ask your friends if they've seen anything unusual around there in the last month or so."

"Like whut?" she asked.

I was throwing a blind net. Ghosts were drawn to ley energy, and with the intensity around St. Martin's, I was hoping one or several in Effie's circle had made their way down there, maybe picked up on something. A shame I hadn't befriended any of the ghosts at St. Martin's, but such things took time.

"Just ... anything that might have struck them as odd," I answered.

Effie appeared to think about that before nodding her head. "A'right," she said. She turned back to her old music box and, in a soft, haunting voice, added words to the tinkling lullaby.

Sweet babe, a golden cradle holds thee
Soft snow-white fleece enfolds thee
In airy bower I'll watch thy sleeping
Where branchy trees in the breeze are sweeping

Ghosts usually required a full day/night cycle to carry out requests, but I was in no hurry to return to my sheet-tangled bed. Ghouls or not, it was a sleepless night. Too many thoughts knocking around my head: at-large shriekers, no-magic decrees, the cathedral murder, the police sketch, the mystery person watching my apartment, my impending hearing at the college. It made the straightforward existence of the undead seem enviable in contrast.

I wound the box for Effie several more times. Sometime after three, her apparition faded along with her solemn notes.

24

It was half past eight the next morning by the time I made it through the pedestrian checkpoint. My NYPD card had worked its charm a second time, but even so, I was thirty minutes late.

I hurried south from the Wall, aware I was challenging Arnaud by returning to his district. I pictured the vampire at his top-story window but doubted the drizzly morning offered him much of a view. The head of his building had been hidden by a drift of low clouds since early light, meaning he couldn't see me. When I peeked up again, my face prickled with current.

Damn. Something told me he could.

I dropped my head and cut west to put a few skyscrapers between us. Soon, I was coming up on the steps of St. Martin's. Beyond the tall bronze doors stood Father Vick, the image of patience.

"Forgive me," I said, hustling up to the other side of the threshold and shaking the collection of moisture from my coat. "Should have known to add an extra hour to the commute."

"It's certainly not what it used to be," he said with a smile. "Please, Everson, come in."

The invitation. I peeked past him to make sure no police were inside—or Detective Vega herself—and crossed the threshold. The wave that rippled through me felt thinner than last time. It didn't induce the same queasiness or deprive me of quite as much power. I wondered whether the shocked and grieving atmosphere of the past two days had something to do with that.

"I'm back here," he said.

I followed his shifting cassock through several doors and across an inner courtyard. The cathedral around us was stone silent. It wasn't until we had reached his one-room apartment that he spoke again.

"How have you been, Everson? I was sorry to hear of your grandparents' passing."

He left the door open a crack behind me, allowing a slipstream of fresh air into the monastic space.

"I'm well," I replied. "Busy. Teaching at Midtown College and now consulting for the NYPD." I intentionally left out that I was doing the second to get six months whacked off my probation—all in the hopes of saving the first. I didn't need to share the wizarding bit, either.

Father Vick moved a pile of prayer books from the seat of a wooden armchair and gestured for me to sit.

"So you're back in the city?" He placed the books on a small desk beneath his lone window and beside what appeared to be a draped handkerchief, then turned his desk chair so he could face me.

I nodded a little uneasily, sensing the question in his raised eyebrows.

"Well, I hope you know you're always welcome back at St. Martin's," he said.

I was pretty sure the threshold would beg to differ, as well as higher-ups in the denomination who hadn't much cared for my published thesis on the *First Saints* manuscript.

"That means a lot," I said. "Thank you."

He studied me for a moment, hand on his cinnamon beard, before breaking into a pleasant chuckle. "I remember when you were in my beginning Sunday school class. You couldn't have been more than five or six. The biblical stories fascinated you, but you never liked to hear about anyone getting hurt." He chuckled again. "At the time, I thought, 'Now here's someone destined for the ministry.' I sense, though, that you help people in other ways?"

"I do my best," I said noncommittally.

His pale blue eyes studied me again until I felt my body wanting to shift.

"Before we get to your questions," he said, "is there anything you'd like to talk about?"

As a shadow exorcist, he could perceive a person's light/dark conflicts—a skill honed through faith and enhanced by the ley energy that coursed up through the cathedral's foundation. By the subtle shift in his tone, I could tell Father Vick had seen something in me. Whether it had to do with my magical bloodline or my darker Thelonious nature, I couldn't say.

"Thank you, Father, but I'm not here for myself."

"Very well," Father Vick said. He set his clasped hands on his lap to signal he was ready to begin.

"Would you mind going over what happened the, uh—" I fumbled for my pocket notebook. "—the night of Father Richard's murder, leading up to the discovery of his body the next morning?"

"Following Wednesday night's Mass, the four of us who live here—the groundskeeper, an acolyte in residence, Father Richard, and myself—we had a late dinner and then retired to our rooms, around ten. Father Richard must have gotten up at some point to go to the sacristy."

"Would that be unusual?" I patted my pockets for something to write with.

Father Vick handed me a ballpoint pen from his desk. "No, he would often spend time there when he couldn't sleep. An hour or so organizing the cupboards, polishing the chalices, preparing for the next day's service."

"Did everyone know about this?"

"Those of us here, yes. Though maybe not the acolyte. Malachi has only been with us for a couple of months. I don't know if Father Richard's habit was ever mentioned in his presence. In any case, nothing was heard that night. The next morning, Cyrus, our groundskeeper, found him..." Father Vick frowned severely as though to prevent tears from forming in his eyes. "Found him on the floor. Just as you probably saw him the other day."

I gave the moment its solemn due before continuing. "Is the cathedral locked at night?"

Father Vick composed himself, then nodded. "It's Cyrus's duty to secure all of the doors and windows, and he's very regimental about it. Our locks are security grade, reinforced by the power of the church. No one's ever broken in, and there were no signs anyone had."

"Was everything locked the next morning, as well?"

"Yes. Cyrus checked."

I finished writing, then tapped the pen against my chin. That seemed to rule out someone slipping in with the day crowd, hiding until he could take care of the rector, and then stealing back out. But it didn't rule out lock picking.

"In the last few weeks, did you notice anyone watching the church, staking it out, anything like that?"

"I stay so busy, Everson. I can't say that I did."

He seemed to be apologizing for his lapse in vigilance, which sent a fresh wave of guilt through me. Here I was, posing as a police investigator, interrogating my bereaved former youth minister, all so I might keep my day job. Despite what I'd told Father Vick earlier, I *was* here for myself.

"Had the rector received any recent threats?"

"Several from the White Hand in Chinatown. The church's commitment to human rights had been butting up against their business interests. The police are supposed to be pursuing that angle."

I nodded. Maybe I'd leave that one to Detective Vega. I still doubted a Chinatown hit man would have left an obscure message in pre-Latin. Why not the White Hand insignia, meant to inspire fear? I decided to go bolder.

"How about threats from less ... mundane quarters?"

Father Vick looked at me thoughtfully before gazing out the window. The drizzle had become a steady rain, splashing over the courtyard's dark-red flagstones.

"Father Richard came from a more conservative tradition," he said after a moment, "one that believed all magic was the work of

Satan or one of his horde. Even sacred magic could open one up to evil forces, he insisted. I tried to help him see otherwise, but he was very rigid in his mindset."

I thought of the violence at the crime scene. "Were his views well known?"

"Well, he didn't seem to think the city was doing enough about the 'occult problem,' as he called it." When Father Vick turned from the window to face me again, it was with a look of apology. He sensed my magic. "He had been preparing to meet with city commissioners and police officials. He wanted them to start cracking down on the 'openly-practicing'—another one of his terms."

I doubted this was something Father Vick had shared with the investigators. If the druid cult had gotten wind of the rector's campaign, maybe they had decided to preempt it. "Have you ever heard of a group called Black Earth?" I asked.

Father Vick frowned steeply in thought. "I'm aware that esoteric groups exist in the city, but my work takes me into the lives of individuals. Those who have lapsed beyond doubt into darkness, aligned with the shadows that dwell there. I've never believed the church's role should be castigation, Everson. We should offer sanctuary and, when possible, healing. Like that young boy in my Sunday school class, I don't like to see people hurt."

He hadn't answered my question, but before I could try again, a sharp pain stole my breath away. Father Vick had raised two fingers, and a force was stabbing through me.

I stared back at him. *What in the hell...?*

But he wasn't causing the pain, I realized, not directly.

Thelonious had been caught off guard and was now burrowing into my energy like a giant tick. Father Vick's powers of exorcism were strong, but not strong enough to dislodge a determined incubus. I raised a hand to show him I was okay. The force and pain relented.

I searched for words to paper over the awkward moment, but Father Vick's pale eyes were gazing past me. I turned and jumped a little to discover someone standing just outside the cracked-open door—a young woman in a white robe, from the segment I could see.

"Come in, Malachi," Father Vick said.

Malachi? The door opened wider, and I saw the person was, in fact, a dude. Though he must have been twenty or so, his nervous, narrow face remained in smooth adolescence. His hair had also thrown me, brown hair long enough to have been gathered into a ponytail in back.

"Malachi is our resident acolyte," Father Vick informed me as way of introduction. "He's interested in St. Martin's history and has been going through our vast archives. Some fascinating items in there."

I stood and shook the boy's pliant hand. "Everson Croft."

The young man mumbled something that was barely audible, his smallish eyes flitting around my gaze.

"Did you have something to tell me?" Father Vick asked him.

"Um, the police are here. They want to see you again."

I knew there was a chance of that happening, but crap.

"Have them wait for me in the nave. We shouldn't be more than another minute."

As the door closed behind Malachi, Father Vick gave me an

ironic smile. “It looks like your colleagues have more questions.” He shrugged as he stood. “Given the circumstances, who can blame them? By all appearances, the murder was committed by someone inside these old walls.”

“What do you think?” I asked.

“Besides no one having any grievances against Brother Richard? Cyrus is too old to have carried out so violent an attack, and Malachi too gentle. There is no malice in either of them.”

Father Vick *did* have that perceptual ability, but I noticed he’d left himself out.

“I have to ask,” I said, already wincing inwardly at what I was about to say. “Did the two of you have any conflicts? I mean, you seem to have been divided on the issue of magic.”

“A fair question,” he replied, holding my gaze. “And yes, we did argue about the matter. But you don’t have to see eye to eye on every issue to be close.” Grief clouded his face. “If you had siblings, you would understand.”

I nodded and lowered my gaze. *Congratulations, Everson, you’ve just leveled up in shittiness.*

Father Vick placed his hands warmly on my shoulders. “It *has* been good to see you, Everson. And I meant what I said. You’re welcome at St. Martin’s anytime. You’re not the exile you seem to believe yourself to be.”

“Good to see you too, Father.”

With a final smile, he stepped past me. “Well, I suppose I need to get to another meeting. And if I read your earlier reaction correctly, you need a back door to depart through.”

“I guess investigators have their own conflicts,” I said sheepishly.

"Say no more. You can leave through the graveyard." He led me out to the covered walk that ran around the courtyard. I noticed he took care to lock the door behind him. "I'll have Cyrus let you out."

I glimpsed something dark and shining in his ear.

"Father, you're bleeding." I pointed to my right ear.

He touched his hair-thatched canal, then inspected the blood on the tip of his finger. "Yes, that happens sometimes." He reached out and washed his finger beneath a string of water falling from the eave of the courtyard. "We are mortals channeling forces far beyond us, after all."

25

I saw what Father Vick meant about Cyrus. The stooped and palsied groundskeeper could hardly heft his ring of keys, much less bring a chalice down on a man's head with enough force to smite him. And I sensed no magic around him.

I followed Cyrus out a back door and along a path beaten in the grass. We were in an older part of the graveyard behind the church. Dark, weathered tombstones rose like crooked teeth. Raised sarcophagi leaned here and there, a particularly mossy one in a solitary corner, beneath a knotted willow. Though the rain had passed, the chill air was stippled with moisture. A good day for a blazing fire.

Cyrus unlocked a door in the iron gate that ran along Washington Street. I thanked him and stepped through the curtain of energy that protected the sanctuary. Definitely weaker, I noted.

My plan was to get home and prepare some spells for a trip to Central Park that night. Yeah, yeah, magic *verboten*. But I'd already worked it out—I was going to play the dumb card: *Ohhh, I thought you meant no magic in relation to the shrieker case.* Cue smacking of forehead.

Would the Order buy it? Who knew, but this was bigger than saving my job. I was thinking about Father Vick now, a man whose paternal concern was still palpable twenty years later. And the way he'd looked when I made him talk about the rector's death and even suggested he might have had a motive in his slaying?

So yeah, screw the Order. I'd deal with the fallout later. The more immediate challenge was going to be putting Detective Vega off for another day. At least until I could—

"Croft!"

—point her in the right direction.

I wheeled to find the one-woman Homicide squad striding up behind me, a black umbrella glistening above her stretched-back hair. She was wearing the same style of suit she seemed to favor, black jacket and pants, blouse opened at the neck. It was a good look for her, and if it ain't broke...

"What in the hell are you doing here?" she demanded.

"Besides enjoying the weather?"

"Were you just inside the church?" When she arrived in front of me, the challenge in her dark eyes told me she already knew the answer.

"Well, I wasn't not in the church, if that's what you're asking."

"I don't have time for this, Croft. Yes or no."

"*Si.*"

"You have no business being in there."

"Look," I said, holding up my hands in a no-harm, no-foul gesture, "my grandmother and I attended St. Martin's when I was growing up. Father Vick was my youth minister. Thursday was the first time I'd seen him in almost twenty years. He invited me to come back and visit him." All technically true. "I had some time this morning, so..."

"Father Victor is a suspect in a homicide investigation—one you're consulting on, I should remind you. You're not to fraternize with him until we've wrapped up. I thought I made that clear."

I was starting to get a little sick of being told what I could and couldn't do.

"Oh, c'mon, it's not like—"

"I'm dead serious, Croft."

"You don't honestly believe Father Vick had anything to do with the murder. Or are you just aiming for 'good enough' again?"

When her eyes glowered, I realized I'd gone too far. "For your information," she hissed, drawing up until her umbrella was dripping water in front of my face, "his trace evidence is all over the crime scene."

"Yeah, and maybe that's because he lives and works there."

"So you're an investigator now?"

"Just..." I took a deep breath and let it out. "Father Vick is a good man. He helps people. Just make sure you talk to those who know him before jumping to any conclusions." I wasn't sure whether I was trying to convince Detective Vega or myself. After all these years, how well did *I* really know him?

"The message," Vega said abruptly. "It's been two days. What do you have?"

I rubbed the back of my neck. "I was actually going to call you about that. I'm going to, ah, need another day."

"That wasn't the deal."

"Right, but I put out a professional inquiry. I'm expecting an answer tonight."

Vega looked at me a long moment, sharp suspicion in her stare, then sighed through her nose. "Tomorrow morning, but that's it. No more extensions or the deal's off. We clear?"

I shifted my cane to my left hand and offered to shake on it.

But Vega's gaze remained on my cane, the suspicion back in her eyes. "Ever been to Hamilton Heights, Croft?"

"I try not to."

"Where were you two nights ago?"

Other than running down a street, being shot at by you? "Home, slogging through student papers. In fact, I received a visit from a couple of your associates. Dempsey and Dipinski?"

She studied my eyes.

"Know them?" I asked.

After another moment, she gave a reluctant nod. "They liked your cat."

I laughed. "I'm pretty sure the feeling wasn't mutual."

Vega's lips pulled to one side, but only slightly. I bet she had a killer smile. "Watch yourself, Croft," she said as she turned to leave. "I'd hate to have to arrest you again."

That makes two of us, I thought as I watched her pace back toward the cathedral.

26

I caught a bus up Broadway, disembarking at the heart of Greenwich Village.

The plan, of course, was to return to my apartment, light a fire, and spend the day indoors, cooking spells. All of that lay west. And yet I felt an urgent pull toward the garbagy, graffiti-bruised East Village and the amateur conjurer who would be rising and shining about now.

"Better think about this, Everson," I muttered, leaning against the cornice of a building on West Third. I might get away with playing dumb on the magic ban, I thought as I observed the funeral flow of foot and car traffic, but the "cease pursuit of the matter" part had been pretty plain.

Still, I'd received no assurance the Order intended to do anything about the "matter" other than call me off it. More likely, whatever they were planning would grow moss before it made it out of committee, by which time our sole lead to the spell supplier could be long gone.

Anyway, the Order didn't have eyes on me twenty-four seven. The perks of being a bottom-runger. Their wards would pick up any magic I cast, sure. So I wouldn't cast any magic. Problem solved.

But there was still that whole violation-of-decree thing.

I peered down Third Street, into a wind stinking of trash and diesel. Then I looked west, toward home.

"Oh, fuck it," I said, and began kicking my way east.

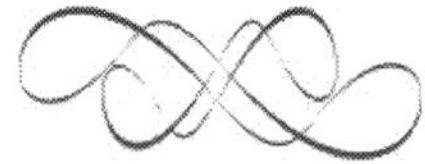

Some neighborhoods looked less menacing in the light of day. The East Village wasn't one of them. Not only were the blackened buildings and trash piles more vivid, but locals were now on the roam, most of them burned out and trashed, too. Beginning at Avenue A, I passed men and women in tatters, yellow skin stretched taut over sharp facial bones, teeth rotten to their roots. A woman with flaking patches of scalp beseeched me for money in a voice that was hardly human. The rest stared from vacant eyes, tagging them as junkies, the soul-eaten, or both.

I chanted to reinforce the strength of my coin pendant.

At Avenue C, I spotted a familiar mountain of garbage and, across the street, the conjurer's apartment building—one of two on the block still standing. Entering the lobby, I hit the stairwell at a jog.

On the top floor, at the end of the hallway, I readied my cane and threw open the conjurer's door.

The room was empty. Against the far wall, the cheap furniture had been piled up, as though someone meant to collect it later, but the line of laundry and spill of canned goods—the signs of habitation—were gone. My one hope was that the conjurer had been robbed while he slept, but he wasn't in his bedroom. Only the spring metal frame and a scatter of books remained.

Balls.

I checked the other rooms to confirm his absence. The table in his makeshift laboratory remained, as well as the mirror, which lay shattered on the floor, but the spell items were missing, probably packed into his trunk and hauled away. I returned to the main room and paced the newspaper-strewn floor in thought.

Had the conjurer left of his own initiative, or been taken? If the second, there was a good chance the mysterious spell supplier had been involved. Finding the conjurer could mean finding the supplier. There were ways to track the conjurer, but they all involved magic, dammit.

At that thought, a low humming shook through the floor and into my shoes. The sensation was followed by the muted cry of guitars.

Maybe someone had witnessed his departure.

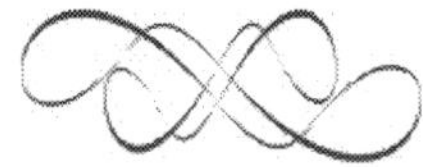

It took a minute for the guitars to die down and shouted voices to decide someone was knocking at the door. The generator idled down next until I could hear a series of bolts being worked. When the door cracked open, a shotgun barrel appeared beneath a squinting eye. The eye widened in surprise.

"Mr. Wednesday Night!" Tattoo Face exclaimed. The door opened until his giant frame was standing over me. "We were wondering if you'd come back!" He leaned his pump-action shotgun against the doorframe and clapped my shoulder with enough enthusiasm to send me into a sideways stagger. "Got another gig tonight, and everyone wants you there."

I braced myself against the wall. "Really?"

"Talk about a show stealer," Blade said, coming up beside him, a rail in comparison. She looked me up and down, her neon-pink smirk reminding me what she'd said the other morning about a strip tease.

Thanks, Thelonious.

"Much as I'd, ah, love to come," I stammered, my face warming like a furnace, "I've got a load of work. I was actually stopping by to ask if you knew anything about your upstairs neighbor."

"What about him?" Tattoo Face said.

"Well, it looks like he cleared out. Probably in the last day or so. Know where he might've gone?"

Blade shrugged. "People come and go all the time. Sort of the character of the neighborhood."

"Did he have any recent visitors?'

Tattoo Face worked his lips in thought. "None that I know of."

"Guy with stringy hair and thick glasses?" someone asked.

Blade and Tattoo Face parted so that I could see the young black man with green hair and skin-tight leathers. He was sitting on a couch, fiddling with the tuning knobs on a battered electric guitar, fingers buried in a spray of wires.

"Yeah, yeah, that's the guy," I said.

"Bumped into him on my way in this morning. He was hauling a trunk out into the street."

"Was he alone?"

"Far as I could tell."

"Did you see which way he was headed?"

"Not really." Green Hair remained fixated on his tuning project. "Screamed when he saw me. Something about the End Times. Then he dragged his trunk to the other side of the street and stared till I'd gone inside. Dude was on something. 'Course, so are most the freaks around here."

So the conjurer had left solo.

"All right, guys," I said. "Thanks."

"Sure we can't talk you into making a cameo tonight?" Tattoo Face clasped his meaty hands to his chest in a fervent plea.

Blade smirked again. "We can probably arrange to have a dancing pole brought up."

"In that case..." I said. "Not a chance in hell."

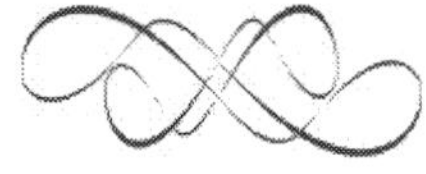

I duly weighed the stupidity of what I was about to do before returning to the conjurer's apartment. Hair made a good target item, and I found several strands in the conjurer's former bedroom. I placed them in the center of a circle of copper filings. Feather of homing pigeon or, better yet, tusk of narwhale made great catalysts, but I was fresh out.

Yeah. I was planning to cast a hunting spell right under the Order's nose.

I took a breath before aiming the tip of my cane toward the tangle of hair. The incantation was basic. White light swelled from the cane, absorbing essence from the smoldering hair. A few minutes later, after the hair had popped into foul-smelling flames, it was done. I'd get a direction by the time I reached the street.

If an agent of the Order didn't swoop down on me before then.

As I was about to leave the bedroom, a book among the scattered pile of them caught my eye. I lifted the Bible by its pebbly black spine and flopped it open to its back page. Sure enough, stamped in the top left corner in black ink:

St. Martin's Cathedral
New York, NY 10006

Now that was interesting.

27

I hustled down the stairs, already putting my discovery in perspective. St. Martin's was involved in various outreach programs for the homeless; the conjurer had likely picked up the Bible at a shelter or soup kitchen. Or maybe a parishioner had seen him on the street and handed it to him.

But call it wizard's intuition, something about the finding nagged me.

I filed the discovery away as my shoes hit the sidewalk and the hunting spell tugged my cane south. I assumed the conjurer hadn't gotten far, given the loaded trunk he was lugging. But blocks later, where the East Village became the Lower East Side, I began to wonder.

My cane pulled me into the shadow of the Williamsburg Bridge. I suddenly found myself dodging through a shantytown that spread from the bridge's massive concrete pylons onto the sidewalk and half the street. Soot-faced residents watched from sagging boxes and tents made from sheets of industrial plastic. The intelligence in their eyes scared the hell out of me. These were the ones who had held jobs and leases but now lacked the means to even leave the city. The ones the Crash had absolutely plowed over.

As I cleared the underpass, I barely avoided bowling over a man who might have been my high school principal. There was no time to check. At an abandoned police precinct, the spell jerked me hard west. I was practically running to keep up now. The conjurer was close.

I saw the trunk first, dirty blue with aluminum binding, then the back of the stringy-haired man dragging it. He was almost two blocks ahead of me and looked to be heading for Roosevelt Park.

"Hey!" I shouted, breaking into a sprint.

He turned his head enough for me to catch the edge of a thick lens, but he didn't slow. The light changed at the next intersection, and I pulled up, craning my neck to keep him in view through the traffic. The surrounding businesses told me I was where Chinatown was growing into the Lower East Side.

"C'mon, dammit," I whispered, looking for a break in the cars.

I was too focused on the conjurer to pay much attention to the group of teenagers stepping from a corner store. They were dressed in loose white suits, wife beaters for shirts, their ink black hair slick with something.

"It's him," I heard one of them whisper. "That's the man."

Shoes scuffed. I wheeled in time to see a collapse of bodies. *What the...?* An incoming fist opened my lower lip. A second blow rammed my temple, icing half my face. The sidewalk slammed into me next. I got my forearms up as stomps joined the descending fists.

The young men, who remained savagely silent, were enforcers for the White Hand. The suits told me that much. But what in the hell had I done to them? When the toe of a shoe nicked the family jewels, I decided I didn't care.

"*Vigore!*" I thundered.

The explosion from my cane threw the attackers in all directions. I gained my feet and rotated, sword and staff in hands. A thug who had eaten a light pole crawled in a crippled circle, blood from his face stippling the sidewalk. But the other four jumped up quickly.

"Stay back," I warned, summoning a light shield.

Pedestrians gave us a wide berth, eyes averted. As a general rule, the less you saw on the streets, the better. It was why I hadn't taken a lot of pains to hide my cane after the police sketch went public. *Is that what this is about?* I wondered now. I hadn't seen anything in the paper about a money reward.

Beretta pistols appeared from waistbands. With subtle jerks of their heads, the thugs tried to encircle me. Naturally, I'd left my own gun at home. The black bores of their weapons eyed my face. Whatever their motive, the thugs had left the street at my back open. Hearing the traffic slow and then idle for a red light, I snorted.

Amateurs.

I was two steps into my retreat when a head blow reduced my world to a ringing fog. I plummeted like a bag of bottles into someone's arms, which hefted me through the side door of a van.

The enforcers had transport, evidently, and a driver I hadn't seen.

I landed on the floor of the van. The thugs piled in after me. A foot forced my face against the gritty metal while sharp knees pinned the length of my body. Not that I had any fight left. I was in Woozyville. As the side door rammed closed and the van jounced from the curb, I found my thoughts fluttering around the conjurer—the key to the demonic summonings—as he drifted farther and farther away.

28

I didn't lose consciousness but would have preferred it to the jack-hammering in my head. Whoever was driving the van wasn't helping. He made several nauseating turns and hard brakes before rearing to a final stop.

The thugs lifted me under the arms and dragged me through a dark garage. In an adjoining basement room, they stripped my jacket and dropped me into a scary-looking chair. A thick leather strap went over my lap and one apiece around my chest and throat, the last cinching until I could hardly swallow.

Instead of struggling, I fumbled for my casting prism. It wasn't there. Brain too bruised.

My wrists and ankles received similar restraining treatment as my torso, the fingers of both hands forced into a pair of metal contraptions attached to the armrests. That couldn't be good. A muscled thug—the driver, I guessed—twisted a series of knobs until my finger joints were pressed straight. His next twists brought them to the verge of bending backwards. Something told me he'd done this before.

"Hey," I mumbled as the first throbs started up, "think you could back off a hair?"

The driver lumbered to a shadowy wall to my right.

Guess not.

I eyed my splayed hands, wondering how long I'd be able to hold out. I'd never been tortured before and didn't think I was going to be very good at it. But *who* was torturing me, exactly—and why?

"Chin Lau Ping."

I squinted at where the voice had come from. Its strained quality sounded like that of a girl on the verge of a tantrum. But the figure looming from the shadows ahead of me was too hulking to be a girl.

"Chin Lau Ping," the high voice repeated. "Why?"

Thick gold rings entered the light first—hands holding the lapels of a velvet smoking jacket. Underneath, a white silk shirt swelled over a loose paunch and the beginnings of man breasts. The emerging head was basketball round, anchored by a double chin and capped with an adolescent spike cut. As the man squinted at me, I wondered if he knew how stupid he looked.

But wait, what was he asking?

"*Chin Lau Ping,*" he screeched.

"I don't know what you're talking about," I said. "And is the screaming really necess—"

"Mr. Ping was my courier, and you murdered him. Why?"

Courier...? Murdered...? Then it clicked. Chin Lau Ping was the Chinatown conjurer. And this man asking after him was his boss: Wang "Bashi" Gang, head of the Chinatown crime syndicate.

I'd found an in with the White Hand after all, but not the one I probably wanted.

"Whoa, whoa, whoa." I tried to raise a hand before remembering they were both bolted down. "I didn't murder anyone, least of all your courier. There's been a misunderstanding."

"Misunderstanding?"

I really wished he'd stopped screeching. It was hell on my concussion. But at the moment, I was more concerned with the glossy black-and-white photo he was shoving in front of me.

"These were taken by the security camera at Hunan's Restaurant."

The photo was actually a split shot, the first showing me about to enter the alley beside Chin's apartment, the second, me leaving at a run—both with date/time stamps. If you looked hard enough, you could just make out the blob-like shadow of the golem in pursuit, but I didn't think that would impress Bashi.

Two of his thugs stepped from the wall, holding up my coat and cane as though presenting evidence in a court of law. I had to admit, the artifacts looked a lot like those in the photos.

I decided there was no point in lying about being there.

"Yeah, that's me." I gave an embarrassed laugh. "I'd knocked off a couple beers earlier. When nature called and I spotted the Dumpster in the alley... Look, it's not my proudest moment."

"Start with the pinky," Bashi said.

The driver stepped forward and twisted a knob over my right hand. My fifth-digit blossomed with fresh pain.

"Wait! You didn't let me get to the part where I was planning to clean it up."

"The day after Chin's murder, you went to Mr. Han's Apothecary and asked if he knew him."

My mind raced. He was right. I had done that. But had Mr. Han informed on me? Though the owner could be hard to read, I got that he genuinely liked me. No, there had to be another explanation.

Then I remembered the shadow beyond the doorway to his living quarters. Mr. Han hadn't been the informer, but his no-good son. He was also an enforcer for the White Hand and probably the thug who had spotted me on the street.

I hoped he was the one I'd rammed face-first into a light pole.

"Right, right," I said, as though remembering. "I'd heard about the murder and was just asking—"

"*That was before it was in the paper,*" Bashi screeched over me.

Right again.

The driver gave the knob a final hard twist. For an instant my pinky felt like the cord beneath a tight-rope walker at its midpoint. And then the finger snapped. A marrow-deep pain speared my senses. I thought I was going to pass out. Instead, I made a sound like nothing that had ever come out of my mouth: part grunt, part shout, part plea—all in the same breath.

"Should we take care of your ring finger next?" Bashi asked, a small smile pursing his lips. My agony was having a cheering effect on him, apparently. Maladjusted much?

"No, no," I panted, sweat breaking over my body. "Give me a minute."

His lips straightened. "Did the Morettis hire you? The Brusilovs?"

He was popping off major names in the city's Italian and Russian crime families—White Hand's competition. I remembered what Caroline had said about Bashi's bloody campaign of revenge. That I had murdered Chin was already established in his mind. He wanted my patron. Problem was, claiming to have no patron would get me my remaining fingers broken, additional tortures I didn't want to think about, and a bullet in my concussed head. A false confession would probably only get me the bullet. Either option sucked.

That left the truth. "I don't work for anyone."

Bashi nodded at the driver, who began twisting the fourth knob.

"I'm a wizard," I shouted, forcing the words out as quickly as I could. "I save amateur conjurers from their spells. Chin was preparing a summoning. My alarm picked it up, but I reached his apartment too late. The demonic creature had already arrived. It cleaned out his organs—it's how they gain strength—and it escaped. That's why Chin's window was blown out."

I'd squeezed my eyes closed as I babbled and was afraid now to open them. Some New Yorkers accepted magic and supernatural creatures with a shrug. Others decried such notions as batshit insane. I didn't know where on that spectrum Bashi's belief system fell, but the still-mounting pressure against my ring finger wasn't a good sign. "There was another summoning in Hamilton Heights," I added through gritted teeth. "Same night, same result."

My center joint was verging on failure when the squeaking knob went silent.

"Where did Chin get the spell?" Bashi asked.

I exhaled an unspoken *thank God* and opened my eyes to find Bashi showing a staying hand to the driver. One more twist and my finger would have joined its neighbor in the very-crooked club.

"That's what I'm trying to find out," I said. "When I visited Mr. Han, it was to see if he knew anything about Chin's casting background. He didn't, but I'm on the trail of someone who was given the same spell."

"Who?"

I let out a forlorn laugh. "Good question. The man was two blocks away when your boy band jumped me."

Bashi narrowed his eyes. I was sure the "boy band" remark had doomed me, damned pain endorphins. Bashi gestured to the driver, who began working the knobs again. But he was twisting them the other direction. The pressure across my joints eased until I could draw my fingers free. My right pinky was already halfway to ballpark frank proportions. I flexed and extended the others.

"When you find out who's behind the spells," Bashi said, "you will report back to me."

I stared at him in confusion before understanding took hold. In his megalomania, Bashi believed the spell to have been a personal attack on his sovereignty. I was careful not to disabuse him of the notion. "You have my word," I said solemnly.

His thugs began removing the belts.

"And you have until tomorrow," Bashi replied.

"Wait, tomorrow?"

He flicked a card with a phone number onto my lap, then turned and disappeared through a doorway.

Another deadline. Super.

29

A letter from Midtown College stood among a clutch of bills in my mailbox when I returned to my apartment building later that afternoon. I tore the envelope open with my teeth and shook open the folded letter. It was a formal notice from the board for Monday morning's hearing, eleven a.m.

Well, good for Snodgrass.

I stuffed it into a jacket pocket, too exhausted and hurt to care, and made the four-story climb to my unit.

After Bashi's men had thrown me back onto the same street corner they'd abducted me from, I had tried to pick up the conjurer's trail. No dice. The hunting spell was spent, and I lacked the focus to return to the conjurer's cleared-out apartment to create a new one. Instead, I wandered Roosevelt Park and the Bowery, squinting around and mumbling inquiries at the few people who would let me approach. No one had seen a bedraggled man lugging a trunk.

I'd lost him.

I closed and locked my apartment door, then leaned against it to get my mental bearings. In my still-concussed state, the shrieker and cathedral murder cases were starting to blur badly—and the next twenty-four hours were going to be crucial to both. I needed to concentra…

I came to in a sitting position. The loft was dark. Between my splayed-out legs, a pair of luminous green eyes stared back at me.

"I thought you were dead," Tabitha said. Though she spoke with indifference, I picked up an undercurrent of concern. Whether for my wellbeing or her own, I couldn't tell.

"How long was I out?" I tried to make out the hands on my watch face.

"A few hours."

"Hours?"

I gained my feet delicately, a force pounding from my brow to the back of my head. When the room steadied, I flipped the switch for the flood lights. My purpling pinky finger looked and felt like a string had been knotted around its base and left on for several days. I hung my coat on the rack, gathered the spilled mail, and shuffled toward the kitchen. Tabitha followed on my heels.

"You all right, darling?"

I couldn't remember the last time Tabitha had asked after my health. I must have looked like hell.

"Nothing a little magic can't fix." I poured myself a glass of water and chugged it. I hadn't had anything to drink since that morning. Or eat, I realized. "But first, let me get some dinner going."

Tabitha made a sound of annoyance as she leapt onto the counter. "You're more likely to pan sear your hand. Just get everything out of the fridge and then go take care of yourself. I'll handle dinner."

I blinked. "You're going to cook?"

It was less that Tabitha had non-grasping paws than she was offering to do, well, anything. Her slitted look told me to back off. Shrugging, I pulled out a couple of New York strips, shredded onion, and some sides. I started to season the pan, but Tabitha swatted my hand and shooed me out.

I would have given anything to stay and watch, but my cat was right. I needed to put myself back together. I started in the bathroom with my pinky finger. Holding a snapped-in-half Emory board to its underside, I straightened my finger, then secured it to the splint with a yard of sports tape.

The next step was to reconstitute my prism. As sizzling sounded from the kitchen, I leaned against the sink and repeated a centering mantra. It took a good fifteen minutes for the prism to emerge from the pink fog and become something solid. The nap must have helped.

With the prism restored, I touched the cane to the back of my head and my pinky, uttering healing incantations. Energy coursed into both, taming the throbbing, knitting bone and tissue back together. It would take time, but I already felt better, clearer.

Good, because I had work to do.

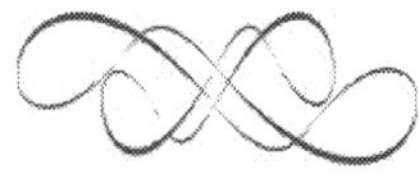

After a dinner that was—I had to hand it to Tabitha—pretty stellar, I climbed the ladder to my library and lab.

The hologram in the corner was dim, which disturbed me. I'd already decided that whoever had supplied the conjurers the shrieker spell was up to something big. What, exactly, I didn't know. But for him or her to stop now?

No, I didn't like it at all.

Best case, the Order had addressed the matter. But apart from disciplining their own, the Order almost never acted with that kind of speed. Even if they had, they wouldn't necessarily tell me. Which left me on the hook with Bashi. No matter how I squinted at the situation, I was going to have to track down the East Village conjurer and find out who supplied the spell.

Right now, though, the cathedral case was the more pressing. There was my job at the college, sure, and needing to get the promised info to Detective Vega by tomorrow. But there was also Father Vick. The more I thought about what Vega had told me outside the cathedral, the more certain I became that the investigative noose was drawing around his neck. If I didn't deliver a more compelling suspect, Father Vick was going to get strung up for something he hadn't done. And given the nature of the crime, capital punishment was *not* out of the question.

My best lead—all right, my *only* lead—was the druid cult in Central Park, who might or might not call themselves Black Earth and might or might not have any connection to Father Richard's murder.

Slam dunk, right?

I set a portable range on my table and placed a cast-iron pot onto each of the two burners. I split a bottle of green absinthe between the pots and set the burners to medium. Given the kinds of horrors that lurked in the Park—and that the druid group was an unknown quantity—my objective was to get in and out unnoticed and to keep anyone or anything who tried to kill me from doing so.

That meant potions.

I didn't have time to prepare the more elaborate ones I'd been planning, but I had a couple of quick and ready recipes to fall back on. Into the left pot I scattered brown clumps of rabbit's hair, a heaping spoonful of baking soda, and about half that of chameleon scales. With a wooden spoon engraved with casting symbols, I stirred the ingredients of the stealth potion.

"Furtiva," I chanted, directing energy through the spoon.

The steaming liquid bubbled and thickened to a gray sludge. Satisfied the mixture was on its way to becoming the potion I wanted, I twisted the burner's knob to low. In an hour or so, it would thin to a liquid I'd be able to drink.

One down, one to go.

I turned to the other steaming pot and took a focusing breath. This would be for self defense, and with a just-purchased vial of sloth urine on hand, I decided to go with an encumbering spell. I uncapped the vial and tipped it over the pot. To the absinthe and foul-smelling urine, I added a nugget of tungsten, a large syringe-full of condensed fog, and some Plaster of Paris. Following healthy doses of energy and intention, the mixture began to sludge and bubble, casting up a rancid odor.

"Christ," I muttered against my sleeve. At least I wouldn't have to drink that one. Woe to the unlucky bastard I squirted it at, though.

With my potions simmering, and an hour to kill, I climbed down from the lab and retrieved the music box and my revolver. It was a longish shot, but maybe Effie would have something for me by now.

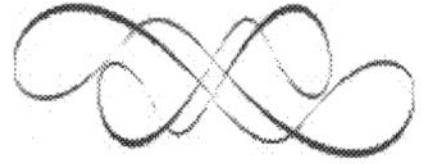

Washington Square Park drifted with the chill mist of recently-fallen rain. I checked to make sure no ghouls were lurking before climbing into the drained wading pool and winding the music box.

"That you, Everson?"

"Hey, there." I twisted to face the entity who would always remain the phantasmal likeness of an eight-year-old girl. Effie's eyes widened as they moved past me.

"You brought me music box!" she cried, running toward it.

It was that whole echo thing. Unless redirected, ghosts tended to repeat themselves from one encounter to the next, and often several times within the same meeting, like video loops or skipping records.

"Hey, did you get a chance to talk to your friends?"

" 'Bout whut?" she asked, focused on the box she couldn't quite handle.

"About whether they'd been down to St. Martin's in the last few weeks and seen anything unusual."

"Oh, thas right." She gave up on the box and started skipping in a circle, her shifting dress and clogs eerily silent over the damp leaves. "Jus' Mary, but you can't believe a word she tells ya."

I frowned. Just what I needed, an unreliable witness.

"What kind of manure is she unloading this time?" I asked.

"Says she was there a fortnight ago, playing hide an' seek with a feller at night."

"Oh yeah?"

"Man with a funny robe and hood. Says 'e was in the graveyard, but 'e wouldn't come from hiding, even when she found him."

"Did Mary say *where* he was hiding?"

"Behind a crypt 'neath a scary tree."

I perked up like an antenna. She was talking about the mossy tomb I'd walked past that morning, in the old part of the graveyard. A fortnight would have been about ten days before the murder. Had the robed man been staking out the cathedral? Plotting his crime?

"Did Mary notice anything else?" I asked.

"Jus' that 'e was easy to find on 'count of his mumbling."

Mumbling? "Could she make out any of the words?"

Either Effie's ghost was tired of the questions or didn't think anything from Mary's mouth was worth exploring, because she didn't answer. She stopped at her music box, and when she began to sing again, it was as though I was no longer there. I made a few attempts to bring her back to Mary's story, but the ghost was too absorbed in her solemn lullaby.

I sat back in thought. Some druids were known to wear hooded robes. Not much of a lead, I admitted, but neither did the ghost's account rule them out. I checked my watch. The potions would be about ready.

30

It was one a.m. by the time I reached Central Park. From the relative safety of West 110th Street, the North Woods looked perfectly forbidding. As my chatty cabbie had been all too enthused to point out (I suspected amphetamine use), the area had become known as "The Bone Yard" because of the gnawed human remains that turned up from time to time.

"So unless you're trying to lose a whole lotta weight, guy, I'd steer clear." His laughter had gone off like machine-gun fire in my face.

Hilarious.

I eyed the dense growth as the cab motored away, finding it hard to believe anyone would choose to venture in there, much less call it home—even a powerful cult of druids. But the bits of info I'd assembled pointed to just that.

"It's just never easy," I muttered, pulling a water bottle from inside my jacket and untwisting the cap. The stealth potion coated my throat as I gagged it down, the aftertaste like something you'd drain from an old car engine.

But as I ducked into the trees, the potion began to work its magic. A tingling force grew over me like a wool glove. An inspection of my body showed that I was blending into the surroundings. My footfalls softened until they made no sound. Though I didn't have an animal's sense of smell, I knew my odor was being suppressed as well.

After cresting a hill, I eased my way down a rocky ravine, where I could hear water flowing. The hidden moon diffused enough pale light through the low cloud ceiling to see by. When I encountered a family of cropping deer, I weaved through them as a test. None of them even raised a head.

"Yes!" I whispered, causing the deer to bolt.

Like much of magic, potion-making was unpredictable. A recipe followed the same way ten times could yield ten varying results, depending on the skill of the magic user. My consistency was improving, but it was nowhere close to Elder-level magic. And even though I'd nailed the stealth potion this time, it had its limits. Time, for one. It would probably hold up thirty minutes before petering out.

Meaning I had to hoof it.

At the bottom of the ravine, I rock-hopped a stream and came upon an old path winding alongside the waterway. That I'd found the path at all told me it was still in use. By what, I couldn't tell. Whether it was a trick of shadow, one set of prints looked awfully trollish.

I followed the path, hoping druids used it, too.

Druids weren't wizards, but they were wizard-like. They drew energy from nature essences, ancestral worship, and, in some cases, ancient gods. They were also big into consulting stars for omens. But that was all generalization. Like any class, druids came in different flavors—and if the group I was seeking *had* bludgeoned the rector, then I was dealing with one of the more homicidal variety. *Nigra Terra* of Roman times was supposed to have engaged in human sacrifice, even using human skin as parchment for its sacred texts. If we were talking about a descendant group, I hoped they'd at least updated to bond paper.

The path passed beneath a crumbling stone archway, fallen stones piled to one side, before seeming to end in a small clearing of boulders. The trees bordering the clearing looked impassable. I expended precious potion time searching the area but found no signs of anything. I was preparing to return down the path when it occurred to me to check for a veiling spell.

"Svelare," I said, sweeping my glowing cane in a slow circle.

One by one, boulders loomed from the darkness and receded into shadow. I had almost completed the circle, when a boulder set back behind some others seemed to ripple.

Hmm?

I was moving toward it when a whisper rose on the wind.

"We see you, fiend."

My heart beat into my throat as I killed the light. I looked around but could make out no one and nothing. Just the shadows of boulders. A chill energy swirled through the clearing. Druid magic? As I returned my gaze to the rippling boulder, it straightened into the silhouette of a hooded, scarlet-robed figure.

I separated my cane into sword and staff. "Who are you?" I demanded.

"We are death to your kind," the figure whispered.

The death part was troubling enough, but *we*? I ventured a peek around.

Okay. I was surrounded by robed figures. I must have triggered a spell planted on the trail. Veiled, the druids had waited for me to walk into their midst. Like a dummy, I'd obliged—and lit my staff. With the druids' attention now focused on me, I could feel the magic I'd pushed into my potion thinning. So much for sneaking in and out. But if dialogue proved more expedient for learning what I'd come to find out...

"Wait," I said as the robed figures moved nearer. "I've come to warn you."

The whisperer, who I took to be the head druid, let out a chilling laugh. "*And he will appear unto mortal eyes as saintly, and earnest and righteous will seem his pleas, but do not be ye deceived, for he ariseth from the darkest pits and bringeth death and ruin*. So the stars have foretold it."

I realized he was quoting from early pagan scripture, an omen that spoke to the return of Sathanas, demon lord of Wrath, the last to be cast from the world by Michael. I'd discovered in my research that the early druid cults defined themselves in part by the stars they consulted. The stars used by one cult in particular pointed to the present age for Sathanas's return. That cult was *Nigra Terra*: Black Earth.

"Whoa, there," I said. "I'm not the death and ruin guy, I promise. I'm a wizard, a magic user like yourselves—"

"Who comes bearing the stink of demon."

I paused to sniff my shoulder. Damn. Not only was my stealth spell starting to wear off, but the smell from my shrieker encounter three nights before lingered like cheap perfume.

"I can actually explain that," I said.

"Can you explain, oh *wizard*, why you were seen fleeing a demonic summoning?"

I hesitated. These guys read the *Scream*?

"Since you ask, yes," I said, "but that's not why I've come. There's talk among city officials of cracking down on magic users. I'm not sure to what lengths they're planning to go—mass evictions, arrests, worse—but I'm trying to warn all of the groups I know before it happens. We need to unify."

It was a whopper of a tale, but if it gibed with the Black Earth's reasons for killing the rector—the voice behind the campaign to crack down—maybe they would reveal as much to someone who appeared sympathetic.

"Yes, we have heard." My pulse ramped up in anticipation of a confession. I'd finally have something for Detective Vega. "But the city and church are not the threat," the druid continued. "It is you, fiend."

My shoulders sagged. *Or not.*

I tried to see the situation from the druids' perspective. Per their star charts, the return of Sathanas was nigh. Now, in the midst of a spate of shrieker summonings, a man wanted by the police, and smelling like demon, suddenly turned up on their doorstep, claiming to offer help.

Sketchy as hell. I got it.

As though picking up my thoughts, the druid said, "Yes, unify us so you may betray those with the power to stop you. We are not so easily fooled."

The bloody message on the rector's robe notwithstanding, I decided this Black Earth wasn't responsible for his murder. The cult was too obsessed with preventing Sathanas's return, and compromising the power of the cathedral would only empower a demon lord. "Black Earth" had either been written as a red herring, or it meant something completely different.

Either way, I wasn't going to fight these guys.

"Great," I said. "Well, think I'll head on home, then."

The robed figures shifted into my path. The head druid spoke at my back, but he was no longer using English. I recognized the language as a variant of Latin, similar to what I used for my own Words of Power.

Which meant—

I threw a light shield up just as searing fire broke around me. In the sudden blaze, the remaining druids became illuminated. From the shadows of hoods, tattooed lips peeled from purple gums and fierce teeth. Wands of what looked like burned ash appeared from billowing sleeves.

Fire casters. And here I'd been hoping for the meadow-prancing type of druid. I aimed my sword at the one blocking my path and shouted, *"Vigore!"*

The energy that coursed down the blade slammed the druid from his sandals and into the trees. The rippling wake knocked two more druids onto their backs. An opening! I hit the gap at a run, calling more energy to my staff and shaping it into a protective dome of light.

I grunted as fresh fire jetted hot against it.

After the day's encounter with Bashi and the White Hand, I wasn't in any shape for an extended battle. Especially not when I was outnumbered by magic users, who, by the force of their casting, must have been calling up power from a god. It also explained how they were able to create a refuge for themselves in Central Park. Trying to match them blow for blow would only bring on Thelonious, which was the last thing I needed tonight.

"Face your doom, fiend!" the head druid called.

Nope. I'd made the trail and had no plans of turning around.

But I'd barely hit my first full stride when a stone from the crumbling arch tumbled into my path. *Damned druid magic.* I managed to leap that one but a second stone materialized beneath my landing foot. I hit it awkwardly, and pain flared through my folding ankle. I stumbled and went down.

Robes shuffled up behind me. I rolled onto my back, ready to nail them with another force invocation. But I couldn't even raise my sword arm. I strained through gritted teeth and tried to assist with my staff arm, but it was like hefting a pair of dead animals. My tongue and lips garbled around a word that hadn't the power to invoke anything.

...the hell?

That was when something warm and wet spread across the front of my pants. *Well, craptastic.* I had carefully loaded the encumbering potion into a squirt gun, which I'd holstered into my waist band—and apparently just crushed. The contact with my skin was releasing the potion's magic, not to mention the god-awful stench, transforming me into a smelly, dull-witted slug.

Fourteen all over again, basically.

The druids swooped around me, ember-tipped wands aimed at my face. With no Words to resurrect my shield, I was as good as cooked. I released my sword and staff at sloth speed and showed my hands.

"Whhuuaaiit," I slurred.

The lead druid emerged through the others and stood over me. The hood had fallen away to reveal a shiny shaved head and strong face, ebony skin patterned with intricate white lines. Like my mental prism, the tattoos were designed to channel energy. The druid's eyes, a fierce turquoise in the light of the wands, searched mine. When the druid spoke again, I realized the person wasn't a man, but a woman—their high priestess.

"Raise it up," she ordered.

It? I thought. *Oh right, the demon.* I glanced around at the others as they stooped down. Though they remained hooded, I guessed by their movements that they were all women.

Several of them seized me beneath the shoulders and hoisted me to my feet. I stepped gingerly, and very slowly, on my twisted right ankle. I should have been terrified, but the potion was fogging my fear. When the priestess looked me up and down, I was more concerned that the leaking potion and smell had them all thinking I'd wet my pants.

The priestess smiled around filed teeth. "A demon is no match for the fire of Brigit."

I was pretty sure a demon as powerful as Sathanas could flick the pagan god to which she was referring like a paper football. But even if I'd wanted to point that out, I couldn't form the words. Plus, she was moving her wand dangerously close to my face, its glowing tip drawing sweat from my pores. I tried to lean away, but it was as though my body were bound in a slow-drying cast. Exactly the effect the Plaster of Paris ingredient had been meant to induce.

"First," she said, wand hovering just above my right cheek,

"we burn out its eyes."

That she was referring to me in third person neutral was chilling enough. But the pain that had begun to build across my cornea and now pierced, searing, to the back of my eye socket was far more troubling. I shut my eyelids to the heat, but she forced them open with a bracing finger and thumb.

I let out a low moan, which made the priestess show more of her teeth. This was *not* good. Arnaud and Bashi were dangerous, but at least they possessed some capacity for reason, however warped. This woman had none. It was written in her staring eyes. Her existence had come to revolve so completely around the return of Sathanas that every interlocutor now looked like a demon.

"That it may no more curse us with its evil sight," she promised.

When my vision blurred, I hoped it was from tears and not the melting of my lens. Either way, it wouldn't be long before my right socket was a smoking crater. When the priestess sucked in her next breath through the sharp spaces of her teeth, I knew it was to summon fire.

And that brought my fear screaming back.

31

I tried again to speak an invocation of protection, but I might as well have been talking through a mouthful of oatmeal. The priestess took her time pronouncing her own Word, the tip of her wand swelling orange hot, strong fingers bracing my eyelids wide.

"*Ustili*—garrh!" she grunted.

Huh?

The heat and glare fell away. She dropped the wand and dug both hands into the neck of her robe, which appeared to be throttling her. I tottered for balance as the others released me. My head rotated slowly from side to side.

The robes were wrapping all of their necks, strangling them like boas.

I didn't know what the hell was happening and didn't much care. My eye was intact, even if a blinding glare remained. Turning, I forced my arms and legs into an absurd underwater run. My sword and staff were on the ground where I'd relinquished them. I was bending in slo-mo to retrieve them when a shaking force nailed me between the shoulder blades.

I reflexively hooked a finger into the front of my shirt collar. But instead of struggling to breathe, I was no longer struggling, period. My limbs were fluid again. I exercised my jaw and tested my voice: "Do-re-mi-fa-sol..." Someone had broken up the effect of the encumbering potion.

Sword and staff in hands, I swung around.

"The animation spell's not going to last," someone said in an Irish brogue. A short, rumpled figure hustled from the gagging druids and seized the sleeve of my coat. "We need to get a move on."

"Chicory?" I asked, stumbling to keep up.

In the year since I'd last seen my mentor, he had gained a bit of weight. Even so, his feet were a blur. Instead of crossing the stream, he led me farther down the path I'd arrived by, his coat flapping around his stubby legs, then up to where the path joined a defunct road. His gray Volkswagen Rabbit sat against the near curb. As he shuffled around to the driver's side, I peeked back, relieved to find no one—and nothing—in pursuit. The diesel engine chugged to life as I dropped inside and slammed the door behind me.

"Man, talk about timing," I said, inspecting my right eye in the visor mirror. It was red and puffy around the rim, but otherwise healthy. "How did you know—"

"Magic," Chicory said, tossing his wand into the back seat, curmudgeonly face set in a frown. Then to clarify: "*Forbidden* magic."

"You mean theirs?" I tried.

He stared at me over a squash-shaped nose. "I mean yours."

I gave a nervous chuckle as Chicory swung the car around. "Yeah, about that..."

"You violated a mandate from the Order. *Two*, in fact."

"Well, their letter was awfully short on details. It called me off a shrieker case without saying why—or what the Order planned to do about it. And cessation of magic? Was that supposed to be a blanket mandate?"

My mentor nodded.

"What the hell, Chicory? If the Order would ever bother to ask, they might learn that I have to make ends meet around here. I also have friends in this city, good people. Keeping my job and keeping them safe require magic sometimes."

I thought I'd made a reasonable appeal, but Chicory was shaking his mop of gray hair. He looked more like a frazzled physics professor than a wizard. "It's not your place to question the Elders."

"So, what, they're gods now?"

"As far as you and I are concerned, yes."

I pushed out an exasperated breath. At our level, the purpose of magic was defending the mortal world from manifested evils. But the Elders dealt in other planes entirely, where linear thought and logic no longer held, necessarily. With their power and knowledge, the Elders *were* very nearly gods. It was what I would become one day—if I lived to be that old. When the Elders issued a decree, there was usually a very good reason for it.

But call it hubris, I still felt like they were missing something. "Do they have a plan for the shriekers, at least?" I asked.

"I'm sure they do, Everson." His response hardly inspired confidence, but before I could press him, Chicory took up his scolding voice. "What were you doing out here anyway?" He skirted a cement barricade and merged onto Central Park West. "Picking a fight with a women's group?"

I rubbed the back of my neck. "I didn't know they were... Look, I thought they might be behind a murder the NYPD asked me to help investigate, all right? The rector was killed at a church I used to attend."

"Oh, yes, about that," Chicory interrupted. "The Order wants you off that case as well."

"*What? Why?*"

"Not our place to ask."

"Well, let me spell a few things out for you, and maybe you can run it up the flagpole." I twisted my entire body toward him. "The church in question sits on the city's most powerful fount of ley energy. The balance of power in the city is already tipping toward darkness because of the crisis brought on by the vampires. We lose St. Martin's, and we may never get that balance back. New York City will become a Romper Room of evil. Father Victor, the man in position to take over as rector? I know him. He's as devoted as they come. He'll safeguard that fount. But he's also about to be slammed for capital murder by a police department short on resources and long on the illusion that they're actually solving crimes."

I hadn't quite put it in those terms before, not even in my own mind, but it wasn't a stretch. Those were the bigger stakes.

Chicory sighed. "Fine, I'll add it to my report." He glanced at the folders and spiral-bound notebooks spread over his dashboard.

I noticed his back seat was jammed with boxes containing more files. I wasn't sure how many of us he was responsible for across the country, but based on the intervals between visits, probably too many. "But until you hear back from me..."

"Yeah, yeah," I said. "No magic."

We rode in silence the rest of the way to the West Village.

As Chicory pulled up in front of my apartment, I peeked around. I still hadn't seen the woman Tabitha claimed to have caught watching the building. I was beginning to suspect my cat had fabricated the story to convince me she was pulling her weight around the homestead.

My gaze returned to Chicory. "Hey, thanks for bailing me out back there." I no longer had a suspect, but I'd managed to keep both eyes and my life, which was something. "And for the lift home," I added.

"Ooh, that reminds me."

I watched cross-eyed as he pressed an ink-stained thumb between my brows. "What the...? Ow!" I cried as a bolt of energy pierced my forebrain. Though the sensation quickly dissipated, a tingling pressure remained behind. "What are you doing?"

"The wards around the city could detect your magic but not your intentions. Consider yourself stamped." He said it matter-of-factly. "If you violate any of the mandates, including pursuing the matter with the church, the Order will know. That should tell you how serious they are."

"And if I do it anyway?"

"You'll find out just how serious."

I sighed and got out of the car.

"Everson," Chicory said before I could close the door. I leaned down and met his eyes, which didn't seem so frazzled anymore. They appeared dark, almost mercenary. "The Order can seem like an abstraction sometimes, but when it comes to their mandates, they're rather black and white. Trust me. I've had to take care of two wayward wizards this month already."

I felt the moisture leave my mouth. "You mean...?"

He nodded once. "Don't test them."

32

I awoke early Sunday morning, having slept decently for someone who faced a deadline with an NYPD detective, another deadline with a mob boss, and a not-so-subtle threat from his mentor of being put to death if he acted on either. It probably explained the shredded feeling in my stomach.

I dressed, fixed an omelet for Tabitha, who was still snoozing, and headed out for coffee. I had some serious mulling to do.

Except for a handful of neighbors out walking their dogs, the West Village streets were quiet. The weather system that had dumped gray clouds and on-and-off rainfall over the city since last week continued to linger like a nagging cold. I wasn't feeling so hot myself.

I hustled the three blocks through the damp to my favorite caffeine stop, Two Story Coffee, and ordered a large Colombian roast with two shots of scotch. I paid for it, along with a folded-over Sunday Edition of the *Scream*, and carried both to a soft reading chair in a corner. Being Sunday, it was too early for the regulars: various artists and practitioners of the esoteric, which the particular energy patterns in the neighborhood seemed to attract.

I took a sip of coffee and sank into the chair in thought.

It seemed all of the decent options were off the table. I was looking at *least bad* now. To avoid the Order's wrath, I would have to back off the shrieker case, which meant hiding from Bashi and the White Hand for roughly the rest of my life. I would also have to walk away from the cathedral case—not that I had any new leads at the moment—but what would happen to Father Vick, not to mention the crucial role of St. Martin's in the city's balance of power?

One thing I had decided for certain was to skip my hearing at Midtown College tomorrow morning. I refused to give Snodgrass the satisfaction of watching me sink. I wasn't sure which hurt more, though: the thought of no longer being able to research and teach the subject I loved, or of not having Caroline Reid as a colleague. Would our friendship survive? And what was she going to think of me for not fighting for my position?

I sighed and unfolded the paper across my lap. The headline that took up half the front page blew all thoughts of the college from my head.

MURDER AND MAYHEM AT ST. MARTIN'S!
RECTOR BATTERED TO DEATH!
PARISHIONERS ASK, "WHO'S NEXT?"

Despite the Church's effort, the story had gotten out. Probably a blackmail job. The paper had wanted more money and the Church had balked. The article contained nothing I didn't already know, the information attributed to a "brave source" who had requested anonymity. I snorted at the irony. I worried, though, what the story meant for Father Vick and St. Martin's.

The cathedral's power as a sanctuary against evil depended largely on a collective faith in, well, the cathedral's power as a sanctuary against evil. Challenging that faith with a graphic depiction of the murder and suggestions that there could be more to come wobbled the central struts.

Maybe exactly what someone was trying to do.

The rest of the article was garbage, something the *Scream* had unabashedly mastered. At least my likeness wasn't featured below the article.

I turned the page. Correction. At least my likeness wasn't featured below *that* article. Because the god-awful police sketch was back, on page two. I raised my eyes to the headline—and nearly spilled my coffee.

THE EVISCERATOR STRIKES AGAIN!
SOHO! CHELSEA! SPANISH HARLEM!
MURRAY HILL!

My eyes rocketed up and down the columns, grabbing the relevant information, slamming it into something coherent. Four more murders since Friday night. Two men. Two women. The info on the victims was sketchy, but they had all been slain in the same manner as the Chinatown and Hamilton Heights victims—hence my reprisal as lead suspect and creep job.

I closed my eyes to a corkscrew of dizziness. Had those same shriekers reappeared to feed? I shook my head. No, these sounded like the just-summoned variety. No signs of entrance, smashed windows for exits.

"Plan for the shriekers, my ass," I grumbled as I recalled the assurance Chicory had given me in the car last night. There were now at least six of them loose in the city, up to God knew what, and the Order wasn't doing a goddamned thing. The thought knotted the muscles in my neck.

And why hadn't my alarm alerted me? The city hologram should have lit up like a supernova. Cold understanding stiffened my spine. The Order had cut me off from their wards. Hence, the hologram's silence the last couple of nights.

I took a large swallow of coffee, more for the alcohol than caffeine, and flipped between the two articles in thought. *Oh, yes, about that*, Chicory had said when I'd brought up my work on the cathedral murder last night. *The Order wants you off that case, as well.*

Now why would that be? I could understand their concern with an incubus-toting wizard getting mixed up with demonic beings, but what danger did Thelonious and I pose to an investigation into a rector's murder?

Unless...

My hand went still, the paper poised between the cases.

Unless there's a connection.

I thought back to the Bible I'd found in the East Village conjurer's apartment. I'd written it off as incidental, but now I wasn't so sure. Had the vagrant been linked to St. Martin's, somehow. Ditto the Chinatown and Hamilton Heights conjurers? The four listed here in the paper? Had the same person who supplied their spells murdered the rector?

There was someone who could probably shed light on those questions—only I was forbidden from speaking to Father Vick by Detective Vega and now the Order. I touched the place on my forehead where Chicory had mashed his thumb. He'd hit me with a binding spell, a psychic tether that created a one-way conduit for my thoughts. The pressure of the spell lingered in my brain like a subsiding headache.

A friend, I told myself—and anyone who might be eavesdropping. *I'm only going to visit Father Victor as a friend.* And then, because I was so fed up with the Order, *If that's a crime, we can discuss it in hell.*

33

Because it was Sunday, the line for the pedestrian checkpoint on Liberty Street was nonexistent. I went through the same motions I'd gone through the last two times, showing my NYPD card and Midtown College ID, even managing to affect impatience. But the longer the guard's impassive shades remained fixed on my ID, the more unnerved I became.

For the first time, I noticed the small black eye of a camera in the corner of his sunglasses. The camera was beaming the info on my ID to a monitor and whichever technician was talking into the guard's earpiece. After another minute, the guard handed my ID back.

"About time," I muttered, going to step past him.

The palm that met my chest knocked me back several steps.

"Hey, what gives?" I shouted, more in surprise than pain.

"You're forbidden entry."

"Why?"

"You're on the list."

"What list?"

"The forbidden-entry list."

"Gee, thanks for the clarification. Can you tell me who put me on it?"

The guard crossed his thick arms to signal he was done talking. One of the perks of bearing body armor and an assault rifle. I peered past him to where the massive towers of the financial district thrust into a gray haze. Arnaud must have known I'd come yesterday morning. He'd put me on his naughty list, alongside the anti-capitalists and bomb-happy anarchists. He must have also included a note to have my NYPD card confiscated, because that was what the guard had done, I now realized.

Shit.

I looked up and down the length of the imposing wall before stepping up to the guard again.

"Look," I said quietly. "Your X-ray didn't pick up anything, right? I'm only going to St. Martin's to meet an old friend, then I'm shooting straight home. You can call the cathedral to check. They'll confirm it."

The guard's arms remained crossed, his gaze leveled above me, as though I was the annoying neighborhood kid who, if you ignored long enough, would eventually slouch off. Maybe I was in luck. Most of the other guards would have beaten me into the pavement by now.

I opened my wallet, removed my remaining big bills—over one hundred dollars—and folded them into the palm of my hand, behind my ID. Though the guard's head didn't move, the tension in his neck told me his eyes were observing me. He was a mercenary, after all. Money spoke.

"There must have been a mistake," I suggested, holding out the ID with the bills concealed underneath. "Maybe you could take a second look?"

The guard remained statue stiff for long enough that I was sure it was a failed bid. But he had only been waiting for the guard off to his right to turn away, because his hand shot out like a piston and seized the ID and tightly-folded stash. He didn't hold the ID to his shades this time. It went in and out of the front pocket of his pants, as though he were cleaning it.

"You don't report back within one hour," he said in a low voice, handing me back the ID sans cash, "and I'll bag you and drag you out myself."

I nodded earnestly. He could just as easily have pocketed the money and denied my entrance a second time, even shot me dead on the pretense of rushing the checkpoint. Now I was only at risk of being shot for failing to return by—I glanced down at my watch—ten after eleven.

"That won't be necessary," I assured him.

But I was sure as hell going to have to hurry.

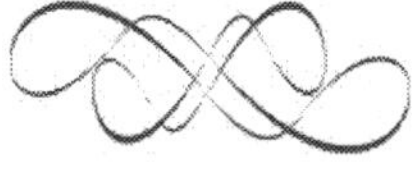

Despite what I'd suggested to the guard, I didn't have an appointment with Father Vick. I arrived at the steep bronze doors of the cathedral, surprised to find them closed and locked. A sign announced that Sunday Mass would not be held. Future services had been suspended "until further notice." Maybe because the wording mirrored my cease-and-desist mandate from the Order, I feared the worst—namely Father Vick having been arrested.

I pressed a button beside the right door. A metallic buzz sounded from deep inside the cathedral. A minute passed. I was preparing to buzz again when I heard the clunking of bolts. After another moment, the right door opened, and the groundskeeper's squinting face backed from the light.

"Cyrus," I breathed. "It's Everson. I met you yesterday morning? I need to have a word with Father Victor. Is he in?"

I spoke with the urgency of someone on the clock and wasn't sure Cyrus had caught it all. Beneath his combed-over wisps of white hair, the folds of Cyrus's palsied face alternately winced and sagged as he studied my lips. "He's unwell," he rasped after a moment.

"But he's here?"

"In bed," the old man confirmed, causing me to exhale in relief.

"Please, it will only take a minute, and it's extremely important."

When Cyrus stepped to one side and waved for me to enter, I hoped the gesture would be enough to temper the threshold. It was, but it might not have mattered. The force that rippled through me was less than half the strength I'd felt on Thursday, and left much of my wizarding powers intact.

Cyrus closed the door behind me and locked it.

"I know the way," I told him, not wanting to wait on his frail lead.

I replicated the route Father Vick and I had taken the morning before, until I was crossing the inner courtyard and standing in front of the vicarage. The door was open a crack, and I could make out a slice of Father Vick's tall figure beneath the white covers of his bed.

I knocked. "Father?"

The bed creaked as he lifted his head. "Is that Everson? Come in, come in."

I entered and returned the door to its cracked-open state behind me. A smell like stale gauze hung thick in the room. By the time I turned back to Father Vick, my eyes had adjusted to the dimness, and I paused to take him in. True to Cyrus's word—though paraphrasing slightly—he looked like crap. His pale red hair was thin and scattered. What I mistook for bald patches in his beard were spots that had gone white, probably less evident when his beard was combed. He blinked with boggy eyelids, but his eyes exuded the same paternal concern.

"Please, have a seat," he said.

I pulled a chair up beside the bed. "I'm sorry to disturb you. I wanted to see how you were doing."

"You read the article?"

I nodded.

As his head rested back on the pillow, he exhaled. "I was to have told the congregation today, in morning Mass. I spent much of the night preparing the service and in prayer."

Holy books stood in stacks on his window-facing desk. Beside the books hung his white kerchief.

"I saw the sign out front," I said.

"The congregation is in a panic. I ... I don't know what to do."

As he spoke, I caught what looked like tissue paper balled into his right ear canal. His nose had bled too, bits of red crust clinging to the top of his mustache. I recalled what he'd said about channeling forces beyond us, and could only imagine the kind of strain he was under. The faith in the cathedral was similar to my mental prism—a converter of ley energy. Right now, Father Vick was having to make up the faith deficit, and it was killing him.

"The Bishop of New York is coming today," he said, but the worry in his eyes confused me.

"That's a good thing, isn't it?"

"Well, the visit is avowedly to chart a path forward, though I think that's a kind way of suggesting the Church wants to conduct its own investigation."

So in addition to the NYPD, he was under suspicion by his own ecclesiastic authorities. I knew the gut-punched feeling. I gave his arm a squeeze of support, which seemed to warm his face.

"And how are you, Everson?" he asked.

"Concerned."

He raised his eyebrows slightly. Though the protective energies of the cathedral had weakened, I sensed it blowing static through the monitoring spell Chicory had placed on me. With that bit of cover, I proceeded.

"There's work I do in the city that not many know about, but I think you would understand." I watched him nod in encouragement. "The Crash rocked the ground under a lot of people. Many fell to vice, but others reached for magic. You help the first group, Father. I try to help the second." Something in his eyes told me he knew, or at least suspected, this to have been the case. "Lately, the kinds of emergencies I've been called to have been especially black—demonic summonings. Lower creatures, granted, but I think something bigger is working its way up the pipe."

Father Vick's gaze shifted to the ceiling. "I've felt it, too," he said after a moment, his voice nearly a whisper. "Like a force eclipsing the sun, casting everything into dire shadow." He shook his head. "I tried discussing it with Brother Richard, but he was preoccupied with the magic use in the city, much of it benign, of course. I'm afraid my concern fell on deaf ears."

I thought about my own appeals to the Order.

"What can we do, Everson?" he asked, his voice possessed by sudden strength.

"If we trace the summoning spells back to their source, we'll know who or what we're dealing with. That would be a start." Not wanting to suggest the church was behind the spreading evil, I proceeded carefully. "I was actually hoping you know or at least encountered the first conjurer. I found him squatting in an East Village apartment. He had a St. Martin's Bible in his possession." I described the man in as much detail as I could.

When I got to the glasses, a look of recognition came over Father Vick's face.

"Yes, yes," he said. "That would have been Clifford Rhodes. We have an outreach group that offers spiritual guidance to the homeless. Clifford was well known to us. When he disappeared, we feared the worst. It grieves me to hear he turned to dark practices. But he's alive?"

"Last time I saw him, yes. The other conjurers weren't as fortunate."

I told him about the Chinatown conjurer next, Chin Lau Ping.

"That was from a summoning?" he asked, sitting partway up.

"You knew him, too?"

"He was an informant, in Brother Richard's campaign against the White Hand."

"So he approached the church?"

Father Vick nodded. "The White Hand pressed Chin into service because he drove a bus and had a clean record. He transported narcotics, and often women, to other cities. Chin wanted nothing to do with it, but the White Hand made it clear it was the cost of doing business in Chinatown. When I read about his murder, I thought the White Hand had found him out."

I took a steadying breath. *So far, two for two.*

"What about Fred Thomas?" I asked. "A young man from Hamilton Heights?"

Father Vick's face creased as he searched his memory for the name.

"He went by 'Flash'," I remembered.

"Flash," Father Vick repeated. "Yes. I read about him, too. Another summoning?" He let out an aggrieved sigh. "He attended one of St. Martin's parochial schools for a time. It was a pilot program for inner-city youths who couldn't otherwise afford the tuition. A prank got him expelled, I remember, but he was good hearted. Afterwards, he showed up to a few of our youth services."

I removed the newspaper I had folded and tucked inside my coat, and opened it to the second page.

"Did you know any of them?" I asked.

Sitting up, Father Vick took a pair of reading glasses from his nightstand and frowned over the article on last night's quadruple slaying. I watched his face go from pale to a blotchy ashen. "Good

God," he muttered. "These three were parishioners, and she participated in the city's Interfaith Council."

"Father," I said carefully, "I think we have to consider that the spells came from someone inside the cathedral."

"From here?"

"It's the common factor." I allowed a moment for the fact to sink in. "I think we also have to consider that whoever supplied the spells may have murdered your rector. Father Richard may have been onto what this person was doing."

Father Vick removed his glasses and set them aside. He looked destroyed.

"Did the rector ever share any concerns with you?" I probed. "About anyone here or in the congregation?"

"Not that I recall," he answered after a moment. "He was a stoic man, praying on problems before acting on them. So even if he'd had such concerns, I wouldn't necessarily have known of them. His concerns tended to be more external, anyway. The corruption he observed in the city. The practice of magic. He *was* uncomfortable with the archival work, though."

"Your acolyte's research?" I asked. "Why?"

Before he could answer, a soft knock sounded at the door. I looked over to find the acolyte himself peering through the crack. I wondered how long he'd been standing there, listening.

"Father Vick?" he asked.

"Yes, what is it Malachi?"

"The, um, bishop called to say they're a half hour out."

Father Vick nodded and pushed the cover from his legs. "I suppose I should get ready, then." When he sat up, blood spattered the lap of his robe. I rose in alarm before realizing it was falling from his nose.

I stretched past Malachi, who was standing slack-armed in the doorway, and reached for the kerchief on the desk.

"No, no," Father Vick said, plugging the bleeding nostril with a thumb. "The tissues."

I followed his finger to the windowsill and pulled several tissues from a plain box of them. He accepted the wad with a grateful nod and, after wiping his bearded mouth and chin, held it to his tipped-back nose.

"That's a heritage item," he said of the kerchief.

"Ah, sorry."

I looked around, but Malachi was no longer in the doorway. His robed form flashed beyond the window, lank ponytail falling over the hood bunched behind his neck. Remembering the hooded man Effie's ghost friend had observed in the graveyard, suspicion spiked hot inside me. I wheeled back to Father Vick.

"What was it about Malachi's work that bothered the rector?" I asked quickly.

Father Vick had gotten control of the bleeding and was now dabbing around it. "Oh, he just believed some things should remain in history. Because of the power of this site, I suspect, the church wasn't always represented by honorable men."

I needed more, but at that moment the church bells began to ring out the hour.

I checked my watch. Crap. I had ten minutes to get back to the checkpoint.

"Can I call you later?" I asked.

"Of course." Father Vick wavered to his feet but embraced me with warm strength. I reciprocated. "You are exactly what Father Richard didn't understand," he said, "that the relative good or evil of magic depends entirely on the channeler. Though darkness clings to you, Everson, your foundation remains as solid and pure as when I first taught you. It is why you were called back here. Remember that."

In many ways, he had been my first mentor—and a great one.

"Thank you, Father. I'll try."

34

Assuming my watch was synced to the guard's, I had less than twenty seconds to spare by the time I arrived, panting, at the pedestrian checkpoint.

I'd risked precious time by having Cyrus let me out through the graveyard again, but I'd wanted to inspect the mossy tomb beneath the willow tree. If Effie's friend was to be believed, someone had been creeping around the site in the dark of night, muttering what might have been an incantation. And I was beginning to suspect that person had been Malachi. I found the raised sarcophagus sealed tight, the ground around it apparently undisturbed.

I read the deceased's name and dates: *Bartholomew Higham, 1772 – 1824*. No other information. It wasn't until I pulled out my notepad that I remembered my small pencil was absent from its spiral binding. I resorted to cramming the info into my memory, hoping it would stay.

“Where’s the fire?” a guard asked as I hurried up to the checkpoint.

I looked from him to his partner. Neither was the one who had let me through an hour before.

“Where’s the other guy?” I asked, breathlessly. “The one who was here earlier?” The last thing I needed was for someone else to be hunting me for having violated some agreement.

“What’s it to you?”

“I, ah, I knew him,” I replied lamely.

“Well, not anymore,” the guard said.

The second guard opened his mouth to join in—it was a slow day at the checkpoint, evidently—but then paused as though someone was speaking into his earpiece. He nodded at the first guard, who, without comment, stepped forward and drove the barrel of his rifle into my gut. I grunted and dropped to a knee, the impact leaving me sick and gasping. From my new vantage, I noticed a smear of reddish oil on the pavement below my face.

Wait ... blood? My bribe had gotten the guy killed?

“If you don’t wanna join your friend,” the guard said, wrestling with my hand now, “you’re gonna give this up.” I realized he was trying to pull Grandpa’s ring off my finger.

Arnaud, I thought. By his reasoning, I had entered his territory; ergo, he had rights to my ring. I balled my hand against the guard’s wrenching fingers. I was risking my life, yeah, but the ring seemed to be compelling me—it had some future role to play, and it wouldn’t do to be in a vampire’s possession. My hand balled tighter, gripped by the mother of all cramps. If my own life played a role, it appeared it was going to be as a footnote.

"Tough guy, huh?" the guard said, ramming an elbow against my ear for leverage.

I was angling my cane toward him, wondering what the penalty would be for magic exercised in self defense, when his partner entered my peripheral vision.

"Stand back," he said, raising his rifle.

Before I could summon my light shield, a pair of explosions sounded. In the ringing aftermath, I recognized the register. I opened my eyes and blinked twice. The shots hadn't come from an assault rifle.

"NYPD," a familiar voice shouted. "Get the fuck away from him!"

I raised my face to find Detective Vega storming toward us. She lowered the nine millimeter she'd fired until it was level with the nearer guard's head. He backed away, palms showing. His partner adjusted his rifle's aim from me to Vega, but he looked hesitant before the tiny tornado in a black suit.

"This man's wanted in an investigation," Vega said, using her free hand to haul me up. The guard who'd been grappling for my ring began to stammer. Before his words could take on intelligence, Vega was pulling me toward her sedan, which she'd left idling at the auto checkpoint.

I wasted no time getting in. She joined me on the driver's side and drove us from the Financial District.

"What in God's name are you doing?" she demanded.

"I *was* making friends," I said. "Sheesh. Now they'll never call." I was buying time until I could determine just how much she knew about my morning excursion.

"Were you at the church?" she asked.

The inflection in her tone told me it was an honest question. I'd caught a break.

"Um, sorry, but were you not just witness to my near-execution?" I jerked my head back. "I was kidding about being pally-wally with those guys, in case you missed that, too."

"You were *intending* to go to the church, though."

"Can you prove it?" I asked, raising an eyebrow.

Ripping off a string of Spanish curses, Vega accelerated around a line of cars, blooped her siren, and shot through a red light. "You're lucky I had business downtown," she said when she'd calmed down enough to return to English. "Those guys could've put two dozen bullets in you, and the NYPD wouldn't have been able to do a damn thing."

"Why not?"

"Official immunity," she grumbled.

I nodded in understanding. Probably one of Arnaud's conditions for bailing out the city. Which also meant that if the guards had gotten it into their meaty heads to gun down Vega, they could have done so without fear of prosecution. Boy, did that make me feel like a dick.

"Hey, listen—"

"Save it," Vega said sharply. "The next words I want out of your mouth are what you can tell me about the message. Today's the deadline. In case you forgot," she added wryly.

"Well—"

She cut me off again. "Not here. My office."

We emerged from underneath the off ramp for the Brooklyn Bridge and into view of One Police Plaza. I had a sinking sense of déjà vu. The last time Vega had driven me here, it was for processing.

She veered into a secure underground garage. We rode an elevator up in silence, stopping every floor or two for plain-clothed personnel and uniformed officers to get on and off. I caught more than a few sidelong glances. It was my six-foot frame, dark brown hair, and cane. I could all but feel my face being lined up with the police sketch and had a feeling Detective Vega was the only reason I wasn't being slammed against a wall and cuffed.

I edged closer to her.

On the eighth floor, I followed her off the elevator and down a hallway to a busy workspace whose cluttered desks and colony of Styrofoam coffee cups shouted HOMICIDE. Of course, I'd been here before, so I was cheating. Vega led me into a windowless office—not an interrogation room this time, thankfully—rounded a desk with piled-up folders and an outdated computer, and sat down hard. I scooted up one of the folding metal chairs.

"Speak," she said as I lowered myself.

I had already decided to be as truthful as I could. I owed her that much.

"All right." I laced my fingers, save my splinted pinky, and bent them back until they cracked. "The message on the rector's back translates to 'Black Earth.' "

"What does it mean?" she asked, jotting it down on a notepad.

"I don't know."

She stared up at me as though there had to be more. I shrugged.

"I gave you three days for *that*?" She threw her pen at the pad.

The pen ricocheted and collided into a propped-up frame, knocking it onto its felt back. When I reached forward to right it, I saw it held a photo of a smiling Detective Vega—white teeth and all—clutching a giggling boy of five or six, her chin propped on his feathery curls.

"Your son?" I asked.

"Yeah," she replied, her frustration seeming to have gotten lost for the moment. She took over the task of righting the frame, angling it toward her, where I could no longer see the photo.

"Good-looking kid," I said. But then so was his mother. And I'd been right about her smile—wow. I blamed Thelonious for flicking my eyes to Vega's left ring finger, which was unencumbered. *Dream on, pal.* I thought at my incubus. *A homicide detective and a probationer?*

"Something funny?" Vega asked, her face creasing with renewed sternness.

I'd snorted at my own thought, apparently. I tried to cover it up with a second snort meant to sound functional. "Allergies."

"I thought you were pursuing some kind of lead." She gestured to the pad. "Is there a group that goes by this name?"

I searched the wall of aged vertical filing cabinets behind her. I didn't want to think about what would happen to Detective Vega if she showed up in that crazed cult's midst. "It turns out there isn't."

"Are you sure?" she asked.

I nodded.

"Guess we're gonna have to see what we can do with this," she said of the message, but without much hope.

I leaned forward. "Look, I know I come off as a smart aleck sometimes, but I meant what I said about Father Victor yesterday. It's not in his nature to raise his voice, much less act violently. And I couldn't find any connection between him and this Black Earth." The image of the vicar's ill face and bleeding nose wavered in my mind's eye. "The man is under incredible strain. Arresting him would ... well, not to sound overly dramatic, but it could kill him."

I was thinking of Father Vick's health as well as that of the cathedral.

Detective Vega shrugged. "We have to go where the evidence takes us."

"Just make sure that's what you're doing." Though I tried to offer it as a suggestion, it came out sounding critical. I expected her eyebrows to crush together, but instead, an odd look came over her face.

"Since we're done here," she said, "I'm gonna need you to hand over your notes on the case."

"Yeah, sure." In my relief, I quickly withdrew my notepad, tore out the pages relevant to the message, and pushed them toward her. My scribblings were mostly illegible, but she wasn't trying to read them. Her dark gaze had remained fixed on my notepad.

"Lose something?" she asked.

"I'm sorry?"

She pulled open a desk drawer, reached inside, and held up a clear Ziploc bag. My stub of a pencil, which used to ride in the pad's binding, was nested at its bottom. I almost asked where in the world she'd found it before realizing the Ziploc was an evidence bag.

"Now, do you want to tell me what in the hell's going on with those *other* murders?"

I maintained a poker face while my thoughts shuffled madly. They stopped on the apartment of Chin Lau Ping. I thought I'd lost the pencil at the downtown checkpoint, but I'd last used it in Chinatown, to jot down Chin's name. I must have set the pencil down when fixing his wallet.

Heat prickled over my face. "If you're suggesting that pencil's mine..."

"You have one just like it," she said. "Or used to. I saw you using it in the cathedral. And you're a nibbler, Croft."

"Nibbler?"

But I knew exactly what she meant. When struggling for a thought, I had a habit of gnawing on my writing utensils. From across the desk, I could see the teeth impressions in the pencil's green paint. My stomach performed a steep dip.

"We have your dental records on file, you know," Vega went on. "Even with our strained budget, given the priority of the cases, I could have these marks analyzed inside of a day."

Man, and I thought she'd been bluffing when she told the guards I was wanted in an investigation. Was she bluffing now? Detective Vega gave the bag a shake, her face frowning in impatience.

"I, ah—"

"*Think* before you answer," she said. "Whether or not you had anything to do with the murder, lying about being at the scene of a crime—either before or after it was committed—is obstruction and a serious violation of your probation. That spells prison, Croft."

"At least I wouldn't have to worry about unemployment," I muttered.

"What?" she snapped.

"My department chair knows about my probation. There's going to be a hearing Monday, which means I'm out of a job." I found my irritation at Snodgrass spreading to Detective Vega, for having talked to him. Or maybe I was just fed up with authority in general. I jabbed a finger at the bag. "That's not my pencil," I lied.

"And if it is, I don't know how it ended up wherever it did. Maybe someone found it on the street and wanted to give it a good home."

"Yeah, the home of someone whose organs were cleaned out," Vega shot back. "Not unlike the victim whose apartment we found you passed out in last year. You know something, *goddammit*."

Though her dark eyes shimmered with anger, I could also see whatever it was I had glimpsed the day she'd driven me to the cathedral. Some deeper intelligence. She blinked rapidly, and the look was gone.

"I'm sorry, Detective," I said, "but I don't know anything more than what I've already told you."

What was the alternative? Telling her who I was and why I had been tracking the conjurers? She wasn't Father Vick. A story like that would land me in a pen with the poo slingers and droolers. And even if Vega accepted my story, I couldn't very well share my suspicion that the spells had originated inside the church. That would only bring more heat on Father Vick.

Detective Vega stared at me another moment. When she saw I wasn't going to answer, she shook her head and craned her neck toward the open office door.

"Hoffman!" she shouted.

A balding man with a greasy red face came hustling in. "What's up?"

Vega scribbled my full name on her notepad, tore the page out, and set it and the evidence bag on the corner of her desk. Her eyes darted to mine as though to say, *This is your last chance.*

When I remained silent, she exhaled through her nose. "I need a priority bite-mark analysis done on this," she said. "It's for the disembowelment cases."

Hoffman, in a brown polyester suit, nodded earnestly. “I’ll run it right over.” He collected the bag and note and hustled out.

Vega turned toward me. “Guess we’ll be in touch.”

My legs wobbled slightly as I stood with my cane, unable to meet her eyes.

“Guess so,” I replied.

35

From One Police Plaza I caught an express subway to Midtown and then hurried the pair of blocks to the New York Public Library.

The looming bite-mark analysis had collapsed my window for finding and stopping the spell supplier, but I had the church in my sights. The next step was finding out what I could about Bartholomew Higham, the man who had been interred in that tomb. Someone at St. Martin's, probably Malachi, had been interested in him in the days leading up to the rector's murder.

I jogged up the marble steps to the library, passing between the iconic stone lions, Patience and Fortitude, and entered through the soaring central portico. Inside the vast stone hall, I paused to get my bearings and strategize. Because the Order was listening in—and without a strong threshold to buffer me—I was trying to veil my intentions with innocent curiosity. Whether it was working or not, I didn't know and couldn't afford to care.

The clock was ticking.

Near the information desk, I eyed a bank of computers, their screens inviting me to search the library's online catalogue. I took a tentative step forward. Almost immediately, the screens began to flicker.

Dammit.

I hailed a slender, smooth-faced man behind the information desk, and he came around. His subtle aura told me he had a little bit of faery in him—not enough to cast glamours or even basic magic, but enough to make him interesting.

"Excuse me," I said. "My eyes are really sensitive to computer glow. Would you mind entering a search for me?"

"Certainly," the part-fae replied.

I gave him the name and dates and stood safely back. A moment later he returned with a neat hand-printed list of sources. "Most of the hits are with the *New York Evening Post*," he said, looking over the slip of paper. "That's going to be in our newspaper archives, on microfilm. Will you need help with that as well?"

Because the microfilm machines were mechanical rather than digital, they would be mostly safe from my wizarding aura. "I should be all right, thanks," I replied. "But if you could tell me how to get there?"

Fifteen minutes later I was sitting in front of a machine, a stack of small boxes holding thick rolls of film beside me. I loaded a roll and scrolled to the March 1814 issue that corresponded with the first hit. Images of aged paper and antiquated print shot past the viewer.

I soon reached the article I wanted. It was an announcement that Bartholomew Higham had been appointed the fifth rector of St. Martin's Cathedral.

So, Father Richard's distant predecessor. I jotted the fact down in my notepad, using a pencil in a box of them beside the machine. The write-up contained info about Higham's studies and past offices, but nothing to indicate who he really was. The subsequent articles were little more than mentions—ceremonies or functions that the rector had attended or presided over.

But the next one caught my eye:

EXODUS FROM ST. MARTIN'S

I read the article with growing interest, mixing in what I knew of Manhattan's history. In the early days, the land north of present-day downtown had consisted largely of farms and fields. Graveyards, too—some of them massive, like the one Effie had been buried in. As development moved up the island, many of the graveyards were dug up and the bones relocated. Unbeknownst to his congregation, Reverend Higham had accepted thousands of remains, for a fee. When the deed came to light, the congregation feared the "fell and malevolent spirits" he had surely brought into their hallowed sanctum. Many parishioners left the church.

Was this the history Father Richard had found so troubling? Father Vick had mentioned something about the church not always having been represented by honorable men.

The final hit was an obituary for Higham, only a month after his actions had been exposed.

Suddenly this morning, in the 52d year of his age, the Right Reverend Bartholomew Higham of Saint Martin's Cathedral in the City of New York, was seized with an attack of apoplexy which proved fatal.

I scrolled past his honorariums to the obituary's abrupt end.

Due to his condition, Reverend Higham will not lie in state. A Rite of Transfer of the Body will be conducted in private.

His condition? I tapped the end of the pencil between my teeth as I reread the obituary. Apoplexy, which was old-time speak for a brain hemorrhage or stroke, shouldn't have affected the man's appearance.

A thought hit me, and I bit down on the pencil.

Had he been Father Richard's predecessor in more ways than one? Murdered, too? And if so, why the cover up? Was someone trying to keep the power of the church, already shaken by scandal, from becoming further compromised?

Or had his murder been sanctioned by the Church itself?

Something told me the answer was in the cathedral archives, and it was *that* which had bothered Father Richard.

The bottom of the page showed an image of the early nineteenth century reverend in a black cassock and stole. He exuded an intense, aristocratic air. I centered the viewer on his face and zoomed in. Parted, graying hair fell to a wiry set of mutton chops growing wild from his jowls. His lips were pressed to his teeth, as though in malice. While the look might have been standard for the time, something about the man seemed ... off. I zoomed in on his staring eyes and stiffened.

I'd seen eyes like that in my own work. They were the eyes of someone entranced.

The part-fae, who seemed to materialize at the very moment I needed him, helped me print off the obituary from the microfilm machine, and I hurried from the library with just enough change in my pocket to call Father Vick.

I needed to find out what Malachi had dug up in the church archives.

With my gaze fixed on a corner payphone, I never saw the man who staggered into my path. We collided, my cane clattering to the sidewalk. Something fell from him, as well. The ragged man dropped to his hands and knees and began slapping the sidewalk for what I quickly understood were his glasses.

"Over here," I said, spotting them beside a tree planter.

I stooped and lifted his glasses by a temple bound in thick tape. I looked from the greasy Coke-bottle lenses to the man, whose stringy hair draped his bowed head, and then back to the lenses.

Well, damned if I hadn't just found the East Village conjurer.

36

I held the conjurer's glasses toward him and watched as he took and pressed them onto his black-whiskered face. In a city of six million, what were the chances? Then again, the nearby park had long doubled as a staging area for the homeless, who shuffled in and out of the library during the day for the bathrooms and newspapers. The conjurer had likely joined their ranks, because it was *definitely* him.

"Hey, are you all right?" I asked.

I drew closer but didn't attempt to help him to his feet for fear he would startle. He blinked as his magnified eyes floated upward. It was hard to tell where they were aimed, exactly. But his head soon cocked to the side, and something like recognition took hold in his swimming gaze.

"Y-y-you-y-*you*!" He stood and shuffled backwards in a pair of ragged tennis shoes.

I was pretty sure he didn't recognize me. The only time we'd been this close, he'd been out like a light, the filaments of his mind blown. This was mental illness talking. I decided to use it to my advantage, ethics be damned. I needed to find out where he'd gotten the spell to summon a shrieker.

"Is that Clifford?" I asked, affecting pleasant surprise. "Wow, I haven't seen you in a month of Sundays."

He hesitated, his grimy fingers wringing between the flaps of an army surplus jacket.

I patted my chest. "St. Martin's outreach service?"

I was trying to present myself as harmlessly as I could, but at mention of the church, Clifford's face contorted in what seemed pain. Tendons popped from his shaggy neck. His thick lips sputtered, but the words, as well as his breath, were trapped in his shuddering chest. When a bluish shade of burgundy spread from his cheeks to his forehead, I reached out a hand.

"Hey, are you—"

"Demon!" he shrieked, stumbling backwards.

Demon? Was he picking up the shadow of Thelonious I carried? Sometimes the mentally afflicted were also endowed with powers of perception.

"No, no," I tried, "I'm with St. Martin's—"

"Demon!" he repeated. *"You are of your father SATAN and he was a MURDERER and abode NOT in the truth because there is NO truth in him and when he speaketh a LIE he speaketh of his own for he is a LIAR and deceiveth the whole world and he was cast OUT into the earth and his angels were cast out with him..."* His words expired in a straining gasp, even as his lips continued to move. But in the mash-up of biblical passages, I'd picked up a theme.

"Who lied?" I asked.

"The demon," he whispered. "The demon in the glass."

"Demon in the glass?"

He jabbed a finger at my chest, the bugging madness of his eyes replaced by the roundness of fear. He babbled and staggered backwards. When he tripped over an ankle-high fence bordering the lawn that hedged the library, he screamed and fell. I rushed to help him, even as his backpedaling heels kicked up chunks of brown sod and his cries grew more piercing.

I only realized a loose crowd had gathered when one of their members spoke.

"Hey, man," an edgy voice said. "What's your problem? Leave the dude alone."

I turned. The dozen or so homeless advancing on me were in their twenties and thirties. They had been working students before the Crash: bartenders and baristas. Cut off from income, they'd given the middle finger to their massive student debt. Even now they wore their scavenged coats and patched pants with defiant pride, as though they were all members of the same clan. A clan Clifford belonged to more than I did. I was the outsider here.

I watched two young women separate from the group to help Clifford up.

"It's not what you think," I said, taking a step toward them. "I actually know him."

The man who'd first spoken drew up in front of me, black discs in his stretched earlobes, fierce judgment in his eyes. "Leave him. The Fuck. Alone."

The others took up positions around me. Geez, what was it about me that inspired a let's-beat-his-ass mentality? Whatever the reason, I had a lot to piece together and not a lot of time to do it.

"All right," I said, showing my palms. "I just caught Clifford on a bad day."

The group let me edge from their circle, then formed a barricade in case I changed my mind and made another go for their compatriot. I watched as, with hard backward glances, they escorted Clifford away. As much as I needed answers, I let him leave. I'd gotten some information, scattered though it was.

I wheeled and strode for the payphone. *Demon in the glass, demon in the glass.* What in the hell did it mean? As my reflection rose up in the phone's steel body, I saw the answer.

The mirror in Clifford's apartment. It had been in the summoning room, intact, the first time I'd seen it. But on my second visit, the mirror was shattered, its round frame a mouth of silver shards. I imagined Clifford driving a fist against it in fear and horror before he clunked off with his trunk.

I thought back to the apartment of the Chinatown conjurer. Yes, there had been a mirror in Chin's summoning space, as well. And the crime photo in the *Scream* showing Flash's apartment? Another mirror.

The spells had never been written down and distributed, as I'd first thought. No, someone had contacted the conjurers, using their mirrors as portals, promising them God only knew what—money, power, salvation—and then dictating spells that would summon shriekers. And I now had a good idea who that someone was. I lowered my gaze to my chest.

Clifford had pointed right at him.

Protruding from my shirt pocket was the folded-over printout of the obituary I'd slid there. For the minute or so we'd talked, Clifford had been at eye level with the reverend's sideways face and dark stare. The reverend was the man he'd been referring to as a liar. He was the demon in the glass, and likely the hooded figure Effie's friend had seen creeping around the tomb—not Malachi.

I pulled the obituary from my pocket and stared at the image.

Bartholomew frigging Higham.

I thought back to the thousands of remains he had warehoused at St. Martin's. One of them could well have held a demon—a demon that took possession of Reverend Higham. The reverend had died, or been slain, shortly after, but if no exorcism had been performed, the demon would still be inside him.

But why emerge now? Had someone called him up, or were there other forces at work?

I crammed some coins into the payphone and punched Father Vick's number. I didn't know what the reanimated reverend was up to, but bludgeoning Father Richard and summoning lower demons? Yeah, it couldn't be good. I needed to warn Father Vick and the others. By the fifth ring, the muscles around my clenched jaw began to ache with urgency.

"C'mon, c'mon, c'mon," I muttered.

The hard male voice that answered sounded like no one I knew. "Yeah?" it said.

"Who's this?"

"NYPD. Who's this?" the voice shot back.

"I'm with the diocese," I lied. "I'm trying to reach Father Victor."

"Well, he's not here. He's missing."

"Missing?" My heartbeats punched through my voice.

"Yeah, him and the bishop both," the officer said. "Got a manhunt going on down here. I'm gonna need to get your name and ask a few questions."

I hung up and closed my eyes to a wave of dizziness. Was I too late?

There was only one way to find out. I hurried west toward the line that would deliver me back to the West Village. I needed to cook up another hunting spell and ready myself for the mother of all banishments.

Assuming, of course, the Order didn't kill me first.

37

"Has anyone been here?" I asked as soon as I'd crossed the threshold of my apartment. I triple locked the door and checked to ensure my magical wards were at full strength.

"No," Tabitha answered, but not from the divan.

I turned, surprised to find her on her feet for a change. She was near my reading chair, and by her posture, it looked as if I'd caught her in the middle of pacing. For some reason, her hair was stiff with static, but I was too focused on my next steps to pay her appearance much heed.

"How about outside?" I asked. "Anyone watching the building?"

I believed now that she *had* seen someone, and I was starting to suspect the long-haired person wasn't a woman, but Malachi. He could have observed me talking with Father Vick on Thursday morning, when Detective Vega brought me to the church, and then followed me home. Even if he hadn't reanimated the demon rector, he could have fallen under his influence, become a spy for him. I thought of him standing outside Father Vick's door.

"I've been out every hour and haven't seen anyone," Tabitha said, her voice edged with something. Nerves? Add that to the static, the pacing, the *very* uncharacteristic touring on the hour...

"Is something wrong?" I asked.

"Oh, it's the bloody demon moon," she replied, irritably. "It's on the rise again. Gets me in a fucking state every time."

I was too stuck on her first line to rebuke her for the last. I wasn't big into consulting the star and moon cycles—my brand of wizardry didn't require it. But I knew from my study of lore that a demon moon was the fourth blood moon in a season and exceedingly rare. It carried End Times portents, if you believed in that sort of thing. But from an energy standpoint, blood moons were opportune times for casting black magic and all manner of devilry, which explained Tabitha's agitation. She was practically a demon herself.

Might the moon also connect to the reanimated reverend?

"Is there one tonight?" I asked, ducking my head to peer out a window. The low clouds had taken on a subtle red tinge.

"My urges are never wrong," Tabitha replied. "They've been screaming at me all day to feast on male energy. In fact, if it weren't for your damned wards, I'd be long gone—and about time."

I disregarded her comment as another empty threat, but at the ladder to my lab, I turned and took in her poofed-out state again. That particular effect hadn't come from the demon moon.

"You tried to get out, didn't you?"

She narrowed her green eyes at me and resumed pacing, which told me she had. I imagined the shock the wards must have delivered. Under different circumstances, I'd be on the floor, choking on my own laughter. Instead, I said, "I warned you they were strong."

"Bite me."

Her insult was actually a reassurance, I thought as I scaled the ladder. If my wards were strong enough to keep a determined succubus spirit in, they would keep all manner of baddies out.

That was when the final pieces snapped into place.

Tabitha must have seen the change come over my face. "What?"

"I don't need a hunting spell," I said. "The threshold."

"What threshold?"

"At St. Martin's Cathedral." I descended and released the ladder. "The reanimated reverend, he isn't hiding somewhere in the city. He's stuck on the cathedral grounds, trapped behind the threshold. He can't get out. He's not strong enough." Tabitha's ears bent in confusion, but I couldn't slow down to explain. The logic was rushing out of me. "He murdered the rector to weaken the threshold. He's planning to do the same to the vicar and bishop. Extinguish two of the remaining bulwarks of faith that give the cathedral its strength. With the added power of the demon moon, he'll get out. And when he does, he'll have a small army of shriekers at his command. Shriekers he's been too weak to summon himself."

Blood pumped hard behind my eyes as I pictured the ensuing carnage. The Church had prevented it from happening in the 1800s by executing the reverend—I was all but sure of that now.

Problem was, destroying the host wouldn't banish the demon. The creature had only to lie dormant in the reverend's remains—for two centuries, in this case—until the conditions were opportune.

I imagined an arriving demon moon would do.

I rushed back to the newspaper I'd dropped on the counter and flipped to the weather. Noting the times for moonrise and moonset, I did a quick calculation. The demon moon would be peaking in a couple of hours. I had to get to Father Vick and the bishop before that happened. I turned over the vicar's business card in my pocket. I'd been planning to use the card for the hunting spell, but it would only lead me to the cathedral, whose threshold would then snuff out the magic.

"So where in the cathedral are they being held?" I asked aloud. From my brief conversation with the officer at the scene, it sounded as though their manhunt had yet to turn up anyone.

A second later, I answered my own question. "Wherever Reverend Higham had room enough to store those thousands of remains without anyone knowing." Panic flashed hot inside me. "Beneath the cathedral."

Tired of being my sounding board, Tabitha began pacing away. "Fascinating," she muttered. A bout of knocking froze her. We both turned. The hard knocking at the door sounded a second time.

38

By the time the second bout of knocking subsided, I had a short list of candidates—none of them good guys, unfortunately.

One, it was someone from the White Hand, wanting to know who had supplied Chin the shrieker spell. The deadline was today. The damned thing of it was, I had an answer, but something told me Bashi wasn't going to accept a two-hundred-year-dead reverend. And I couldn't afford to be dragged into his basement and finger-cranked again. There wasn't time.

Two, it was the NYPD, coming to arrest me for my chewed-on pencil ending up in Chin's apartment. That would be worse. With Bashi, there was at least the chance he'd take me at my word. After all, he'd accepted that dark magic was at play. The same wouldn't fly with Vega. I'd be looking at incarceration.

Candidate number three? Arnaud's goons. I'd strolled into the vampire's territory twice now after he'd warned me away. And he clearly wanted Grandpa's ring. He wouldn't think twice about having me killed to get it. Unlike Father Richard, I was a nobody in the city.

Finally—and the one that scared me the most—was plump little Chicory, coming to execute me for violating the Order's mandates. Bullets I could handle. A dissolution spell? Not so much.

I waved Tabitha back as I stole up to the door. Gripping my cane, I peered through the peephole. My list of candidates erupted in smoke—it wasn't any of them. A thin back was to the door, brown hair falling down a khaki coat, as though the person was contemplating leaving.

Malachi?

With energy crackling around my prism, ready to cast, I twisted the bolts and opened the door a crack. Fully expecting a man's narrow face to round into view, I started to discover a woman's instead. A young woman's, and one I recognized from Midtown College.

"Meredith Proctor," I said, opening the door to my overachieving student.

"Hi, Professor." Her face looked strange, almost sinister, and then I realized I'd never seen Meredith without her glasses—or in makeup. She'd gone especially heavy on the eye shadow and lipstick. "May I come in?" she asked.

The timing couldn't have been more horrible, but before I could give the polite version of that answer, Meredith was stepping past me. She unfastened her coat in the front and turned for me to draw it from her shoulders. It was an awkward gesture, unpracticed, and like the makeup, looked forced on someone who couldn't have been older than nineteen.

I snuck a peek at Tabitha. Over the years, we had developed a body language for when I had visitors. Her staring eyes told me everything. This was the person who had been watching the apartment building.

"So, ah, what brings you here, Meredith?" I asked, deciding to ignore the invitation to remove her coat. I reached around her to close the door.

She turned abruptly so she was inside my arms. Thick tendrils of perfume climbed my nostrils, triggering an asthmatic cough. She managed to shrug her coat away, and it thudded to the floor. The sparkling black dress that had been hiding underneath was low-cut, high riding, and completely inappropriate for a student visiting her professor.

"I'm going dancing with friends later," she explained, as I stooped for her coat and hung it on the rack. "Your place was on the way, so I thought I'd stop by. Hope that's okay."

Not rehearsed at all.

"Actually, Meredith, you've caught me at a bad time," I said, trying to sound professorial. "I'm rather preoccupied."

"That lecture on Thursday, about the *First Saints Legend*?" she continued as though I hadn't spoken. "Wow. I just have *so* many questions. About your trip to Romania, your research, your published paper."

Suspicion prickled through me at the strangeness of her voice, the timing of her visit. Aside from being a stellar student, I knew nothing about Meredith. Was she connected to the shrieker summonings, somehow? To the resurrected reverend?

I followed at a safe distance. But when she peeked back over a bare shoulder, I saw it wasn't either of those. There was another explanation for why she'd been staking out my apartment. The trance-inducing effect of Thursday's lecture? Well, it must have lingered—and judging from the batting of her mascara-caked lashes, gotten mixed up with her amorous centers.

I had a groupie on my hands, basically.

"Listen, Meredith," I said. "I'm going to have to answer your questions another time."

She clicked to the center of the loft in a pair of strappy black heels, my words once again sailing right past. "Shall we relax on the couch?" she asked.

I tried to circle around to the front of her. "It's not as relaxing as it looks, actually," I stammered. My priority now was getting her back to the door. Which I'd left ajar, I realized.

While Meredith lowered herself, cooing over the soft cushion, I beat it back toward the foyer. The partially-opened door rattled in the doorframe, as though the window beside the staircase was open and pulling air from the corridor. That had never happened—

Something large landed in the hallway.

—before.

I got my shoulder into the door, forced it closed, and was snapping the bolts home when the thick wood shook against me. A moment later, a familiar pain jagged to the depths of my eardrums.

Only this shriek sounded more adult.

And there were two of them.

39

I backed from the shuddering door and turned to check on Meredith. I found her across the couch, palms clamped to her ears. I'd chosen index fingers to block my own. Thanks to the wards, the demonic register of the shriekers couldn't penetrate the threshold, sparing my mental prism.

But the screams still hurt like hell.

During a brief lull, I shouted, "Get into the bathroom! Lock the door!"

When Meredith squinted up, I could see that terror had shattered her trance. She was probably beginning to wonder what the hell she was even doing here. She nodded rapidly and wobble-ran toward the back of the apartment.

I looked around for Tabitha, but she had taken off somewhere—maybe out onto the ledge, and who could blame her? With her feline hearing, the sound would have been doubly piercing.

A splintering crack sounded, and I wheeled around. I had enough time to note my front door bowing out before it was flying at me in two halves. The larger piece slammed into my left shoulder, spinning me halfway around. It took a moment for the rude clunk of dislocation to register, the bruising pain spreading from my shoulder into my neck.

I retrieved my fallen cane. In the next moment, light shields covered my ears like muffs. With the horrid sound stifled, I rammed the front of my shoulder into the steel beam that anchored the end of the kitchen counter, popping the humeral ball back into its socket. The shoulder was a recurring thing, the only upshot being I knew how to fix it. But that didn't make it any less agonizing.

The world behind my closed eyes spun, and I clenched my jaw to the throbbing pain. With a cane tap and a spoken incantation, I initiated the healing to the strained and torn tissue. At last, I turned to confront my visitors.

Sweet Jesus.

If you took a man-sized bat, crossed it with a gargoyle molded by a demented sculptor in bloody tar, you'd be in the neighborhood of the kind of creature—correction, creatures—I was facing. The two were taking turns throwing themselves into the field that covered my threshold, sparks spattering their thorny black wings and screaming faces.

Their juvenile selves were almost cute in comparison.

But as big, powerful, and hideous as the grown shriekers were, they weren't spell casters. Against my wards, it was force against force—and, like any wizard worth his salt, I'd infused my wards with years of cumulative energy. Out there, I'd be in a world of hurt. Inside my apartment, I was safe as houses. I had only to wait until dawn for the shriekers' power to wane, whereupon they would flap off to their dark, damp hiding place to regenerate.

Problem was, I didn't have until morning. I needed to get to the reanimated reverend before he killed Father Vick and the bishop and escaped into the world. I hesitated on that thought.

The shriekers showing up now wasn't a coincidence. The reverend must have known I was a threat to him. My thoughts returned to Malachi eavesdropping on Father Vick's and my conversation that morning. He would have heard us connecting the recent summonings, as well as Father Richard's murder, to someone inside the cathedral. But how had the reverend known where to direct the shriekers, especially since Malachi *hadn't* been staking out my apartment?

Working backwards, I searched my memory for anything I might have left at the cathedral for the reverend to cast from, some specimen that would have held a piece of my essence. I was usually exceedingly careful about such things.

I came up empty, empty, empty—until I arrived at the morning I'd viewed the crime scene. Before entering the sacristy, I'd donned a pair of latex gloves and had had a net pulled over my head.

Sweat and hair.

Assuming the reverend had accessed the bag, he would have been able to cast from either specimen. But mine hadn't been the only bits of protective covering. Who else might the reverend have deemed a threat to his—

My heart missed a beat, then slammed twice as hard to catch up.

The lead detective. Vega.

I angled the phone on the counter toward me, already fishing Detective Vega's card from a pocket before realizing the second I removed the shields from my ears, I wouldn't be able to hear a thing over the shrieking. I lifted the phone, looked around, and then ran toward the bathroom, cord spooling out behind me.

As instructed, Meredith had locked the door. I waited for another break in the shrieking before knocking. "It's me!"

The knob turned tentatively, and I dispelled my ear shields just before one of Meredith's eyes appeared in the door space. Once inside the bathroom, I shut the door against a renewed cycle of screaming. Meredith had pushed a towel against the space at the bottom of the door to stifle the sound, and I shoved it back into place with a foot. It helped a little.

"What's going on out there?" Meredith asked, hands back over her ears.

"Building put in a new alarm system," I shouted. "It's having some problems."

I set the phone on the lid of the toilet tank and dialed Vega's number. A light dome around my head would have helped, but I didn't want to cast in front of Meredith. Instead, I cupped the mouthpiece and clamped the receiver to my ear with my good shoulder. I could just make out a faint ring.

"Vega's office," a man answered.

"Is she in?"

"Who's this?" he asked.

I recognized the out-of-breath voice from earlier that day. "Is this Hoffman?" I asked in a tone I hoped sounded high ranking.

"Yeah, but—"

"There's no time for stupid questions," I shouted. "We've got a situation. Where is she?"

“Home,” Hoffman said after a moment. “Kid’s sick.”

I remembered the little boy in the photo, and my heart rate kicked up again. I had to think fast, act fast.

“All right, listen,” I shouted above the shrieking. “This is”—I gave a garbled name. “I’m working homicide in the Bronx. Got a case that’s looking like some of yours down there. Gonna need to run a car by Vega’s place to ask her some questions. She’s over in Queens, right?” It was a shot in the dark, but I needed to get to her before another pair of shriekers did.

“Wrong borough,” Hoffman said smugly. “And I’m not giving you an address. You gotta call personnel for that.”

“Listen to me—”

“No, you listen to me,” he shouted back. “I don’t give a ratshit if you’re the pope and the four horsemen are charging down Broadway. There’s a protocol for getting info on our detectives. How do I know you’re not some scumbag wanting to settle a score?”

As a breed, New York cops were hard to cow. Despite my initial read on the man, Hoffman was no exception. “Can I get her cell at least?” I asked, the authority deflating from my voice.

“Personnel,” Hoffman repeated, and hung up.

Shit. I eyed Vega’s business card. I could cast a spell to locate her, but that was going to take too much time—not only in the casting, but the tracking. No, I needed an address.

I had one more card to play. Literally.

I swapped Vega’s card for the one Bashi had flicked onto my lap before having me hauled off. I peeked over at Meredith, who was sitting on the side of the tub, hands still over her ears, and dialed the number.

“Yes,” a voice answered evenly.

“This is Everson Croft.” I shouted to be heard. “I need to speak to Mr. Gang.”

“Then speak.”

“Is this him?”

“*Speak*,” he said shrilly.

That I’d been given a direct line to the boss himself told me how badly Bashi wanted to nail whomever had arranged for a shrieker to be conjured in his neighborhood. I needed to use that to my advantage.

“I know where the spell came from,” I said.

“Tell me.”

I checked my reasoning before answering. “St. Martin’s Cathedral.”

Bashi repeated the name, his voice dripping with venom. Telling him the truth was a risk, but a conservative one, I concluded. The officials were missing and the church itself was crawling with NYPD. There was no one there for him to exact revenge on. Not tonight, anyway.

“Here’s the thing,” I said quickly. “We’re dealing with a supernatural being. A powerful one. Bullets won’t do anything. A job like this is going to require serious magic.”

The use of *we* and *job* was intentional. I needed to get him thinking collaboratively.

“You said you were a wizard,” he screamed.

“I am, but my magic’s not cheap.”

“Maybe I’ll just have you killed. How about that?”

“Wow.” I’d been expecting a money offer, but either way… “Or how about payment in information,” I countered. “An address and phone number, that’s all, but I need them up front.”

"Whose?"

"Detective Vega in Homicide."

Any of the major crime syndicates in New York would have that kind of information—for levying bribes, threats, or to eliminate a troublesome investigator—but I only had access to Bashi. Who had gone silent.

Outside, I could hear the shriekers continuing their assault on my threshold. I only hoped the reverend had perceived me as the greater threat and cast my spell before Vega's.

"Fine," Bashi said at last. "But the job gets done tonight."

Like I had a choice. Demon moon ... hello?

"You have my word," I assured him.

"Or I have your head."

Fair enough, I guessed.

I was put on hold. Two minutes later, another voice came on and gave me Vega's number and address. I jotted them down in my notepad. The address was in Brooklyn, not far over the East River. Good, because from there I would need to hightail it to St. Martin's before the moon neared its zenith—which would mean getting past the Wall again.

But first I had a bigger challenge, I thought as I eyed Vega's cell number. Convincing the good detective she was in mortal danger.

40

"Croft?" Vega said, not nicely.

"Detective," I called into the cupped mouthpiece, "I need you to listen—"

"Where in the hell did you get my number? Were you the one who just called my office?"

Crap. The second that jerk Hoffman had hung up on me he must have called and alerted Vega. Fortunately, she was too irate to let me answer.

"And what's that racket?" she went on. "Are you at home?"

"Yes, but listen—"

"No, you listen," she shouted. "The analysis came back on the pencil. The marks are yours, Croft. I gave you a chance to come clean. Remember that. Dempsey and Dipinski are on the way. Try to run, and I'll up your case to felony fugitive so fast it'll make your ass hurt."

"You're in danger," I yelled into the brief space she allowed me. "You need to get your son someplace safe and then—"

"Are you threatening my family, you piece of..." The rest was lost to the noise outside.

"I'm trying to *help* you," I shouted.

Detective Vega fell silent. "I'll see you tomorrow," she said at last, coldly. "In your cell."

The line clicked off.

I hung up too, my heart pounding with anger and futility. There was no sense calling back. I would have had to go to her either way, but I'd hoped to convince her to usher her son someplace safe in the meantime. Vega wouldn't be able to hide herself. With the binding nature of the hunting spell, the shriekers would draw a bead on *her*, not where she lived. The only positive to glean from our chat was that the creatures had yet to arrive. I still had time.

But first I had to face the nightmare version of the Bobbsey Twins and then get out before Dempsey and Dipinski arrived.

I squeezed Meredith's arm until she opened her sealed eyelids. "I want you to lock the door after I step out and then stay here until well after the alarm stops. Do you understand?"

"Can't I just leave?" she asked, tears threatening her mascara.

"The alarm probably went off for a reason. You'll be okay as long as you stay in here."

She didn't need to see her professor battling a pair of creatures from the pits of hell, I decided. I only prayed that if I failed, those same creatures would bugle a mission accomplished and sail home, sparing Meredith and the others in the building a messy fate.

I gave my student a nod of reassurance, then slipped from the bathroom and closed the door. I waited for the knob to jiggle, indicating she had locked it, before replacing my ear shields. In the ringing of the sudden quiet, I took a steadying breath. Then I rounded the kitchen counter until the front door came into view.

At the sight of me, the shriekers went spazoid, scrabbling up the field with taloned feet, swiping it with gnarly hands, beating it with black-veined wings. The wards held, knocking the creatures against the far wall of the corridor, which was faring far worse. Blown-out plaster and sections of wainscoting littered the floor. Thankfully, no one from the building had come up to investigate. No bloody remains among the detritus, anyway. In post-Crash New York there was a name for those who had learned to keep their heads down: survivors.

Not an option for this New Yorker.

I strode forward until I was ten feet from the door, then drew my cane into sword and staff. Under most circumstances, I would be no match for these guys. I'd barely handled their kid brother. But wards and years of cumulative energy? There was my ticket.

"Soglia," I whispered, aligning my energy with the defenses over my threshold. My plan was to release the pent-up power into the shriekers. A daisy bomb of magical energy. If that didn't destroy them, it would weaken the creatures enough for me to finish them off.

I fixed my feet in a swordsman's stance as I watched the shriekers, waiting for them to hit the threshold at the same...

"Liberare!" I boomed.

For a moment all of the energy seemed to be sucked from the room. I leaned back, the force pressing my coattail flat to my calves and flapping the sides toward the warping threshold. Hanging pictures rocked on their nails. Something shattered in the kitchen. The furniture began to slide toward the exit en masse. My leg muscles screamed as my planted soles stuttered.

An instant before I could topple forward—and conclude that this had been the worst idea ever—the doorway flashed like an exploding star. Mostly away from me, thank God.

I staggered from the violent release, blinking at the bursting afterimage. Then I righted myself and powered into a run. Through the dust of demolition, I could see the doorframe hanging from the wall. Beyond the threshold, a hulking shadow twitched on the floor.

Down, but not out, dammit.

I tossed my sword up to switch to an overhand grip. Arriving above the shrieker, I plunged the blade between the spot where its wings erupted from a back just human enough to be grotesque. A mewling cry sounded as black fluid bubbled over the striated muscles. Its wings flapped crookedly, the left one twisting around to get a hooked horn into me.

I leaned away and shouted, *"Disfare!"*

With a final mewl, the shrieker exploded in a torrent of black ectoplasm.

A gusher caught me in the face, the demonic scent blasting up my nose. Pawing for a clean section of coat to wipe away the mess, I could hear the remaining gobs pelting the length of the corridor.

I'd pushed more energy into the shrieker than necessary, but with the amount of adrenaline pumping, who could blame me?

Plus, I needed to make sure it did the job. I just hoped I'd kept enough in the tank. There was still one shrieker to go, and it was clawing its way to its feet.

Sponging the remaining gunk from my eye sockets, I backed from where the shrieker had landed, down the corridor. I could hear it stumbling from wall to wall, its wings like the slapping of canvas sails, the beginnings of a wail from its nightmarish mouth an approaching squall.

I thrust my sword toward it and shouted, *"Vigore!"*

The middling force was sufficient to send the shrieker clattering back. I staggered over my threshold into the apartment to allow the last of the gunk to evaporate from my eyes. I had just blinked my sight clear when the shrieker appeared in the doorway, clawed hands gripping the blown-out frame. Its eyes, milky and goat-like, fixed on mine. There were no wards to keep it out. With a fresh scream, it shot forward.

I slid right and slashed my sword through one of its unfurling wings, tearing sinew and vessels before notching a black horn. The impact of metal on exoskeleton rang to my elbow. I grunted and spun away as the shrieker snapped its jaw of hooked teeth at my head. Its toxic breath hit me instead.

"Buddy, you've just redefined halitosis." I swung for its neck, but only nicked it.

Through the ear shields, I made out Meredith's straining voice. "Is it okay to come out now?"

"Not yet!" I called back.

The shrieker went for me again, its talons scrabbling over the slick of its spilled fluids like someone trying on a pair of roller skates for the first time. Under different circumstances, the sight might have been comical. I skipped to one side and, with a hacking slash, cleaved the other wing. The shrieker fell past me into a crouch, ruined wings hugged to its body.

"All right," I panted, drawing the tip of the blade to my hip. "Let's call it a night, shall we?"

I focused on a spot between its wings—and slipped on a spatter of gunk. The cement floor rammed into my side, angering my injured shoulder. From my new vantage, I watched as the tears in the creature's wings began to fuse, black tissue knotting along the repair lines.

The damage from the wards was running its course. The shrieker was healing itself.

We rose at the same time and faced off. I didn't wait for it to make the first move. Too many precious seconds had already ticked away.

Lowering my head behind the shield that crackled from my staff, I charged. If I could get my sword through the shrieker's core, I would hit it with a dispersive force powerful enough to get Thelonious licking his lips but not quite diving in. The still-weakened shrieker wouldn't be able to hold itself together.

That was the theory, anyway.

In a rapid one-two, the shrieker seized my thrusting blade and brought its head down. My good shoulder exploded in white-hot pain. The creature's teeth sunk in deeper as the horns on its wings collapsed toward me.

"*Respingere!*" I cried.

Energy from my shield shoved the shrieker off and into a wall, a bloody flap of my coat, and probably skin, jiggling from its mouth. As the shrieker righted itself, a segmented tongue emerged to grab the scraps and pull them into its gullet. I didn't need to see that, I thought, pressing my staff hand to my torn-open shoulder—a shoulder the wormy appendage had just touched.

But more worrying than its tongue was the creature's regenerative powers. I wasn't sure any level of blast, short of one that would invoke my incubus spirit, was going to do the job now.

And if Thelonious *did* escape my containment, I would be done for the night. Detective Vega? Her son? Father Vick? All dead. And if the possessed reverend succeeded in escaping the church threshold, who knew how many others would die with them? Through it all, Thelonious would drink and dance the night away, happy as a clam. And I'd awaken tomorrow to the mother of all hangovers in a city that would make the current version seem like Paradise.

Never mind whose bed I'd shared.

The shrieker flew at me. Claws raked over my shield. The impact knocked me to the floor. Flapping above me, the shrieker scrabbled its taloned feet against the shield, its foul air buffeting me in great gusts. Ignoring the pain in my shoulder, I drove my sword at its torso.

Without my legs beneath me, though, the thrust was weak, the contact glancing. I brought my sword back in time to block the horned wing diving for my neck. I had the shrieker where I wanted it, close enough to run through. But with the direction things were headed, it was going to run me through first.

Need to get the son of a bitch off me, I thought. *Regroup.*

I hit it with a force blast, which was barely up to the task. The shrieker rose, flapping, and circled the high-ceilinged room twice before I realized what it was doing: sniffing out sustenance.

I aimed my staff at the locked bathroom door. *"Protezione!"* I called.

The shrieker crashed into a shield of light energy. With another blast from my sword I could ill afford, I knocked the shrieker away from Meredith's sanctuary. It lifted off again, coming to a flapping perch on the rail that ran along my library/ lab. It stretched its wings until they were gripping ceiling and wall, like some grotesque parody of the crucifixion.

As the creature stared down with evil, unblinking eyes, I could all but feel it reconstituting the last of its lost strength. Me? I could barely keep my sword and staff aloft.

The shrieker was above my hologram, though. If I could detonate the energy inside it, as I had with the wards, I might be back in business. After all, the hologram was bound to the city-wide wards set up by the Order.

The thought deflated like a sputtering balloon. *Had* been bound to the wards set up by the Order—who had duly unplugged me from their grid when they sidelined me. A quick check confirmed this.

Damn.

The shrieker's next scream shook my ear shields. I backpedaled as the shrieker tore a wing from the ceiling, sifting plaster down. It was unhooking its other wing, preparing to dive, when a hairy pumpkin landed on the back of its neck.

Tabitha!

She must have been crouched on the top of the bookcase, because now she was sinking a mouthful of teeth into the shrieker's tarry flesh. It reared back with a cry, flailing to get one of the horns on its wings into her. Tabitha flattened her head and sank in deeper.

She wasn't just wounding its physical form, I realized. Being a succubus, Tabitha was draining the creature's essence, weakening it.

The shrieker's talons scraped over the iron railing, lost its grip, and fell. With wings still writhing to dislodge Tabitha, its torso was an open book. Seizing my chance, I scrambled underneath it. Right shoulder screaming, I thrust up my sword. The blade passed cleanly through the heart of the shrieker—so cleanly, the creature's plummeting weight flattened me.

We hit the floor together, my head cracking cement. The sensation of warm tar oozing over my hands pulled me from a daze, and I realized in horror the shrieker and I were cheek to cheek. Tabitha's green eyes appeared from behind its neck. *What the fuck are you waiting for?* they asked.

I drew air into my shocked lungs and shouted the Word for dispersion. *"Disfare!"*

The shrieker jiggled against me for several seconds, then erupted in ectoplasm. Tabitha went airborne in a yowling series of somersaults. She hooked her claws into a set of drapes, bringing the whole apparatus crashing down behind her divan. A string of choice words told me she was all right.

Panting, I rolled in a small pond of black gunk onto my side. As the tail end of the geyser spattered down, a creamy white light fluttered around my vision. I'd come really close to my limits with that invocation, but I'd know in a few seconds just how close. I could all but hear Thelonious's smooth, jiving voice, anticipating his night of carousing.

"Not now," I begged as his light washed in like the surf. "I'll let you out another time. I promise."

I'd begged before, but it never did any good. Thelonious was a force beyond sympathy, beyond reason. But whether it was for the urgency of my plea, or that I had just enough fumes in my tank to forestall him, the creamy white light began to withdraw. At last, it fluttered out entirely.

Thank God.

I pushed myself up, groaning. But did that mean I *would* have to let him out another night? I wiped my sword against a pant leg and sheathed it in the staff. I'd worry about whatever bargain I might or might not have struck with Thelonious another time. Right now, I had to get to Detective Vega and her kid and then to the cathedral.

"Wh-what in the world happened out here?"

I turned to face Meredith, who was standing in the bathroom doorway. As she stared over the trashed and tar-splashed apartment, it looked as if she was considering retreating back into the bathroom and relocking the door.

"Everything's fine now," I assured her. "Just a couple of pranksters."

"Pranksters?" Her gaze fell to my right shoulder. "You're bleeding!"

I looked down as if noticing the sopping mess for the first time. "Well, I'll be damned."

"We need to get you to a hospital!"

"All right, but let me grab a few things."

I climbed the ladder to my lab. There was no time to cook potions, but I dropped the bottle of holy water and a few spell implements into my coat pockets. Otherwise, it was going to be my sword, staff, necklace, and whatever power remained in me, which was almost none.

By the time I descended the ladder, Tabitha had extricated herself from the drapery and was perched on the divan, trying to smack the taste of shrieker from her mouth. The black pools had all but evaporated, but the scent hung in the air like an evil mist. I gave my cat a thumbs up before striding toward Meredith, who was exclaiming over the ruined hallway.

"I'll be here when you get back," Tabitha murmured, referring to the lack of wards.

It took me a moment to realize she had also voiced her confidence that I *would* be coming back. My eyes threatened to well up. Sometimes all a person needed was the begrudging love of his cat. I opened my mouth to say this, but her slitted eyes suggested I not push it.

"And I'll have goat's milk," I amended. "You've more than earned it."

That got half a furry smile.

41

Meredith and I arrived on the street at the same time police lights appeared down the block. Before the car's jouncing high beams could hit us, I pulled Meredith around the side of the building, into an alleyway.

"What are you doing?" she asked. "That's a police car."

I peeked around the corner. Though the shrieker battle felt as though it had lasted an hour, it had only been ten or so minutes since I'd spoken to Vega on the phone. And here were Dempsey and Dipinski, as promised. With a finger to my lips, I signaled for Meredith to keep behind me.

Confusion creased her young face. "They can help us," she whispered.

"Trust me," I said. "They can't."

The squad car jerked to a stop against the opposite curb. Dipinski emerged from the passenger side and squinted around. I had absorbed a little light from our space to be safe. The boy-sized officer looked past the alley, then adjusted his too-large hat as he waited for Dempsey to kill the engine and join him.

They started across the street at a jog, Dempsey snapping his keychain to his duty belt. With the point of my cane and a soft incantation, I undid the leather clasp, then caught the keys before they clattered to the street. Using the same low-level force, I lowered the keys gently the rest of the way. Dempsey didn't break stride. I waited until the building door knocked closed behind the officers before pulling Meredith into the street.

"Know how to drive?" I asked her.

"Yeah...?"

"Good." I scooped up the keys and handed them to her. "I need a driver."

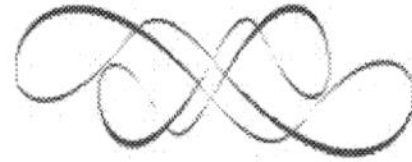

At about the time I estimated Dempsey and Dipinski were emerging from the apartment building, Dempsey slapping his empty key holder, I had Meredith take a sharp left onto Delancey Street.

"Where are we even going?" she asked.

She was driving the police cruiser only slightly faster than my late grandmother, but at least she was driving. That had taken a little convincing, but she had consented—for no other reason, I suspected, than I was a favorite professor. I was abusing the teacher-student relationship big time, but seeing as how tomorrow's hearing was going to be career ending for me anyway,

I didn't feel I was risking an awful lot. And with tonight being potentially *life* ending...

"The Williamsburg section of Brooklyn," I answered.

"Brooklyn? Is that where your primary physician is?"

"It's where a police detective lives."

She stole a glance over her shoulder. "Couldn't those guys back there have...?"

"It's a long story, but no."

"What about your arm?"

"It's not as bad as it looks."

When I didn't offer anything more, Meredith trained her frowning face on the approaching suspension bridge, hands at ten and two. I sat back. The shoulder that had dislocated throbbed in a cold ache. The one that had been gnawed on flashed with hot barbs. I managed to put a little healing energy into both without Meredith seeing, then watched her work the pedals, having already taken note of what she'd done with the gear shift. My wizarding aura had knocked out the dashboard computer and GPS system, which would keep us cloaked.

"The inner roadway's clear," I said, pointing at the lane running beside the train tracks. "How about a little pedal to the metal?"

She hesitated, then depressed the accelerator. The cruiser jumped forward, plunging into the tunnel of scaffolding as the bridge lifted us up. When Meredith leaned over the wheel, something on her face told me she was starting to enjoy this. If nothing else, I was giving her permission to bend a few rules.

Five minutes later, we found the street, and a minute after that, the address. Meredith cruised past Vega's skinned-up sedan and pulled in front of the modest-looking apartment building.

"I want you to drive straight home," I told her. "Park the cruiser wherever but leave the keys in the ignition." A straight-A student like Meredith would never be suspected of boosting a police cruiser, I figured, but if someone else stole it afterwards, so much the better.

Her eyes staggered with disappointment. "What about you?"

"I'll be fine." I got out of the car, then turned around and stooped to the open door. "Thanks for your help."

"See you in class tomorrow?"

The hope in her voice made me hesitate. "You bet," I said. "See you in class."

I closed the door and slapped the roof of the cruiser twice. She wheeled around and took off the way we'd come. I was gambling that Dempsey and Dipinski were still debating whether to call in their stolen vehicle, given that Dempsey's missing keys would suggest negligence, not to mention gross stupidity.

I hustled up the stone steps to the apartment. Like many buildings in the current era, an entrance that had once likely consisted of swinging glass doors now featured a steel monster. I tugged the handle. The door didn't move, its bolt guarded by a thick metal plate.

I looked around. At this late hour, there was almost no chance of anyone showing up for me to pull the "hey, mind holding the door? forgot my keys" routine. Given my bloody state, I was far more likely to send them screaming in the other direction, anyway.

I dug through the spell items in my pockets until I found the vial of dragon sand. I sprinkled some into the palm of a hand, then used a licked finger to lift the dark granules and press them into the keyhole.

When I was done, I whispered, *"Fuoco."*

Smoke curled from the keyhole followed by the hiss of white flames. Within seconds, the locking apparatus sagged in like a half-baked cookie. When I yanked the door, it swung open, the melted bolt plopping to the ground.

I stepped over the threshold and into an anteroom. A locked set of glass doors separated me from an empty lobby. A buzzer panel to my right listed the apartment numbers in two tall columns, with the punch-out of a speaker underneath. Almost immediately, the speaker began to crackle and buzz. Sometimes all these systems took was a little hexing, and for that I wouldn't need a spell medium. As a wizard, I *was* that medium.

I pushed a little more energy into the metal panel, then tried the door. The magnetic lock gave up its failing hold, and I was inside.

I consulted my notepad before hitting the half-lit stairwell. Vega's unit was on the third floor. Fatigue weighed down my legs as I climbed, making me think of the exhaustion I'd observed in Vega's eyes the morning she drove me to the cathedral. Twice now, I had glimpsed something else in those eyes. Some deeper knowledge.

And then the obvious slapped me upside the head.

At her door, I pressed an ear to the cracked lacquer paint. No shrieking or sounds of struggle. I raised a fist, took a second to review what I was going to say, and knocked four times hard. When twenty seconds passed, I wiped the sweat from beneath my nose and knocked again, heart pounding in anticipation.

"Drop the cane, and lock your fingers behind your head."

Not in anticipation of that, though.

I did as Detective Vega said and turned slowly. She was approaching from the staircase I'd arrived by, both hands on the grip of the nine millimeter she was aiming at my head.

"Will you at least let me talk this time?" I asked.

Though she was wearing dark jeans and an untucked white V-neck, Vega was all business. She eased beneath the dim lights of the corridor in a practiced approach, eyes level with her line of fire. Her bottom lip swelled out, and she blew a loose strand of hair from her left eye.

"Face the wall," she said. "Get on your knees."

I turned until I was looking cross-eyed at a pattern of cheap wallpaper. I thudded to one knee, and then the other.

"I imagine someone in Homicide sees a lot in this city," I began, working out the epiphany that had hit me in the stairwell.

"I didn't say you could talk."

"And some of it, maybe a good amount of it, you can't explain. Not to yourself, and certainly not to your higher ups—they want cases cleared, period. Start going to them with things that don't conform to that goal, much less reality?" I gave a rueful laugh. "Next thing you know, you're standing in traffic with a whistle between your teeth, right?"

Detective Vega, who had begun a search of my pockets, didn't respond. I heard her set my wallet and keys on the carpeted floor behind me, the blackberry scent of her shampoo mingling with the sour smells of my sweat and blood.

"So you shut away the things you've seen," I said, "the things you *know* to be out there. And it's not because you're a bad detective—far from it. It's because you're not given a choice. You believe in the mission on your shield, and you can only fulfill it from inside the system, blind and broken as it may be. Making the city safer. Protecting the vulnerable. Protecting your son."

She had moved to my coat pockets, turning out the spell items, but now I thought I felt her slow.

"It's why you listened to me tonight," I said.

"The hell are you even talking about?" she growled.

"You took your son someplace safe, like I asked. That's where you're coming back from." It was an educated guess. She could just as well have been staking out her apartment to see who might show.

"Or maybe I just want to keep him safe from you," she shot back.

I gave a knowing chuckle as she resumed her rough excavation of my remaining pockets. "Why did you bring me in on the St. Martin's investigation?"

"*That* was a mistake," she muttered.

"I'm not the only authority on ancient languages in this city. You could have gone to any number of experts, none of them carrying the stain of probation. Care to hear my theory?"

"No."

"You wanted to size me up. You knew I had no hand in that murder last year, because when you followed the evidence, it didn't point to me. In fact, it didn't point to anything explicable. But like a good soldier, you obeyed the orders of your higher ups. You went deeper, looking for any angle that would implicate me in the man's death. What you found instead were strange rumors about who I was and what I could do. When you connected the dots, you realized I'd been trying to help the victim, even if it was in a way that didn't make sense to you."

She finished her search. I craned my neck around until our eyes met. And there was the look, the one that spoke to deeper knowledge. What I'd missed before was the angle of curiosity.

"The decision to arrest me for obstruction didn't come from you. You followed orders—and felt bad about having to, I'm sure—but you didn't forget what you'd found out. So when you needed an expert on ancient languages, you came looking for me. To see what I was all about."

Vega narrowed her gaze, though whether because I'd made her feel transparent again or that I was way off the mark, I couldn't tell. "Stand up," she ordered in a voice that could have suggested either.

"None of this changes the fact that you're in danger," I said.

"You want to tell me what you were doing at Mr. Chin's?" The pistol she held on me drifted from my head to my midsection as I rose. "Or up in Hamilton Heights, for that matter?"

"Trying to help," I said, looking directly into her eyes. "And you know that."

Her gaze moved to the torn and bloody shoulder of my coat. I could see her trying to work up her anger again, and it wasn't because she thought I was a degenerate. No, her anger originated from a struggle between her wanting and not wanting to understand a world that challenged the more rational, order-based parts of her mind, which was most of it.

"Who killed them?" she asked.

"*What* killed them," I amended, "are the same creatures that came after me tonight—and that could show up here any second."

The spell items arrayed across the floor between us seemed a boundary between the rational and the irrational, the mundane and the magical. I imagined the struggle behind Vega's hardened face. To trust me meant throwing a radical switch in her head, altering her thinking, her language.

"If you're fucking with me, Croft, so help me God..."

"I'm not."

She assessed me for another moment. An urgent timer ticked down in my head, but gaining her trust was the more immediate need. If I failed, she would arrest me, and my warning would go unheeded.

"You can lower your arms," she said at last, giving a small nod.

Relief swam through me as I unlaced my hands and let them down.

"On whose order were those people killed?" she asked, holstering her pistol into her pants in back.

"The same person who murdered the rector."

Her hands froze at her back, and she blinked up at me. "Come again?"

"I'll explain, but we should probably go inside. I'm going to need to demonstrate some of what I'm about to tell you." She didn't stop me when I started scooping the spell items from the floor and returning them to my pockets. When I retrieved the vial of copper filings, I assessed its weight. I should have topped it off, but there was enough inside to protect Vega.

She wasn't going to like it, though.

42

"A *spirit* is behind all of this?" Detective Vega watched dubiously as I sprinkled the last of the copper filings from the vial.

To her credit, she'd remained mostly silent during my explanation.

"A demonic entity," I reminded her. "I know how that sounds, but think about the evisceration cases, all the evidence you've had to explain away. The summoning circles, for example." I stood up from the one I'd just completed. "They were in the same room as every one of the victims, contained the same casting elements. You concluded the slayings were ritualistic, but how do you explain the absence of forced entries—just forced exits?"

"We have some theories," she said in a defensive voice.

"Yeah, and I bet they require feats of mental gymnastics. But do they have the explanatory power of what I've just told you?"

Instead of answering, she glanced around her two-bedroom unit. The apartment was simple and functional, with a few potted plants. Framed photos of her son and what I guessed to be extended family lined the walls, infusing the space with color and warmth. I had chosen a spot in the corner of the living room for the circle, scooting out a small table and standing lamp. Now I followed her gaze across the room to the lone couch, one end littered with toy trucks.

When she looked back at the circle, I could see her mind working. She still didn't want to believe me, but could she afford not to? "All right," she said at last, sighing through her nose. "Show me."

I was very limited with what I could demonstrate, not only for time's sake but that my powers remained in a slow state of recharge. I reached into a pocket and pulled out a bag of clematis buds.

"The creatures we've been talking about were summoned from a place humans should never attempt to access." I crushed the bag and emptied its contents into the casting circle. "An evil place." I spread the fragrant buds around with the tip of my cane. "Rest assured, I won't be summoning from there, but this will at least give you an idea of how it's done."

Detective Vega crossed her arms and cocked a hip.

I returned the crumpled bag to my pocket and stood back. I appraised the circle, which would need to do two jobs tonight. Deciding it looked up to the task, I pushed enough energy into the circle to close it. I trained the cane on the crushed buds next, focusing until they rustled, as though a light breeze had passed over them. With the strong scent of vanilla drifting up, I began to chant the name of something that inhabited a plane very close to our own.

"Susurle," I repeated.

"Can't believe I'm standing here watching this," Vega muttered after a minute.

In the next moment, her breath caught. A twist of light, and there it was: a small creature with a magnificent butterfly's body but intelligent blinking eyes. It fluttered around the casting column with thin orchid-colored wings before descending to the buds and picking over them.

"How in the hell did you do that?" Vega whispered, arms fallen to her sides.

"That's what a summoning looks like," I said, unable to suppress the triumph I felt.

"And it's not an illusion? That thing is real?"

"For our purposes, yes." I waited another minute. "Seen enough?" I didn't want to rush her, but I couldn't afford to expend any more of my power than necessary—especially since I still had her to protect.

Vega stared for another moment, then straightened and nodded.

I called back the energy from the buds and spoke another incantation, this time banishing the creature. With no particular designs on our world, it dissipated without a fuss. Its orchid wings glimmered out last.

"And the demonic entity talked to the victims through their mirrors?" Vega asked, still studying the spot where the delicate creature had been. She affected a hardened, professional tone, even as I sensed her mind trying to shift blocks around to accommodate this new reality. I had to hand it to her, though. She had taken it better than most people would have.

"Yes," I replied. "He would have used what's called a scrying mirror."

She repeated the word quietly. "And he had the evil creatures summoned to escape the church?"

"No, he killed the rector for that. He plans to do the same to the vicar and bishop when the moon reaches its zenith in..." My heart sped up when I checked my watch. "In less than an hour. The shriekers are to help him once he's free. The phalanx of his demon legion. He'll summon more beings, I'm sure, once he's no longer confined by the power of the church."

"Assuming this is all true, how do you deal with a spirit like that?" She gave a small snort. "Ghostbusters?"

"The only person you're gonna call is whoever's in charge of the search at the cathedral. I need you to suspend it, terminate it—whatever. Just get everyone the hell out of there."

"Call it off? You're asking a lot, Croft."

"They're not going to find anything," I said. "And if they do, they'll be massacred."

"So who's—?"

"Me," I said, anticipating the rest of her question. "Alone."

She shook her head, loose hair flipping over her shoulders. "Forget it, Croft. I've already given you the benefit of the doubt tonight. No way am I letting you go to a major crime scene unescorted. And with the perp and hostages on the premises? Unh-uh. I'm going with you."

No, you're not, I thought, *but I do need your authority.*

"Fine, first call off the search."

She frowned at my order even as she fished a smartphone from a back pocket. “If I find out you’re playing me for a fool,” she said, her collapsing brows promising more violence than her voice, which was promising plenty, “I’m taking you down, Croft. Hard.”

“They’ll be no need,” I assured her.

She relented, scrolled for the number, and tapped it. I backed away so her phone wouldn’t go funny, and listened to her tell whomever was in charge at St. Martin’s to order everyone out of the cathedral. She was bringing in a “specialist,” she explained. A definite upgrade from “probationer,” I thought—as short lived as that upgrade was going to be.

She hung up and disappeared into her bedroom. “What’s your plan?” she asked from beyond the closed door. I heard metal hangers screech and clothes landing on a bedspread.

“It depends on what kind of entity I’m dealing with,” I called back. That was the one thing I hadn’t been able to determine, and yeah, it mattered. Certain demons were susceptible to religious artifacts and scripture, which I was sort of counting on. There would be plenty of both at the church.

“So that message on the rector’s back,” Vega said. “ ‘Black Earth.’ You weren’t lying about not being able to connect it to anything?”

I thought about the fanatical cult in Central Park and started to open my mouth to reiterate what I’d said earlier—no connection—then stopped. An ice floe slid into my stomach. What if the message hadn’t been meant as a threat or a red herring, but as a warning?

“Christ,” I whispered.

"Croft?" she called when I didn't answer.

"You interviewed everyone at St. Martin's, right?"

"Yeah." I could hear her questioning frown.

"All of them over at Police Plaza?"

"Yeah—" She stopped. "Well, all except one. Gave some weak excuse, but then got frantic when we pressed the issue. We ended up doing his interview at the cathedral, which was no biggie."

I swallowed dryly. "Who?"

"Your buddy," she replied. "Father Vick."

The name horse-kicked me in the chest. For a moment, the apartment tilted. I clasped my cane in both hands, as though to anchor myself. But it made sense, didn't it? The illness, the bleeding, and now this revelation of Father Vick's unwillingness—or more likely, inability—to leave the cathedral.

The demon hadn't reanimated the long-dead rector. The demon had found a new host.

Vega emerged in her professional attire, hair stretched back and banded off.

"Ready?" she asked.

"I'm sorry, Detective," I said, then whispered a Word. The force from my cane shoved Vega into the corner of the living room. A second force straightened the scuff her shoes had made in the copper circle.

"Croft, what—!"

I closed the circle with a more powerful incantation. When Vega lunged forward, she rammed shoulder-first into an invisible force and rebounded. *What the fuck?* she mouthed, looking up and down the field that bent her image slightly. She slapped the field twice, then drew her pistol. The shots sounded like distant fireworks, flattened bullets falling to her feet.

“I’m really, really sorry,” I said so she could read my lips.

You son of a bitch, she mouthed, murder in her dark eyes. She drew her smartphone, but the circle’s energy had killed it.

Confident she’d be safe, I wheeled and jogged toward the door. The field was strong, but temporary. Two hours, tops. If the demon went down—no, *when* the demon went down, I amended—so would the phalanx of shriekers, who were bound to him. One more reason to not fail.

My gaze moved over the framed photos and scattered toys.

Actually, two reasons, when I considered a young boy would be without a mother.

I stopped at the kitchen to collect the keys Vega had dropped on the counter. Now it was a matter of seeing if what I had observed Meredith doing in the police cruiser would translate into my being able to drive the detective’s sedan. I could only imagine the knives Vega was staring into my back. Hopefully, she would forgive me when this was all over.

Two more shots sounded as I locked the door behind me.

Then again...

43

The car's accelerator and power brakes took getting used to. I had put too much weight on both starting out. Fortunately, the roads were clear at this late hour and Vega's car was already banged up. By the time I skidded south onto Broadway, the Wall and the Financial District rising ahead, I had the driving thing down, more or less.

With a straight shot to my destination, I leaned toward the windshield to check out the sky. For the first time in almost a week, the low cloud ceiling was breaking up. The hovering moon it exposed was red, frightfully large, and—behind a foreground of moving clouds—appeared to be rising fast.

A distant shriek made my gorge rise. I swallowed against the cloying taste that still tainted my palate. Now two shrieks. Whether they were headed to Brooklyn or the cathedral, I couldn't tell. I started flipping switches on the dashboard until one flashed red and blue lights between the headlights. I picked up speed, blowing through the dozen or so intersections south of Canal Street.

At the checkpoint at Liberty, two blocks ahead, an armed guard moved into my path and held out an arm. A series of squat steel columns, meant to block vehicles, rose from the street behind him.

Crap, I hadn't seen those before.

I held my velocity steady at forty, blooping the siren, like I'd seen Vega do that morning. I was hoping the guard would understand this was a police emergency and lower the bollards. The alternative, stopping and allowing him to put that camera on my face, was a nonstarter. I'd be detained for sure, if not shot.

With a block to go, the guard thrust his palm forward twice, then raised his rifle to his shield sunglasses.

He could also shoot me before I even got there.

I powered my window down. But instead of slowing, I pressed the gas. The guard barked a halt command before the muzzle of his rifle began flashing. A hailstorm lit up the front of the sedan. Sparks flew and bits of bulletproof glass stung my face. I ducked until I was peering beneath the top of the steering wheel.

The guard moved to one side, and a second guard stepped in from the other, rifle blasting. Amid the growing storm, something thumped deep in the engine, sending a jet of steam from the right seam of the hood.

I grabbed my cane from the passenger seat and aimed it out the window.

"Vigore!" I shouted.

The force threw the guards back, automatic fire bursting skyward. The car needle had jumped past seventy, and the bollards were fast approaching. I pointed the cane at the street, angling it behind the front axle.

Please, let this work, I thought.

I called power to my mental prism and, with the glaring lights of the checkpoint feet away, boomed, *"Forza dura!"*

The force that shook down my arm and into the cane emptied against the street. I was going for Newton's third law: for every action, an equal and opposite reaction. The reaction, in this case, was immediate. The front of the car vaulted up and angled to the right. Something slammed the undercarriage hard enough to rattle my spine—the tops of the bollards. When the same columns hit the back tires, the sedan was thrown onto its front fender.

My forehead cracked against the windshield, and my view of downtown Manhattan became asphalt and flying sparks. The car skidded on its nose for a good hundred feet, ever on the verge of upending, before slamming me hard into the seat, downtown Manhattan bouncing back into view. But the hailstorm had returned, this time lighting up the back of the car.

I steadied my shaken-up eyes on the street ahead and pressed the accelerator. Movement! Crippled, granted—and something large and metallic was dragging beneath the car—but a check of the rearview mirror showed the checkpoint falling away, the flashes of muzzles getting smaller.

I cranked the wheel right. The flattened tires thudded us behind a skyscraper and out of firing range. I slowed to get my bearings, then steered a stepwise route to reach the cathedral.

Humping the sedan over the curb, I aimed the one functioning headlight at the front of St. Martin's—and immediately saw my error. The bronze doors were closed and certainly locked. Worse, by having everyone cleared out, there was no one to invite me over the threshold. Assuming I could even force my way inside, my powers would be stripped to the bone and then some.

I hammered the steering wheel. "Idiot!"

I fought with the damaged car door, finally kicking it open. Red moonlight burned bright around me as I limped toward the cathedral. To my surprise, when I moved the police tape and pulled the right door, it swung outward. That was something, anyway. But now I had the humming threshold to consider. It had been weakened, but if it was keeping a demon caged, it remained plenty strong.

"Hello?" I called into the darkness. Nothing moved beyond the closed glass doors inside.

I had some spell options, none great, but if that was what it was going to take...

"Everson Croft," someone called from behind me.

I stiffened at the voice. If it was Chicory, I was a dead man. I'd thrown around enough magic tonight to power Yankee Stadium. And that was to say nothing of having defied the Order's other mandate of staying off the cases. The fact I was standing at the cathedral threshold was proof enough of my disobedience. The Order would go straight to sentencing.

But the voice that had called my name was younger than Chicory's, more hollow-sounding. I turned. *Oh, hell.* Roughly a dozen young men in tailored suits and gelled hair were arrayed in the street in a semicircle, closing toward me. Vampire Arnaud's freaking blood slaves.

"You have something owed us," the foremost blood slave said. It was Zarko. Even in the dimness, I recognized his short monk's bangs. His jaundiced eyes dipped to Grandpa's ring.

"Look guys," I said, "now really isn't the time."

"Give it to us, and we will leave you in peace," Zarko said.

"How about just skipping to the leave me in peace part?"

One side of Zarko's mouth slid up as he stepped from street to sidewalk. I felt Arnaud's venomous presence. "We will take it one way or another," Zarko said. "And you do not appear in any shape to stop us."

I brought my fingers to where he was looking now. A wet gash smarted at my hairline, where my head had smacked the windshield. I looked past Zarko to the car's pock-marked glass. With the high adrenaline of the encounter at the Wall winding down, pain pulsed in every part of my body. I felt as banged up and broken down as Vega's poor sedan.

"Can't I set up a meeting with Arnaud to, you know..." A cold wind hit my sweat-soaked shirt and pants, shuddering out the rest of my sentence "...d-d-dis-cuss this."

Zarko and the rest of the blood slaves began to laugh. They had already seen my blood; now they heard my weakness. I was succumbing to shock. I aimed Grandpa's ring at them.

"Keep on g-giggling," I warned, fighting to hold my voice and fist steady.

Zarko hesitated for a half-step before striding on. "You haven't the strength to overwhelm us all," he—or more likely, Arnaud—decided. "Even with your family trinket."

He was right, of course. Though the ring was throbbing with the same urgency I'd felt in Arnaud's office, I wouldn't be able to channel the kind of juice needed to cripple this crew, much less destroy them.

Which meant it was time to bluff. "Care to test that theory?" I asked, forcing my lips into a puckish grin.

Before I saw him move, Zarko darted in, seized my throat, and lifted me. I choked on the crunch of cartilage and kicked weakly, tears springing from my surprised eyes. He hoisted me higher. I seized his ice-cold wrist in one hand and used the other to swing my cane at his head. But without leverage, I couldn't land a solid blow. The contact mussed his hair—which was actually an improvement—but that was about it. Zarko didn't even blink.

"The ring," he said.

The other blood slaves pressed closer, but I noticed they kept a respectful distance from the threshold at my back. That respect wouldn't necessarily hold up. They were at Arnaud's command. The second he gave the word, they would be on top of me, fighting over my wings and drumsticks.

Meanwhile, my vision was doing strange things. I fought to focus down the length of Zarko's arm to his waxy face.

"The ring," he repeated, the lines of his mouth a growing blur.

A warm fog of sleep began to drift over my oxygen-deprived brain. But rather than seduce me, the sensation sent down an alarm. I hooked my cane over a thumb, extended the remaining fingers, and used my free hand to tug on the ring. It clamped down, as though refusing to be relinquished, but I refused to let up. With a final twist that nearly sloughed the skin away, I felt the ring release. I drew it from my finger and held it up for the blood slaves to see. I then threw my arm forward as hard as my throbbing shoulder would allow. Heads turned simultaneously and swiveled back to face me. I showed them my empty hand.

Zarko released his grip, and I collapsed to the pavement. Leaving me in a heap, the blood slaves spread out into a search. The towers above me spun as my breaths returned in bruised gasps. I rolled to my side and shook the ring from my sleeve back into my hand.

One of the first sleight-of-hand tricks Grandpa had taught me.

I swayed to my feet. I'd bought myself a little time, a little breathing room, but not enough for spell-casting. As the blood slaves searched the street, I began calling energy to my prism. I was spent but not empty.

I backed from the church threshold on shaky legs.

"He still has it," Zarko announced.

Time's up, I thought.

With the rapid patter of leather soles closing, I launched into a run and shouted, *"Penetrare!"* Light in the form of an arrow's head took shape around my cane. Holding it in front of me, I stooped low, shoved with my right foot, and plunged head first into the roaring threshold.

44

I didn't hurt. There was nothing *to* hurt. I was disembodied, detached. Anchored to no one and nothing. I drifted without sight, sensing darkness all around. The darkness seemed to shift like the black sands of a far-off shore—or the folds of the Grim Reaper's robes.

At that second image, I paused. *Wait a second...*

I'd been under no illusions my invocation would pierce the threshold—I had just needed the field to yield a little at the point of contact. I was even prepared for some god-awful pain. But straight to death? Seriously?

Son of a bitch.

So now what? Was there supposed to be a light or something?

At the thought, one appeared. But it wasn't the divine illumination I'd imagined. This light was pale yellow and fluttered like a candle's flame. It seemed to turn a corner before drifting toward me.

I blinked twice. I had eyelids, apparently. And a cheek, which was flattened to something hard and cold. I wasn't dead, just badly stunned. The effort to lift my head opened the storm gates of hell. I writhed around my gnashing teeth and gnarled cries, disembodied no more.

Oh crap oh crap oh crap oh crap...

It felt as though someone had flayed me open, pounded my insides to liquid, shoveled in hot coals, and then stitched me back up again, poorly. Death would have been a mercy. I stomped the floor and punched the air, as though to beat back the agony. Exhaustion eventually did the job.

I lay panting on my back as the pain slipped off by degrees and a coolness settled in.

I raised my head. Beyond my outstretched legs, energy hummed over the open doorway and night. No sign of Zarko and the blood slaves. They had either left me for dead, or Arnaud had recalled them to pursue me another day. Either way, he wasn't going to have them test a cathedral threshold. I only had a little demon-like energy in me; they carried it in spades.

I remembered the candle flame and turned back to the glass doors. The light was gone now, but I hadn't imagined it.

I found my cane and pressed myself to a knee. While I waited for the room to stop spinning, I performed a self check. I was crippled, bleeding, in shock, and stripped of all powers, save the small reserve holding Thelonious at bay. Otherwise, I was fine.

Standing all the way, I brought my face to the glass door. I could make out the cathedral's cavernous nave, rows of pews proceeding to the raised chancel. Above, the stained-glass faces of saints were being tinged red by the demon moon, as though possessed themselves.

The candle-bearer was gone, but I knew who it was. That Father Vick was still trapped inside was a good sign. It meant the demon hadn't carried out the sacrifice yet. But he'd seen me, I was sure.

There was no time to lose.

I tried the doors. Locked. The plate glass didn't look very thick. I stepped back and brought my heel forward with everything I had. The glass shattered to my knee, taking some more skin with it. Reaching a hand through the opening, I fumbled for the bolt, turned it, and stumbled inside.

Glass crackled under my soles as I got my footing and looked around. I staggered down the corridor to the interior courtyard, crossed the blood-red flagstones, and pushed open the door to Father Vick's apartment.

I flipped the light switch, but the power must have gone out. By the ambient moonlight, I could see he wasn't here. I took a leather-bound Latin Bible from Father Vick's desktop and then rifled the drawers of the desk until I found a silver crucifix. Turning to leave, my gaze fell to his white handkerchief. I lifted it from the object it had been draping and stumbled backwards at the sight of a nightmarish face.

My own, I quickly realized, staring back from the foggy glass of a scrying mirror. But the flame that fluttered up over my shoulder did not belong to me. Neither did the hooded head it illuminated.

My heart slammed as I spun, but it wasn't Father Vick I faced.

"What are you doing here?" Malachi asked.

45

"No one's supposed to be in here," Malachi said in a cold monotone. The light from the candle swam in his watery gray eyes. His gaze was bolder than it had been that morning. I dropped my own gaze to his other hand, but it was hidden by the sleeve of his robe. A black robe, I noted.

"Where are they?" I demanded.

"Who?"

"Father Vick and the bishop?"

"Haven't you heard." He drew nearer. "They're missing."

His voice held its monotone as his narrow face fluttered in and out of the hood's shadow. I caught a whiff of sour breath. With the backs of my legs pressed to the desk, I was boxed in.

"Why didn't you evacuate with the others?" I asked, looking for his hidden hand again. He wasn't who I had expected to find, and there was something off about him. He seemed ... haunted.

"I hid," he said, pressing nearer. "I needed to atone. I think I'm the cause of what happened."

"What you found in the archives," I said.

He stopped, his eyes seeming to sharpen in surprise.

"Bartholomew Higham, the fifth rector," I continued. "The Church believed he'd become demon possessed. They killed him, but didn't perform an exorcism, or didn't perform it correctly."

"Father Vick didn't seem to think it had been done right," Malachi said. "But Father Richard said to leave it alone. They argued terribly. And then—"

The flesh of Malachi's other hand hit the glow of the candle. I lunged forward, managing to catch his wrist. Even in my sorry state, I was able to drive Malachi back. We toppled over the corner of the bed and landed hard on the floor. The candle clattered off somewhere and went out.

"Help!" Malachi cried in the darkness, trying to pry my fingers away.

Teeth clamped around one of my knuckles, and I stifled a yell. I climbed my fingers to his hand, finding it empty. I proceeded to pat him down as best I could, which must have felt to the kicking, writhing acolyte like a sloppy grope. Satisfied he wasn't holding anything dangerous, I used the bed's footboard to pull myself up. Malachi scooted back before stopping to regard my offered hand.

"Sorry," I said, breathing hard. "I thought you had a weapon. And with everything that's happened..."

He looked at my hand another moment, his hood fallen away from his long hair, and then let me help him to his feet. As he recovered the candle and relit it, I watched him closely, trying to make sense of his presence. In the light of the new flame, I saw what I had misinterpreted moments before.

It wasn't possession written on Malachi's face, but the dull lines of inebriation.

The atonement he'd mentioned apparently involved helping himself to the communion wine I smelled on his breath. The kid was one shade shy of blotto. And who could blame him? He believed he'd set in motion a chain of events that had led to Father Richard's murder and now the disappearances. I guessed that around the time I was crashing through the threshold, he was downing his fourth or fifth chalice of St. Martin's red. The light I'd seen was him coming to investigate the noise before ducking away. As someone who knew the cathedral better than most, he would have had plenty of hiding places to choose from.

Which meant he could help me.

"The place Higham stored the bones," I said. "Where is it?"

"The catacombs," Malachi answered. "But the entrance was closed off after Higham's execution. The site was decreed a sanctum of evil. I've already checked it out. There's a solid wall over the entrance."

"Show me," I said.

He picked up the urgency in my voice and nodded quickly. Cupping a hand around the flame, he wheeled toward the door. As I shambled after him and across the courtyard, I was afraid to look up. Afraid the demon moon had reached its zenith. Afraid I had lost Father Vick for good.

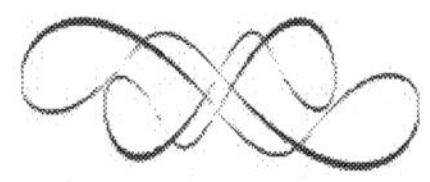

The air seemed to thin as we hurried down a stone stairwell in the corner of the cathedral, but that was my phobia at being underground kicking in. The darkness wasn't helping. A nauseating blend of heat and cold prickled over my tightening chest. I began to wheeze.

Malachi turned his head. "Do you need to rest?"

I shook my head. As long as I could breathe, I had to keep moving. If the demon was the one I feared, we were dealing with a big-time baddie. He could not be allowed to escape, under any circumstances. Underqualified or not, I was assigning myself the task of stopping him.

Which was infuriating when I thought about it. I'd risked my neck tracking leads, taking shots in the dark, getting shot *at*—not to mention fire-blasted and finger-cranked—to eventually connect the dots. With the monitoring spell Chicory had thumbed into my head, the Order should have had the same information as me. And yet, where in the hell were they?

It was the kind of critique I wanted to stuff into the Elders' flabby ears, but with the interference from the energy surrounding the church, I doubted even my thoughts were getting through.

I was truly on my own.

Fresh anxiety snuffed out my anger as the stairwell deposited us into a low-ceilinged basement. Malachi held up the candle. Light swelled through a suspension of dust and over storage trunks and mounds of covered furniture.

"It's in the back," he said.

I studied the stone floor as we walked. Its powdery surface was marred by prints. Some from the search team, no doubt, but perhaps not all of them. I raised my eyes to the far wall emerging from the darkness. I made out what had been an arched doorway, since filled in by uneven stone bricks and chunky mortar. The former entrance to the catacombs.

Malachi stood to one side. “See what I mean?”

I pressed both hands against the impeding wall, then tested the individual bricks. A metal ringlet, too dull to determine its age, had been bolted into one of the central bricks. I pushed and pulled on that, too. Nothing budged. I pressed an ear to the wall, but it was too dense to hear through.

“You think they’re inside?” Malachi asked in alarm, catching on.

I nodded distractedly and searched my pockets. I still had Father Vick’s card but without my wizarding power, I couldn’t locate him. None of the other spell items were worth a squat, either.

My gaze roamed the floor in thought, until I noticed something: faint lines.

I asked for the candle and knelt. The lines were abrasions left by stone. I touched them and noted the grit on my finger. I stood again and moved the candle around the door frame. The texture of the mortar here and there told me what I’d begun to suspect. The bricks were secured to one another, but no longer to the frame of the doorway. Someone had chiseled out the mortar, then hidden his work. I searched around for a handhold, a place to pull.

“Here,” Malachi said, tapping something.

Of course. The metal ringlet.

“There’s some cord over there,” he said, a step ahead of me again. Where panic was making a confusion of my own thoughts, inebriation seemed to have cooled and steadied his.

Malachi ran to an old piano, its closed lid secured with twine, and began to unknot it. I set down the Bible and cross, standing the candle on the ground beside them. The length of twine Malachi returned with looked sturdy enough, but I doubled it over before threading it through the ring. I passed the folded-over end to Malachi and took the loose strands in my own hands. We backed from the door at an angle until the cord was taut and even.

"Ready?" I asked.

He nodded, and we began to pull. Our strength was well short of demonic, but working together, pained grunts bouncing off the basement walls, we managed to walk the door out a few inches. I handed my end of the twine to Malachi and wedged my cane into the narrow space. With him pulling and me prying, we created an opening that looked large enough to edge through.

I held the candle inside and groaned. Rough-cut stairs spiraled down into a strangling darkness.

"Want me to carry these?" Malachi asked, stooping for the Bible and cross.

"Hand them to me once I'm through. You've got another candle, right?" I'd encountered one during my pat-down of him. "Good. Use it to see your way back up, then get as far from the cathedral as you can."

"But I—"

"Forget it," I interrupted. "You have no idea what's down there."

I peeked through the opening once more. If I failed, which felt almost certain, I didn't want Malachi to be in the path of an emerging demon lord. The apocalypse that followed would likely consume him along with the rest of the city, true, but I was still holding out hope that the Order would get their heads out of their collective asses before that happened.

"Where should I go?" he asked.

I fished through my pockets until I found Detective Vega's card. "Call this number. Someone named Hoffman will probably answer. Tell him you got left here, and he'll send someone to pick you up."

He nodded as he accepted the card, emotion trembling through him for the first time. I slid my cane inside my belt and squeezed through the opening. The effort left me dizzy. Malachi passed me the Bible and silver cross. I took them and then touched the flame from my candle to the wick of his.

As the light suffused his young face, I saw in his eyes something I recognized. "Listen to me," I said. "Passion led you to uncover those things in the archives, not sin. You've no fault in this."

The words seemed to fortify a layer of my prism. Maybe because they were words I would have liked to have been told ten years ago. Instead, the Order black-marked me. I didn't want Malachi shouldering the same guilt.

He nodded and wiped his watery eyes with the back of a hand. "Please help them."

"I'll do everything I can. Now go."

I turned from his diminishing scuffs and peered down the steps. *Better to perish in conviction than live in cowardice, right?* I felt too queasy to answer. Drawing a diver's breath, I started down.

46

The spiral staircase ended at a cave-like corridor that diminished into darkness. I struggled to control my gasping breaths so I could listen. Easier said than done. The pressure in my chest wasn't just my anxiety talking now. The air was heavier than in the basement, from being shut away for so long, no doubt—but an oppressive evil lived here as well.

Noises began to take shape. Things skittering here and there, and farther away, what sounded like speech, low and garbled.

It wasn't human.

"You wanted to join the big leagues, Everson?" I whispered over a tremulous breath. "Batter up."

I raised the candle and proceeded down the corridor. Within several paces, I saw what the corridor really was—an ossuary for the remains Reverend Higham had piled down here. They sloped toward the floor in great drifts: dusty-brown arm and leg bones, tossed-off pelvises, sections of vertebrae. And skulls. Everywhere. No matter where I looked, a host of them stared back with ghastly sockets and withered teeth.

My heart slammed harder. As decent as these people may have been in life, I wasn't ready to join their ranks. Especially not when a shiny red centipede slid from one of their ear canals.

Ahead, the corridor bent around a corner, and the speech I'd heard earlier picked up again. The words were nonsensical, guttural grunts in a language I'd never heard or read. And they warped the atmosphere, twisting up my guts and making my eardrums ache. Though I couldn't interpret them, it was clear the incanted words were intended to gather power.

I stopped to make sure I had everything I needed: religious text, silver cross, holy water, cane. Four checks, even though the last wasn't much good in my weakened state. I would attempt the exorcism alone if I had to, though I was counting on Father Vick's help. Assuming enough of him remained.

Where the corridor ended, I peered around the corner. The candle light swelled into a large grotto, revealing the missing church officials.

The bishop was a woman, I saw. She lay supine on the floor, gray hair piled under her head, back arching in spasmodic thrusts. Her closed eyes suggested she was either unconscious or entranced. The black-robed figure standing over her swayed with his back to me, those awful sounds emanating from his bowed head. He'd been incanting in the dark this whole time, which felt freaky as shit.

I swallowed hard on a knot of fear and grief. Man, I had wanted so badly to be wrong.

“Father Vick?” I called into the echoing space.

If he heard me, he gave no sign. His robe continued to shudder with his guttural chants. Steeling my nerves, I stepped into the grotto. Off to one side were the blue bits of protective clothing Vega and I had donned and the demon had used to guide his shriekers. They would be at the detective’s apartment by now.

I reached up with a shaking hand and inserted the candle into the eye socket of a dome-gazing skull. The swelling light revealed an elaborate bone pattern over the floor, one I recognized. The grotto had been made into a demonic casting circle, the convulsing bishop at its center.

The demon was preparing an alchemy spell, taking the potent faith of the bishop and warping it into a black wrath that would empower him and enable his escape from the cathedral’s weakening hold.

Like rape, there were few acts more evil.

“I know you’re in there, Father,” I said to his back. I reached into my right jacket pocket and loosened the screw-on cap to the bottle of holy water. “I know you can hear me. The night the demon murdered the rector, you wrote the message on Father Richard’s back. You couldn’t name the demon. He wouldn’t let you. So you did the next best thing. You named a druid group, Black Earth, whose beliefs revolve around the imminent return of Sathanas, demon lord of Wrath.” The esoteric Latin had likely come from an old prayer book. “You were trying to warn us.”

The garbled incanting rose in pitch and urgency. I could feel Sathanas’s rage now, could feel how badly he wanted to tear me apart. But to turn from the spell would be to sever his connection to the bishop. I followed the dark, twisting umbilicus of energy from the demon's head down to the aging woman's heart. I would have to be careful. At this stage, any violent disruption—such as driving my sword through the demon or dousing him in holy water—could kill her.

I needed Father Vick to work against Sathanas. And to do that, I needed to call him forth. Problem was, Father Vick's hold, which had already begun to fail during the daytime, would be all but absent after dark. Demons ruled the night. And with a demon moon nearing its zenith?

But Father Vick had wrested back enough control once to leave the "Black Earth" message. I hoped that walking him through what had happened would spur him to rebel again.

"Yes, you're possessed, Father," I said. "The fifth rector of St. Martin's took in the remains of thousands, to enrich himself, but he succumbed to the demon Sathanas in the process. The Church executed the rector and performed an exorcism. Malachi found the account in the archives and shared it with you and Father Richard. You weren't convinced the exorcism had been done properly, though. You may even have sensed a shadow around his tomb. When Father Richard forbade you from performing a second exorcism, you attempted the rites at night, in secret."

I thought about the robed figure Effie's ghost friend had seen muttering around Reverend Higham's tomb. I was sure now that had been Father Vick. And that had been his mistake—attempting the exorcism at night.

"The demon was more powerful than you anticipated," I continued. "He overcame you and put you under his control. He had you retrieve Higham's scrying mirror from the heritage room so he could contact those you sensed dabbled in magic." It was the same mirror Father Vick had kept covered with the handkerchief. A mirror that would have shown the image of Reverend Higham to those on the receiving end. "Clifford, Chin, Flash, the others," I said. "Sathanas dictated to them the spells to summon the shriekers. The night the demon contacted Clifford, Father Richard must have seen a light on in your room or overheard you. Not understanding your possessed state, he chastised you for practicing magic. In wrathful response, Sathanas followed Father Richard to the sacristy and murdered him."

He'd also had Father Vick leak the murder to the press later.

Sathanas's breaths gurgled in Father Vick's throat. Was the struggle beginning?

"I can only imagine your horror," I said. "But you *fought*, Father. You named a demon who didn't want to be named. And as long as there's any will left in there, you have to fight again."

"Go away," the figure garbled in an inhuman voice.

Sathanas? Father Vick? I couldn't tell.

"Father, listen to me—"

With a final eruption of words, something appeared above his head. A dagger. He was going to finish the spell by driving it into the bishop's heart, releasing the last of her energy. I dropped everything and scrambled forward. With bones rolling underfoot, it felt as though I was running in a dream. But the space separating us collapsed, and my lowered shoulder struck his ribs in the back. His incantation broke off in a wet roar that shook the grotto.

I wrapped my aching arms around his waist and continued to drive with my legs. He was larger than Malachi, more solidly built, but I managed to topple him. We crashed down into the bones that edged the casting circle.

When he rotated his head, I delivered a bone-crunching right to his jaw.

He fell limp, the dagger tumbling from his outstretched hands. I turned quickly to the bishop. She'd fallen into quiet repose, but I couldn't tell whether she was breathing or not. In either case, I could no longer sense the warping energies of the spell. What that meant, I wasn't sure.

"Father Vick," I whispered, shaking his shoulder.

He stirred, and I helped him onto his back. When his face rotated into the candlelight, I recoiled in horror. In addition to his ears and nose, blood had been pouring from his eyes. He hadn't just been fighting to maintain the faith of the cathedral these past days. Father Vick had been fighting to maintain himself. How he'd lasted this long, I had no idea.

"Everson?" he mumbled. He blinked, then stared in a way that told me he couldn't see through the red skein that coated his eyeballs and gummed up lashes.

"It's me, Father," I said. "But we have work to do." I left him to retrieve the holy items I'd dropped. When I returned, I arranged them quickly beside him. Remembering I'd loosened the cap to the holy water, I pulled the bottle from my jacket pocket, relieved to find only a little of the water had dribbled out.

Father Vick pawed for me. "Are you still here?"

"Yes." I clasped the back of his hand and squeezed it. "You're under the possession of a demon lord, Father. We need to exorcise him. I have all the implements here. Tell me what to do, what to read. Quickly."

His eyes winced in agony, then seemed to fix on mine. "I'm so sorry, Everson," he whispered. "I wasn't deceiving you when we spoke. I just ... I didn't know the things I was doing..."

"*Sathanas* was doing," I corrected him. "But you're back now, and I have your Bible. We can drive him out."

After another wince, he nodded heavily. "Yes, yes ... all right." Father Vick sounded ripped up inside, but more like himself, the awful garbling gone from his voice. "Begin with the prayer."

I flipped open the Latin Bible to the section he indicated and began to read. *"Exorcizo te, omnis spiritus immunde, in nomine Dei Patris omnipotentis..."*

As I moved the silver cross over Father Vick's chest, a part of me felt like a fraud. I wasn't ordained. I hadn't even attended a Mass in ten years—during which time I managed to contract an incubus spirit and challenge a core belief on which St. Martin's was based. But I shut that all away and focused on the power of the words, driving them into Father Vick. I concluded the opening prayer, making the sign of the cross twice more.

Father Vick's next wince turned into a grunting cry. His head whiplashed back, bloody teeth bared. But for the first time, hope stirred inside me. It wasn't pretty, but the exorcism seemed to be working.

"C'mon, Father," I whispered as I checked the next steps. "Hang in there."

I opened the bottle of holy water and wet the first two fingers of my right hand. I touched the moist pads to his right ear and then his left, saying, "*Ephpheta, quod est, Adaperire.*"

Steam hissed up, and Father Vick released another cry. I was reaching for his lips when my hand hesitated. Had he just cried ... or laughed? The sound hardened and took on a cruel rhythm, until there was no longer any doubt. I backed onto my haunches, ice water breaking through me.

"Father Vick?" I asked.

His grinning face shot up like a Jack-in-the-box, but it was no longer his. The smile was too large, too mocking. His irises had blackened and spread, taking on fierce glints of red. And the skin between his brows was fissuring, as though someone had laid into it with an axe.

"Fight him, Father," I urged, splashing him with holy water. "Fight, dammit!"

The wet laughter became riotous as, with blood streaming down his face, the demon rose to his full height. I stumbled backwards, the holy items falling from me. Though I couldn't see it, I could hear the water glugging from the tipped-over bottle. I imagined it seeping through layers of bones, lost.

"Stupid wizard," Sathanas taunted in that awful voice. "You cannot banish a demon lord."

I watched as his robe began to shift and jut out in places, as though something were emerging from Father Vick's body. Something was, I realized in horror: the massive form of the demon. The fissure growing along his forehead broke through his nose in a crackling burst and then split his grinning lips. *Oh God, Father.* His ears sloughed off next. When horns erupted through his red-bearded cheeks, the little strength in my legs gave out, and I collapsed to the floor.

47

The last vestiges of Father Vick dropped away, and a demon lord crouched inside the grotto, horrid wings scraping the walls. Horns studded his face, including two black blades that erupted from his temples like a Brahma bull's. A clawed hand tore away the remains of the robe, revealing a grotesque fusion of muscles and exoskeleton. At the demon's back, a barbed tail raked the bones.

I struggled to see the being analytically, even as I began shoving myself away. Demon lords were elementals, expressions of our darkest emotions and urges. No pure embodiments of the elemental virtues remained to oppose them—only the lineage of Saint Michael. Me, in other words. And right now I was about as dangerous to this thing as a chewed-up sock.

Sathanas's laughter died off. "Alone," he rumbled. 'The poor wizard is all alone."

I eyed the bishop, who had begun to stir. Had the demon pulled enough power from her to break the cathedral's threshold? The million dollar question. If I managed to escape with the bishop while the demon remained entrapped, I could alert the Order, bring in Elder-level magic.

Assuming they listen, I thought.

Sathanas's fiery red eyes tracked mine. Bones crunched under his hoofed foot as he stepped over the bishop, separating us.

"Alone," he repeated. "All alone. How does that make you feel, wizard?"

His words penetrated my mind, cracking like flint against my resentment toward the Order. Dark sparks kicked up inside me.

"Yes, angry," Sathanas said, hungrily. "And rightfully so. You have been threatened, dragged over jagged stones, abandoned like a pathetic pup. And by the same ones you have so dutifully served."

I struggled to suppress my crackling rage.

"And what about those who prattle of cultivating knowledge, delivering justice, and yet who gleefully deny you both?"

He was speaking of Midtown College now, the NYPD. Despite my efforts, the sparks inside me swelled and broke into flames. I watched them climb the administration wing of the college, the walls of One Police Plaza. And as the flames blackened the institutions and pulled them down, an ecstatic energy beat with my surging heart. I was becoming the powerful wizard I knew myself to be. Before I could recoil from the dark fantasy, Sathanas spoke again.

"And this holy place," he sneered. "You know what they did to your forebears. Rounding them up like animals. Beheading them. Burning them at the stake while they screamed for mercy."

Fresh images of the Inquisition slashed through my mind's eye, too horrible to watch, too horrible to look away. I witnessed a woman I knew to be a direct ancestor pursued and hacked to death, her head paraded on a pike. Fury roared through me, searing my injuries closed, shaking hot tears from my eyes.

"Make no mistake, they hate you, wizard. *Hate* you. They will come for you again." I didn't recoil as Sathanas extended a grotesque hand toward me, horned wings looming above. "I feel your power," he said as he pulled me to my feet. "But it can be so much more, wizard, if you would only claim it."

Ugly or not, Sathanas was speaking to emotions that had been swirling inside me like combustible fuel. I was sick and tired of being marginalized and threatened. Take the Order, a bureaucracy with a God complex. Everything I had learned since my earliest training had come from my own initiative, not the Order. They hadn't assigned me a mentor in Chicory, but a goddamned warden. Now the Order was threatening me with death, and for what? Being a wizard? Why should I feel any allegiance to them? Why shouldn't I seek power elsewhere? To defend myself—and, if it came to it one day, to overthrow the Elders?

"Yes," Sathanas hissed, "you know it to be true."

Whoa, cowboy, I thought from a distance. *This is a demon talking, a master manipulator. And you're letting him inside your head.*

I took a step back, but Sathanas quickly closed the space, his nightmare face bowing low. "There is no sin in passion," he insisted, his eyes like stoked coals. "No sin in righteous anger. I will teach you to cultivate it, bring it to its glorious expression. You have no idea the power, wizard. All who once stepped on you will come to cower at your feet."

Over the years, I had resorted to wisecracks and self-deprecating humor to deflect my anger. But the anger felt so much richer. So much more ... *redemptive.* I ached now to punish those who had wronged me, even if it meant destroying them. I burned for them to know my terrifying power. A malicious smile broke across my face. Yes, *that* was true redemption.

And yet...

"What do you get from the deal?"

"What do you mean, wizard?" Sathanas demanded.

The flames inside me began to thin, as though reason were pulling oxygen from them. "A demon does not give selflessly," I said, my voice strengthening. "There's something you want."

Huge black knuckles cracked inside the clenching fist he held out. "Like you, wizard," he boomed, "I wish to exist according to my nature." Fire breathed inside him. His body turned an incandescent red, and smoke plumed from his horrid wings. "I wish to be free."

That's all? I thought dryly, the anger guttering lower, the fire it had stoked leaving me. Mortal pains broke throughout my body, and I staggered against my cane.

But why is Sathanas appealing to me?

My gaze slid from the demon to the bishop, who remained down. Her faith, twisted from her, had given the demon form. But because I had ended the ceremony prematurely, he must not have acquired the power to break his confinement. He needed fresh fuel. He was trying to stoke my wrath into a force he could command. He would use it to free himself, then he would destroy me.

Unless I used that wrath to destroy him first.

I met his blistering gaze.

"Tell me more," I said.

48

I listened as Sathanas stormed above me, recounting the times I had been slighted, shoved aside, stepped on. I opened myself to the dark, manipulative fingers writhing through my mind, twisting my thoughts. I nodded at the rush of charges and insinuations he leveled—some against those I loved. I allowed the flames of indignation to rear up again, to roar through my compassion, my reason.

And with the frothing wrath came power. God, the power. It didn't require a mental prism to channel. It was already raging inside me. The demon Sathanas hadn't lied about that.

But amid the exhilaration, I clung like sin to a single mantra:

He'll use you and then kill you. He'll use you and then kill you. He'll use—

"Drink in the power, wizard," he said. "Let it become you."

At the potent suggestion, something withered to ash inside me. The last of my will. Flames gushed into the space, and I lost the mantra. A beautiful weightlessness overcame me. I was levitating, phantom fire roaring around my flapping coat. I'd read of magic users becoming demigods, but holy hell. Why would someone *not* elect this power, already latent inside him?

Sathanas cackled in delight as he poked a single talon against my shoulder, rotating me until I was facing away from the grotto. "Now, train your vengeance on those who wronged you."

Their faces flashed through my mind's eye—Professor Snodgrass, Detective Vega, Chicory, others from my past—and yes, I hated them all. I drew my sword and staff apart. The steel blade glowed red hot, orange flames licking up and down its length. I would break from the cathedral, climb into the red-lit night like a glorious archangel, and rain hellfire on my enemies.

But there was something I was supposed to remember.

"Go now," Sathanas said. "Break the hold of this wicked, wretched place."

I flew forward several feet, then wheeled with a thundering *"FUOCO!"*

The forces that roared down my sword and staff were more concentrated than anything I'd ever commanded. Like jet fuel, they merged into a single column of fire that broke against Sathanas's chest. In blissful release, I watched him blast across the grotto. Flames plumed as Sathanas's form drove into the rear wall, bones and skulls erupting around him.

When the catacombs fell still again, Sathanas was buried, save for a black flap of wing and his serpentine tail, which lay limp beside the bishop. My wrath spent, I fell to the grotto floor, weary smoke rising from me. But I couldn't rest. I sheathed my sword and crawled to the bishop's side.

"Are you all right?" I asked. "Can you walk?"

She looked from the demon's tail back to me, her face creased with fear. "I believe so."

I helped her up, wrapping an arm around her waist, even though I wasn't in much better shape. Her first few steps were uncertain, but by the time we reached the grotto entrance, she was walking under her own power. By some miracle, the candle in the skull's socket had remained lit, and I removed it and handed it to her.

"You lead," I said. "I'll watch our rear."

I followed her from the grotto. As we turned the corner, I saw that Sathanas's impact had jarred the bones from the corridor walls such that we were facing larger drifts than when I'd arrived. With her short stature, the bishop had to crawl over the first pile. I peered nervously over a shoulder.

"Father Victor brought me down to the basement," she said in a gravely voice, "allegedly to show me something. Then he pressed a cloth over my nose and mouth. Chloroform, I suspect."

"That wasn't Father Victor," I said as I helped her over the next drift. "In trying to exorcise a malevolent presence from these grounds, he became possessed. It wasn't his fault. He didn't know what he was facing. The creature back there is an ancient demon lord. He murdered Father Richard and was preparing to do the same to you. Were it not for the will that remained in Father Victor, the demon would have succeeded and escaped. So please, remember him in that way."

As had happened with my parting words to Malachi, another layer of my prism seemed to harden. More of my magic-born power returned.

"And who are you?" the bishop asked.

I thought for a moment. "Father Vick was a teacher and friend."

We were halfway to the staircase when the catacombs began to shake again. A roar erupted from the grotto. Even as I tried to speed our pace, the bishop peered behind us, eyes huge.

"Wizard," Sathanas's voice boomed.

"Go," I told her. "Those stairs lead to the basement. Climb them and get out of the cathedral. Then put all of the faith you have into the sanctity of this place. It will prevent him from escaping."

"What are you going to do?"

I drew my cane apart and called light to my staff. "Delay him."

A hand, strong and maternal, pressed between my shoulder blades. "I've never met you," she said, "but I recognize you now, Everson. Father Victor spoke of you. He praised your benevolence. He said you would become a powerful ally one day, and he was right."

Her warmth and words undermined my fear. For a moment, I glimpsed Father Vick beside us, a white robe swimming around him. When I turned to look, though, the illusion vanished, and there was only a mound of skeletal remains.

"Stupid wizard," Sathanas boomed over his growing footfalls.

The warmth between my shoulder blades swelled with a gentle pressure that lingered even as I heard the bishop climbing away behind me. Cinching my grip on sword and staff, I stepped forward.

"I hear you, demon," I said.

With any luck, my blast had weakened him. I couldn't destroy him, but with the power I now possessed, I could offer a large enough speed bump for the bishop to escape. The demon would have nothing to draw on following my death. He would remain trapped. What happened next would be up to the Order, but hopefully I'd stirred up enough dust to get their attention.

When Sathanas rounded the corner, I staggered back. What I'd just said about him being weakened? Forget it. He was larger than ever, his horned and ripped physique radiating fiery power. He stooped into the corridor, bones smoking to black dust around him.

"Yes," Sathanas said. "I saw into your feeble mind. I turned your wrath into mine."

Feeble, indeed. Believing you could outwit a demon was like believing you could best the guy on the subway platform at three-card Monte. Sathanas had laid a trap inside of a trap. First by manipulating my wrath, then by getting me to believe the power of that wrath could harm him. Instead, he absorbed it. Now he commanded the strength to break the cathedral's hold.

And I was all that stood in his way.

"Stop," I shouted, setting my spent legs apart, sword and staff held out.

Sathanas stormed closer. "Do you wish to make me stronger still?"

Before I realized he'd thrashed it, his tail was driving toward me. I grunted out a *"Protezione,"* but my summoned shield shattered before the barbed tail. The hooked tip, diving for my heart, sunk beneath my left clavicle instead. With a sick crunch, it punched out my upper back.

I screamed, hands wringing my sword and staff, forearms hugging the tail.

Sathanas laughed as his tail lifted me from my feet and

slammed me into the corridor wall. Remains tumbled around me as the pain cast me into a gray world between excruciating waking and bone-aching sleep. From far away came the piercing cries of shriekers.

"Do your hear that?" he asked. "My legion is circling."

With another lash, he slammed me into the opposite wall.

"Soon, your world will belong to me."

Into another wall I went, the corridor flickering in and out.

Sathanas curled his tail around until I was struggling to hold his looming horned face in focus. "You will be gone in a moment, wizard. But be reassured, when I emerge into the world, it will be known that Everson Croft freed me. What power you lacked in your pathetic life, I will grant you in death. A demon may not give selflessly, but he gives."

In my hazy state, I could see the ley energy coursing up around us, warping the air. Any attempt to channel it would be suicide. The flow was too pure for me, too potent. It would blow my prism before destroying my mind. But if I wanted to slow Sathanas, it was the only option left.

Anyway, I thought with a wince, *I'm already toast.*

But first I needed to forgive all those I had sworn vengeance and death upon. Detective Vega, Chicory, the Church, even Professor Snodgrass. I would never wish on them what would befall humanity with Sathanas's escape.

I also thought of my friend and fellow professor, Caroline Reid. A woman who, I could freely admit now, I was kind of, sort of in love with. If I somehow managed to get out of this, I would tell her. But whatever happened, I hoped Caroline would have some sense that I tried. That I never gave up.

That determined, a pervasive calm settled over me. It was time.

"Hey, Sathanas," I mumbled, holding his blazing eyes, "Take your gift..."

I drove my sword arm forward and watched the blade plunge into the demon's throat.

"...and choke on it."

I threw open my prism to the torrent of ley energy. It smashed through me, white and raging, like dam waters. I strained with all I had to contain it, to channel it into the demon, whose angry eyes flared wide. But my prism was breaking up like a paper straw. I didn't know how much longer—

Silence hit me.

I was a young boy again, sitting in the middle row of pews, looking on the great stained glass window. Head titled, I had come to a stop at Michael. He was depicted as an angel, but I knew that wasn't quite right. He had been an elemental, a First Saint. Someone occupied the seat beside me, but not my grandmother. I tried to turn my head, but I was *in* the stained glass now, light pouring through me.

Sathanas's horrid scream wrenched me back to the present. Or maybe that was my own cry, the final expression of a blown mind, because I felt myself crashing into a blackness of collapsing bones.

49

I woke up to a cliché, which was to say in a hospital room. I did blink around, but no confused murmurings leaked from my lips. The antiseptic smell, sounds of distant monitors, and blue curtain that encircled my raised bed cued me in immediately.

I looked down to the right, where a pair of IV tubes fed blood and saline into the crook of my arm. On my left side, thick padding hugged my chest and shoulder, a spot of red striking through its center.

I remembered Sathanas's tail piercing me and struggled to sit up, but something restrained my left wrist. I pulled the cover away. I was handcuffed to the bedrail.

"Do you know the punishment for imprisoning a cop?"

Someone stood from a chair beside the head of my bed. A second later, Detective Vega stepped into view. I looked her up and down. Same serious face, pulled-back hair, and black suit as just about every time I'd ever seen her, but man did she look stunning. Maybe it was just the fact she was alive.

"You're all right," was all I could think to say.

"Are you?" she asked.

Except for a little pounding in the back of my head, I wasn't in nearly as much pain as I should have been, considering. "Just foggy," I said. "How in the hell did I end up here?"

A corner of her mouth smirked. "Your buddies brought you in."

"Buddies?"

"Dempsey and Dipinski. The acolyte at the cathedral called my office late last night and spoke to Hoffman. When Dempsey and Dipinski arrived to pick the kid up—in a taxi, for some reason—the whole cathedral shook. Like a bomb had gone off, they said. This kid, Malachi, insisted on going back inside for you. They dug you out of a boneyard in the subbasement. Boy, the officers just loved that."

"And the...?" I almost said demon, but stopped myself. That Detective Vega was alive—that *I* was alive—told me all I needed to know. Somehow, someway, Sathanas had been destroyed.

My body relaxed into the mattress.

"Do you want to tell me more about my visitors last night?" Vega asked. "Or should we save it for another time?"

"Definitely another time," I said wearily. "But you were ... protected?"

She looked at me a long moment before nodding. "Around the same time the cathedral would've been shaking, those screaming creatures fell apart, evaporated. And then that field, or whatever you put up, disappeared."

"And your son?"

"Safe as can be."

I nodded at her softening expression. The dissolution of the shriekers occurred when their source, Sathanas, was destroyed. The subsequent breakdown of the shield was me tumbling into la-la land—and under a pile of bones, apparently. I remembered the centipede I'd seen crawling out of the ear canal of one of those skulls and fought the urge now to check my own.

Vega lowered her voice. "So what happened down there, Croft?"

I thought back to the experience of becoming Michael in the stained glass window. In that final instant, the power of the cathedral and my magical bloodline had aligned. And it was all because...

"I forgave," I said.

"Forgave?" Her face scrunched up. "Who?"

"Um..." I looked down. "A few people. But I had help, too."

"There was someone with you?"

"Yeah. Father Vick."

His had been the presence beside me on the pew. I was certain of that now. Like strong hands over the backs of mine, he had helped me hold the prism together long enough to destroy the demon. Without him, I was sure I would have perished instead. And Sathanas would be loose in the world. I took a moment to compose my face before raising it again.

I expected Vega to say something skeptical—she had that look in her eyes—but she sighed in what sounded like accession. "The bishop told me what happened. Father Vick ... the demon ... how you saved her butt."

"Then what's with the handcuffs?" I gave them a little rattle.

Vega snorted and shook her head. "You woke up a few hours ago and tried to dance a tango with the night nurse." She separated a small key from the others on her chain as she circled the bed. "The cuffs were put on for her sake as much as yours. She wasn't amused."

Thelonious, I thought with an inward groan. At least it settled the question of whether I owed him a night out.

I watched Vega unlock the cuffs, conflict furrowing her brow. I didn't need to read her mind to know what was going on upstairs. She was considering just how in the hell she was going to explain to her higher ups what had happened at the cathedral. I didn't envy her.

"You were right," I said.

She looked up, eyes bright with surprise. "About what?"

"The evidence leading you to Father Vick. I don't blame you for that. Two very different approaches led us to the same person, though for different reasons. When you write up your report, I hope you'll consider that."

The last thing I wanted was for Father Vick to be vilified, especially after having made the ultimate sacrifice. I doubted Vega would be given a choice, though. But as she pocketed the cuffs in her jacket, she looked as if she was debating whether or not to tell me something. She stepped back, establishing a professional distance.

"I'm working on a request," she said at last, "for a special unit in Homicide. Crimes that don't fit the typical mold, that sort of thing." She hesitated. "I could use a consultant."

"Well, that all depends on what you're offering, Detective," I said with a smirk.

She folded her arms. “How about not citing you for trashing my vehicle?”

Heh. I’d forgotten about that.

“No, look, I’d be honored,” I said, as her face relaxed into an almost-smile. “I’m just not sure what kind of a future I have in the city.” *Or whether I have a future, period.* I glanced down at my left wrist, finding a hospital band instead of a watch. “What time is it?”

Vega consulted her own wrist. “Quarter till eleven.”

“Monday morning?”

“Yeah, why?”

I drew the IV tubes from my arm, lowered the right bedrail, swung my legs over the bedside, and stood.

“Croft!” Vega whispered. “What in the hell are you doing?”

I steadied myself, not nearly as weak or sore as I had expected, then realized with a flush my gown was wide open in back. No wonder Vega had thrown a forearm to her wincing face. “I’m, ah…” I said, holding the flaps closed behind me with one hand and batting past the curtain with the other in search of my clothes and personals. “I’m late for something.”

50

The hearing was already underway when I arrived at the conference room at Midtown College. The distinguished faces of the board members turned at my entrance. And then there was Professor Snodgrass, who I had apparently caught in the middle of his presentation.

He cleared his throat and peered over his little oval glasses. "How nice of you to join us, Mr. Croft. Wardrobe problems?" He gave a self-satisfied sniff. "Well, go on, have a seat."

I looked down at my bandaged shins poking beneath the hem of my coat. With my clothes blood-stained and filthy, I'd donned a second gown on my back instead, then buttoned my punctured coat to the throat. At least it wasn't inside out. I grunted and took the empty seat at the end of the table, hanging my cane over the armrest. In my peripheral vision, I noticed several faculty members seated around the edge of the room. I felt like I'd walked into a trial.

"As I was saying," Snodgrass continued, with a final glance of reproach my way, "Mr. Croft's criminal status, coupled with his failure to disclose said status to you, the esteemed board, is more than sufficient, I should think, to have him terminated from the college and forbidden from teaching or conducting research here ever again. I urge you to also consider that since the college renewed his contract under the false impression Mr. Croft had a clean record, he be fined the equivalent of his salary going back to his arrest date."

Ouch. That would definitely land me in a cardboard box beneath the underpass. I watched the board members flip through the stapled packets in front of them—copies of my arrest record and court papers—and tried to read their expressions. That all eight were frowning wasn't encouraging.

"May I say something?" I asked, raising a hand half way.

I wasn't going to try to convince the board of anything. My plan was to give a brief account of the events that had led to my arrest, leaving out the magical parts, of course, admit fault for not informing the board, and then ask that they consider probation instead of termination. I would even accept a pay cut. If they terminated me anyway, I had tried. I think Caroline would look on that at least somewhat kindly.

When my gaze returned to Snodgrass, I remembered my other reason for racing over here in a pair of hospital gowns. I had forgiven him last night, sure, but it didn't mean I was going to allow the twerp the last word.

Snodgrass met my gaze with a haughty *this should be good* look.

"If I can say something first," a voice intervened. I turned to Chairman Cowper, a bald man with large, sagging lips that smacked every few words. The chairman of the board directed his smacking lips to Snodgrass. "For all of our sakes, I wish you would have been a little more thorough."

Snodgrass blinked rapidly. "More thorough, sir?" he asked. "I'm not sure I understand. It's all in the—"

"A follow-up phone call at the least," Chairman Cowper continued. "When I spoke to the detective of record this morning, she said that Professor Croft here..." He smacked again as he opened a hand toward me. "...has no criminal history. His arrest was in error, and it is all being taken care of, per the detective's own words. She admitted that it should have been expunged a long time ago, but the court system being in its present state..."

I suppressed a smile. *Detective Vega, you little lynx.*

Professor Snodgrass's lips began to twitch between his reddening cheeks, but the chairman showed his palm. "Your motion that he be terminated, Professor, is based on the assertion that he is on probation. Well, that is hardly the case, now is it? Some due diligence would have established this—and spared us all the toil of yet another pointless meeting," he added in a mutter.

"I spoke with the detective just the other week!" Snodgrass exclaimed.

But Cowper had already started to stand, the other board members joining him.

"And what about his class size?" Snodgrass continued, arms pumping. "Six students!" His titter verged on hysterical. "And his grants? We haven't seen any of those lately!"

"Oh, that reminds me." At the door, Chairman Cowper turned his head. "Just this morning, the college received its largest grant to date—double the amount, in fact, that Professor Croft requested." He nodded at me, appreciation gleaming in his eyes. "It seems someone is very taken with your work."

"A grant from who!" Snodgrass demanded.

"*Whom*," the chairman corrected him, then smacked his lips in recall. "Ah, yes, the Obadiah Rockledge Department for Esoteric Research. Or was it Rutledge?" He waved a hand as though it hardly mattered.

I worked out the acronym and smiled openly this time. It seemed I was back in my magical society's good graces.

Before I could work my lips straight, Snodgrass's eyes jerked from the departing board members to me. "Oh, there's something funny going on, all right," he said. Without dropping his menacing gaze, he gathered his papers into a sloppy pile. "I'm going to be watching you, Croft. I'm going to get to the bottom of this. And you are *not* going to be smiling when I do."

I leaned toward him. "A little advice, Snodgrass? Next time you want to crap on someone, try pulling your pants down first."

His lips screwed up so tightly, I thought he was going to foul himself right there. Instead, he jerked the papers to his chest, stood abruptly, and marched from the room. When the door slammed behind him, I sagged in my chair, triumph giving over to weariness.

So I had my life, my job, a future with the NYPD that didn't involve a probation officer, and the blessings of the inscrutable Order. Was there anything that *hadn't* fixed itself in the last hour? Arnaud and the ring remained a point of contention, I guessed, and there might be some issues with Bashi, though I *had* dealt with the spell supplier. Word would get to Bashi eventually, if it hadn't already. The vampire I would worry about another time.

I patted the bandage on my left shoulder. Though it seemed the energy at St. Martin's Cathedral had jump-started the healing, I had my injuries to take care of. There was also the matter of a trashed apartment and exhausted wards, not to mention a succubus cat expecting goat's milk. With a deep sigh, I pushed myself up from the chair. The more things changed...

"I'm proud of you."

I wheeled in surprise. Caroline Reid, who must have been in the audience, smiled as she made her way toward me. Golden hair spilling over one shoulder, she looked angelic. I felt my cheeks flush as I remembered the pledge I'd made to myself while in the clutches of Sathanas—telling Caroline how I really felt. It had seemed such a good idea at the time.

"Hey, thanks for coming," I said.

She looked me over, fingers touching the bandage on my forehead. "Should I ask?"

"Probably not."

"Word at City Hall is that there was a break in the St. Martin's murder case." She laced her fingers into my right hand and swung it lightly. "Thanks to a mysterious consultant."

"I had some help," I said, squeezing her hand. If there was a moment to tell her, it was right now.

Her dimples reappeared. "So, where are you off to?"

She released my hand, and with the lost contact went most of my nerve.

"Um, I was planning to head home to take care of a few things. Change of clothes, of course," I said with an embarrassed laugh. "Then I'll be back for my afternoon class. I promised one of my students I'd be there." I thought of Meredith, hoping she'd made it home safely.

"Aren't you forgetting something?"

I glanced around to where I'd been sitting.

"Right here, sport," she said. "You owe this girl a lunch."

"Ahh, in that case..." I looked at my wristwatch. It was just shy of noon. "How does now sound?"

"It's a date."

We left the college together, stepping out into the stir of Midtown. Not running late for a change, I had a moment to inhale and take everything in. The sky was a bold blue for the first time in what seemed months, and warm sunlight sparkled up and down the block. Whether it was from the brilliance of the fall day or Caroline holding my arm, chatting happily, or the lingering high of whatever pain medication the nurses had shot me up with—or the simple fact I was alive—I loved my beautiful, broken city more than ever.

"Wow, stunning day," Caroline said.

"Perfect," I agreed, admiring the sun against her face.

As we entered the thick of the lunchtime crowd, though, I caught myself gripping my cane a little more tightly, invocations at the ready. After all, even on the finest of days you never knew who—or what—might be prowling the streets. And wizards made tempting targets.

Especially the wiseass kind.

THE SERIES CONTINUES...

BLOOD DEAL (PROF CROFT, BOOK 2)

On sale now!

About the Author

Brad Magnarella is an author of good-guy urban fantasy. His books include the popular Prof Croft novels and his newest series, Blue Wolf. Raised in Gainesville, Florida, he now calls various cities home. He currently lives and writes abroad.

www.bradmagnarella.com

BOOKS IN THE CROFTVERSE

THE PROF CROFT SERIES

Book of Souls

Demon Moon

Blood Deal

Purge City

Death Mage

Black Luck

Power Game

Druid Bond

THE BLUE WOLF SERIES

Blue Curse

Blue Shadow

Blue Howl

Blue Venom

MORE COMING!